# Honesty Works Best When It's the Truth

Tales by Emma Gladstone

Ron Hosea

iUniverse, Inc.
New York Bloomington

**Honesty Works Best When It's the Truth**
**Tales by Emma Gladstone**



*iUniverse books may be ordered through booksellers or by contacting:*

*iUniverse*
*1663 Liberty Drive*
*Bloomington, IN 47403*
*www.iuniverse.com*
*1-800-Authors (1-800-288-4677)*



*ISBN: 978-1-4502-4878-5 (sc)*
*ISBN: 978-1-4502-4879-2 (ebook)*

*Printed in the United States of America*

*iUniverse rev. date: 08/30/2010*

*To Ella*
*My wife; my friend; my rock*

*"The eyes are the window to the soul, and the nose is the doorway to influenza."*

Emma Gladstone

# Table of Contents

# Acknowledgments

The list of people to thank would easily fill a book all by itself, but I do want to name a few special people.

Shirley Carter helped me in so many ways during this process, not only proofreading but also cooking suppers and making Emma's dress for the book cover. Shirley never said no.

Robert McMullen provided the cover photograph; he went out of his way to accommodate every shot and angle I wanted.

Adele Brinkley's edit work tweaked my stories into a presentable fashion.

Jeannie Walker read, reread, and reread this book to polish up my flow when it went a little awry.

And, of course, my family. Rick, you encourage me more than you will ever know. Randall, thank you for laughing at everything I write (even when it's not meant to be funny). Mom and Dad, I feel your support daily, and as the saying goes, I wouldn't be here without you; thank you. My dear Ella, you tolerated this grumpy writer who complained nonstop about everything, and you always managed to keep a smile on your face.

# Introduction

What comes to mind when you think *small town*? Chances are, the same words pop into our heads. Warm. Friendly. Quaint. All those fuzzy feelings ring true, but what would happen if we pulled on the fabric that held those towns together? Okay, forget pulled. Let's say we yanked on the thread until the soft underbelly was fully exposed. Eureka! We just found envy, backbiting, and—dare I say it?—pettiness. Of course, humor with a strong sense of irony lives within those ungodly characteristics. My simple motive behind this book was to give the fictional town of *Forbye* a good yank and see what unraveled beneath its foundation.

While Emma Gladstone lives in my imagination, I assure you that her spirit lived in many of the women I grew up around. They were solid, God-fearing women, blessed with Southern roots and entrenched in the Baptist faith. Maybe they weren't always right, but they were never in doubt when it came to their convictions or the latest gossip.

I don't have a degree in human behavior; however, I am well qualified in church politics and the characters that drive its engine. My dad was the Baptist preacher in a small Florida town. From the pews, and from the streets, I witnessed many unique situations that taught me a lot about human nature. I remember those days fondly, and while writing this book, I drew on those experiences that shaped my childhood. I set out to recreate the humor, drama, and comfort I found while living in an ... ahem, let's call it a warm, friendly, and quaint small town.

This is the first volume in a series of stories told through the narrative of Mrs. Gladstone. The second volume is in the works and should be finished soon. They are really a joy to write.

# The Church Social

Although it happened years ago, that day was as clear as yesterday. I guess time is irrelevant when it comes to thievery, spiritual corruption, and a church social that ends in fisticuffs. Normally, I wouldn't speak of such things, but I'd rather you hear the truth from me instead of hearing lies by the bushel from Nelly Dalton. Yes, *that* Nelly Dalton. I'll tell you this: if Satan ever wanted to marry, there wouldn't be a doubt that Nelly Dalton would be high on his courtin' list.

I'm sorry. How rude of me! Let me introduce myself before I continue. My name is Mrs. Emma Gladstone. I prefer the name Sister Gladstone when discussing church business, and shortly I will get to that business.

I'm a Southern lady, born and raised in a small Florida town called Forbye. It's just ten miles south of the Georgia line. You see, 'long about the early eighteen-hundreds or so, Scottish settlers cleared out a patch of land and so forth to create a town. Forbye came to mind because *forbye* is a Scottish word meaning "near or beside." As I said, the town was near Georgia, hence the name Forbye; those imaginative Scots. Anyway, I hate to rattle on, but a little background was in order to stifle your curiosity when I refer to the township of Forbye or the First Baptist Church of Forbye. I'm a detail type of woman, as you're about to find out, and I wouldn't want you to ponder over the simple and trivial name of Forbye.

Somehow, I've managed to stay married to the same man for years. Earl, my husband, will make appearances in my story, and you, too, will question why I'm still married to the rascal. For instance, there's not a sailor alive who knows more curse words or sips more whisky than my Earl. Earl, of course, blames it all on the Korean War. We can't even go into Wal-Mart without Earl looking over his shoulder for the Koreans. Lord help us if there's ever a short Oriental man standing in the frozen food section.

I have many wonderful stories, but first let me tell you about the church social that took place in the year of our Lord, 1956. What's that? Gossip, you say? There's no gossip here! What I'm about to tell you is the truth.

Anyone who lived in Forbye knew the summer social was the event of the year. Not only church members, but also regular town folk—you know, the unwashed—came out to feast on God's buffet. Calvin Tibbs, a reporter from the *Forbye Telegraph*, always covered the occasion in his "Talk of the Town" column. If a lady wanted to be known for her culinary skills, all it took was a mere mention from Mr. Tibbs, and she and her recipe would go down in the annals of Forbye folklore. Here is an example of Mr. Tibbs' work:

> In my life, I've had more macaroni and cheese than I care to remember. However, Doris Humfinger brought such excitement to this dish that it gave new definition to pasta and pressed curds. My taste buds wrestled each other just to be the first to savor Mrs. Humfinger's classic creation. To say that this is just macaroni and cheese is like saying the Mona Lisa is just a painting. This dish should be served at the Waldorf—it's that good!
>
> Forbye Telegraph
> July 6, 1953

After that, Doris Humfinger became the macaroni and cheese queen. No other clear-thinking woman would ever darken the social hall door with that dish in hand.

Mr. Tibbs dubbed several queens over the years: Martha Bennett for her pecan fried chicken, Ida May Long for her tuna soufflé, and Grace Mobley for her Hungarian succotash, just to name a few. I don't know what was more enjoyable, the social itself or reading the reviews on Monday. In any event, to get noticed you had to make it through Mr. Tibbs' stomach, and that is what I set out to do.

About six months before the summer church social, I started dickering around with different recipes, but nothing worked. I just couldn't come up with something new. The queens of Mr. Tibbs already had a lock on so many wonderful dishes. Meat products were pointless;

salads never set Mr. Tibbs' taste buds on fire; and casseroles were for old ladies. I needed something to put me in the circle of famous dishes. Keep in mind, I was a young gal at the time; with one great dish my status in Forbye would be solidified. However, my mind went blank. I had nothing, no idea of what on earth I could concoct.

One day I looked to heaven and asked, "Lord, what can I make?"

Almost instantly I heard, "Boysenberries." That's right. The word *boysenberries* echoed around my kitchen table. The voice was so loud, so clear, and so recognizable. It was Earl's voice; he was talking to me as he came in from the garden. "The boysenberries will be blooming soon. I bet we'll have a mess of them by June," he informed me.

Okay, God didn't say boysenberries outright, and picking Earl as his messenger seemed odd. But the Lord does work in mysterious ways. "Boysenberry pie... boysenberry pie," I thought out loud. "That's it, Earl!" I screamed. Earl looked at me funny and then shuffled off to find a ballgame on the radio.

Although fresh boysenberries were out of season, I spent all spring perfecting my piecrust. Don't tell anyone, but I used canned blueberries through the trial phase. The crust mattered most during the early stages. I spent weeks adjusting the lard-to-butter ratio. And not just any lard; I'm talking high-dollar leaf lard, which comes from the fat around a pig's kidneys. Also, of course, I used Goldfields baking butter. Is there any other? Oleo? Please, dear. I'm Emma Gladstone. So anyway, by the time I had the crust just right, the first boysenberries were falling off the vine. Earl was right. We had a mess of them, but each one was precious, so none could be wasted.

One day I sent Earl out to pick a bagful. I was standing over the kitchen sink singing "Just a Closer Walk with Thee," when I glanced out the window and happened to see Earl pop a boysenberry in his mouth. *That rascal! Now I'm about to get a closer walk with Earl,* I thought. I grabbed the slingshot we kept by the back door for shooting tomcats, loaded up my apron with cherry tomatoes, and set my sights on Earl's backside. As soon as he raised his hand to his mouth again I let the tomato fly. *Smack!* Right in the seat of his britches! Earl leapt forward and then went into a defensive crouch. "Earl Bartholomew Gladstone, you eat another one of the Lord's berries, and you'll wish you were back in some Korean foxhole!" I yelled as I lined up another tomato. But before I could let it fly, Earl dropped the berry into the bag.

With a month to go before the summer social, it was time to get down to the serious business of sorting berries. I separated each by ripeness, aroma, and color. Anything not up to snuff was tossed. Earl stood by like an old hound dog waiting for discarded scraps. Nothing but the best made the grade for my prize-winning pie.

The pie filling itself became a thorny issue. If this pie was to stand out, it couldn't be just sugar, cornstarch, and boysenberries. That would never make Mr. Tibbs's "Talk of the Town" column. No, sir! My pie filling needed to exhibit a combination of style, comfort, and imagination. I wanted Mr. Tibbs's taste buds to wrestle each other over my pie. I wanted to be the talk of the town. I wanted to be the Queen of Boysenberry Pie.

I explored several options to find the perfect ingredients to complement the boysenberries. I tried just a hint of vanilla, a pinch of nutmeg, and so forth. The pies were all good, mind you, but nothing to cause a body's taste buds to wrestle. I added a little coconut—well, that one was no good; in fact, it was awful. I even went as far as spritzing the berries with a little of Earl's sipping rum, just for flavor, of course. Earl loved the stuff, but it tasted horrible mixed with boysenberries. I was beside myself. The social was only two weeks away and I had accomplished nothing more than a perfect crust.

My pride wouldn't allow me to sulk, but it did take a toll on my spirit. My desire to cook had deserted me, causing poor Earl to get by on cold cuts and peanut butter. Since the war, all he wanted was home cooking and a soft bed. Now, because of that elusive pie, Earl didn't have either one.

I guess he got tired of the cold cuts, because Earl finally went off on me. I remember it so clearly: I was sitting in my chair doing my crosswords when Earl stomped in. "Emma, quit your moping and make me something to eat," he barked.

His tone caught me off guard, but I liked that he needed me. He was a helpless caveman in the wilderness seeking some sense of civilization, bless his heart. Little did I know the Lord was about to use Earl as his mouthpiece again. I put down the crossword puzzle and made my way to the kitchen. Earl followed close behind me. "What would you like, Earlee?" I asked (that was my pet name for him).

"How 'bout some warm gingersnaps," he replied.

"Of course, dear." I went to the cupboard and then stopped. "Eureka! Earl, you glorious caveman—ginger—ginger—ginger—oh, dear Lord—ginger!"

"What the...?"

"Never mind the gingersnaps, Earl. Mamma's gonna make you the best boysenberry pie ever."

Earl muttered something like, "Here we go again," before shuffling out to find a ballgame.

Now I must have passed my hand over the ginger box a thousand times without thinking what delight it would bring to a boysenberry pie. To my knowledge, no Southern lady had ever used the two together. I know what you're thinking: "Two opposite flavors competing in the same dish? Absurd!" Oh, ye of little faith. This was the combination I'd been seeking. I could taste my prize-winning pie before I made it.

Do I really have to tell you how it tasted? Let's just say that my coronation waited for Mr. Tibbs. I carefully transferred all my chicken-scratched notes into one legible recipe. Before going off to bed, I baked the pie again just to make sure. And to tell you the truth, the second one was better than the first.

I remember lying in bed saying my prayers. "Dear Lord, if you could find some way for me to make the 'Talk of the Town' column, I'd rightly be grateful." Of course, I said that after I prayed for Earl's soul, the orphans, and the infirm. I drifted off, and for the first time in three weeks I slept peacefully.

The Tuesday before the social was when this story turned. Nelly Dalton, remember her? Well, she stopped by that Tuesday for her monthly gossip and lies session. I never much cared for Nelly. We had a history, but that's another story. Anyway, she popped in for a visit, which was more like a holy inspection. She'd just love to catch me with a pinch of snuff, or maybe find Earl all liquored up. She always nosed around mendaciously, looking for anything that might conjure up a raised eyebrow before prayer meeting.

We kept the conversation light. I didn't speak of my boysenberry pie. The last person I wanted to know about the ginger was Nelly Dalton. In fact, we did not discuss the social at all. She was either holding her cards like I was, or she was planning a boring casserole. I'm sure somewhere in her imagination Nelly was a good cook, bless her heart.

Nelly was wrapping up her visit with her usual request. "Oh, Emma, by the way, could I have some cold water before I go?" she asked, all syrupy. This was her technique to peek into my icebox, looking for Earl's beer.

Why, sure, Nelly." I opened the icebox door all the way back to the hinges because I never allowed Earl to put beer in there. "There you go, Nelly," I said as I poured a glass of cold water while letting the fridge door hang wide open for a full investigation.

Suddenly I heard, "Emma, come here!"

It was Earl's voice coming from down the hall. About twenty minutes earlier I had witnessed Earl walk through the house with a newspaper under his arm. By his tone and schedule I knew what he wanted. "Emma, I said come in here!" Earl called again, a little louder.

I briefly excused myself while Nelly drank her water. How do I put this delicately? Let's just say Earl had a paper shortage and was disinclined to retrieve a new roll on his own. I went down the hall. "Here, Earl, and don't flush until Nelly leaves. I'll let you know," I whispered as I handed the necessities through a cracked door.

As I came back around the corner, I noticed Nelly jamming a pen and note pad back into her handbag. *Making a list of dirty dishes*, I thought. I'm quite sure she found something awry in my kitchen. Anyway, all loaded up with prayer meeting gossip, Nelly said a quick good-bye.

I stood there for a good ten minutes wondering what she had been up to. Earl finally broke my concentration. "Emma?" he quietly called out. Oh, dear Lord, I had forgotten about Earl waiting to flush.

What a glorious morning I woke up to on the day of the social! I checked the pie first; it looked absolutely perfect sitting next to my *Holy Bible*. Norman Rockwell couldn't have painted a better picture, and certainly not a better tasting one. I told Earl it was all because of him and his craving for gingersnaps. He said nothing, but I could tell he was proud.

I got dressed: new nylons, floral blue dress, matching shoes, pearl necklace, pillbox hat, white gloves, and white handbag. Earl threw on a dress shirt and polished hard shoes, and away we went. We only lived a few blocks from the church, so I left the pie at home until after services.

We had a normal attendance for Sunday School, but the preaching service was filled to the rafters. The regular townsfolk came out just to have a clear conscience before partaking of God's food. We must have run two hundred in meeting service. This was a particularly hot July morning, so Brother Johnson from Forbye Funeral Parlor stood in the foyer handing out fans. They were lovely fans indeed, with a beautiful print of Jesus herding a flock of sheep.

Preacher Babcock delivered a wonderful sermon on sins of the flesh. He told us how prurient thoughts lead to deviant behavior. He touched on all the topics of lust and perversion—you know, mixed swimming, drive-in movies, and Elvis Presley. Then the preacher railed against dancing as he strutted around the podium like a banny rooster, gyrating and swinging his hips as if to mock Elvis. Half the congregation gasped while the other half snickered as the preacher jiggled from head to toe. Suddenly, he stopped. It was so quiet. He gazed into the congregation. He waited... waited some more... and then swung his fist high in the air before bringing it down on the pulpit. *Thwack*! That woke Earl up. The preacher shouted, "Lucifer wants you to dance because he knows it's a vertical movement looking for a horizontal opportunity!" I glanced over at Nelly Dalton; she was going to town with a fan. *You can fan all you want to, Nelly, but sin sticks,* I thought. It was no secret that Nelly and her husband liked to sneak down to the Elks Club for some rug-cutting, and they'd been known to switch dance partners.

I reckon Preacher Babcock figured on getting the most out of a packed house, because he went a full thirty minutes beyond a normal Sunday meeting. Eventually, Brother Campbell said the last amen, and the holy morning of obligation was over.

On the way out, I couldn't help but notice a flock of ladies surrounding Calvin Tibbs. Talk about a hideous outpouring of vulgarity. Well, I never! You should have heard the flirtatious innuendos sprouting about. "Oh, why Mr. Tibbs, you might have to undo your trousers after filling up on my brown-sugar-glazed meatloaf," Linda Humphrey said. She giggled and then sort of brushed by Mr. Tibbs while ever so slightly touching his elbow. While I was watching this, another woman, June Miller, got extremely close to Mr. Tibbs and whispered something into his ear. Keep in mind all this went on while standing just outside the church—technically still in God's house! Not more than five minutes earlier, Preacher Babcock has spoken for the umpteenth time about sins of the flesh, going to hell, and prurient thoughts. Nevertheless, these hens had visions of Mr. Tibbs undoing his trousers while they whispered who knows what kind of favors in his ear. Honestly, I'd witnessed enough. I turned curtly on my heel as a statement of disapproval and removed myself before lightning struck. Besides, I had other pressing needs.

I grabbed Earl before he lit another cigarette, and we quickly headed home. Earl kept the car running while I ran inside. The smell of boysenberries and a wisp of ginger wafted through the house as I grabbed the pie, retrieved a gallon of sweet tea from the fridge, and said a quick prayer—I figured it couldn't hurt. Then it was back to the church for us.

We pulled into a packed parking lot, and suddenly the magnitude of the event gripped me. I felt dampness filter through my gloves. I had rehearsed this moment over and over in my mind, but the gravity of it became all too real. My nylons bunched up; my dream was about to come true. Boysenberry, ginger, the *talk of the town*—it was all about to happen.

We parked in the back, two slots over from the cemetery. Maybe it was a sign of things to come, because guess who pulled up next to us? That's right, Nelly Dalton. And before I knew what was going on... it happened. Some things in life never escape one's memory. A thousand Sundays can come and pass, brain cells can fade away, and dementia can riddle this old lady's mind, but never, never, will I forget what happened at that very moment.

As I stated, Nelly pulled up with her litter of brats. There must have been five or six young'uns all jammed into Nelly's Buick. One little typhoid-carrying miscreant jumped out of the car and started roughhousing with another dirty-faced lad. Suddenly, the entire Dalton clan surrounded me. I tried to balance the boysenberry pie with my *Holy Bible*, white handbag, and gallon of sweet tea. Where was Earl? Forget it. He was still behind the wheel of our car, swigging the last drop out of his Sunday flask. Then one boy ran into my right arm. I was still trying to steady myself when another kid ran into me going the other way. I violently swung around, my movements inducing a mammoth twirl. I'm no scientist, but the velocity caused such centrifugal force it propelled my pie out of my hands and turned it into a flying saucer. When I finally stopped spinning, I stood stock still, motionless. The vision seemed to last forever: the pie, suspended in air, rotating, rotating, rotating with gravity nowhere in sight. The saucer sailed past the cemetery gate while appearing to leak purple oil. I watched in disbelief as my pie crashed into the tombstone of old Doc Potter.

Just like that, the pie, the ginger, the talk of the town—all were gone. Although I was all shook up, I managed to hear a giggle (or was it a snicker?) coming from Nelly's direction. Too crestfallen to chastise her boys who caused the ruckus, and too humiliated at the moment to look at Nelly, I slumped forward to catch my breath. I hung my head, my white gloves now stained purple; one little boysenberry clung to the gallon of tea before mercifully dropping to the ground.

I don't know how long it took to gather myself. I don't even remember walking into the social hall. At some point, the fuzzy haze left me and I found myself sitting on a metal chair with arms folded. Anger—that's right, anger—set in.

One by one the ladies entered. Martha Bennett with her fried chicken, Doris Humfinger with her macaroni and cheese, Ida May Long with her tuna soufflé, Grace Mobley with her Hungarian succotash, and on and on, a parade of food. Calvin Tibbs sat off to the side viewing this sickening procession like a peacock waiting to gather his harem.

I heard somebody say, "Look at that pie." My eyes cut to the doorway and guess who came sashaying in with a big grin and an arm full of boysenberry pie? You guessed it, Nelly Dalton! Not only did she methodically coordinate a disturbance that brought destruction to my pie, but she had also stolen my recipe! I knew something was up with that woman when she hurried out of my kitchen a few days before. Now the proof was in the boysenberries. The nerve, the gall, the audacity of it all!

I sat there and stewed. Then I tried to reason with myself. *Maybe she didn't steal the recipe itself, maybe just the idea. After all, there are several boysenberry pie recipes; surely she wouldn't use my unique creation with ginger—would she?*

While all the other sisters placed their dishes on long tables, Nelly went about the room putting the pie under all the men's noses. You should have heard her talking openly about her recipe. What an embarrassing spectacle. She went right up to Mr. Tibbs and said, "Mr. Tibbs. You must try my boysenberry pie. It's made with ginger."

*Okay! That's it! She used ginger!* All the ladies gasped, and then "ginger" was whispered throughout the dining hall.

What would you do? You didn't have to be Agatha Christie to solve this caper. Well, I had had enough! Nelly had just lit the fuse to the powder keg I'd been sitting on. I bolted from my chair and dashed toward the thief who was spinning a tale of lies.

"Nelly Dalton, just who do you think you are?" I said.

"Why, Emma, what on earth do you mean?"

"Ginger! Really now! You expect me to believe you came up with ginger all on your own? You stole my recipe!" I accused.

The social fell silent. We stood with only the boysenberry pie between us. Preacher Babcock tried to step in. "Now ladies—"

"Hold on, Preacher," I interjected. "You spoke all morning about sin, but I guess it didn't work! Now it's my turn. Not only did this woman steal my pie, but her children attacked me in the parking lot."

"Baseless allegations," Nelly puffed back.

"I'm not in the habit of saying things that aren't true," I replied.

All parties concerned have debated what happened next with vigorous elaboration. But this is what occurred.

Nelly tried to nudge me out of the way, but I stood my ground waiting for a confession. You know, being Sunday and all, I figured confession would be good for her soul. However, she nudged a little harder, so I nudged back. The preacher, still trying to diffuse the dispute, touched both of our shoulders to calm the rising tempers in the room. Nelly resisted and led with a finger-poke to my pillbox hat. I whipped my arm up to stop her, and by chance my thumb caught the rim of her pie plate, and for the second time that day a boysenberry pie was airborne. I'm not sure who threw the first punch, but Nelly and I ended up on the floor.

Bloomers flew and girdles ripped. Doris Humfinger, who always found Nelly to be quite haughty, rushed to my aid. She yanked off Nelly's wig and threw it into Grace Mobley's Hungarian succotash. A melee of the highest order ensued. Earl flashed back to the Korean War, immediately went into combat mode, and started rounding up all the short men for torture. Nothing was sacred. Hymnals were used as missiles, Bibles were used as shields, and the whole church erupted into a holy war. The preacher shouted, "Order!" which was ignored as fisticuffs continued at every corner.

I was sitting on top of Nelly pulling at her legs when I glanced over at Earl. He had Mr. Tibbs belly-down and hogtied with his necktie. Food covered the floor, walls, ceiling, and most of the two hundred guests. Forbye hadn't seen this much action since General Alfred Colquitt beat back the Union Army during the Civil War.

Finally, Luther Hunt fetched a shotgun from his pickup truck and fired off a round into the ceiling. Everyone stopped. I let go of Nelly's leg, stood up, and straightened my dress. The preacher asked us all to leave and not speak to each other for fear of another outbreak. Nelly slid out the back door, and the crowd slowly dispersed. Earl untied Mr. Tibbs as well as four other men. I tried to stay behind to clean up, but the preacher said, "Go, Emma. Just go."

Before I went out the door I glanced back to see Mr. Tibbs walk over to a heap of boysenberry goo. He bent down and pushed his finger into the center. He plucked up a glob to his tongue, rolled the substance around in his mouth, and then shrugged his shoulders before walking out the side door.

On the way to the car I groused at Earl, "You just had to have gingersnaps, didn't you!"

The next morning Earl came running in with the paper. "Look, Emma!" he exclaimed as he held up the paper for me to see. Lo and behold! There in black and white was a front-page photo of me smearing boysenberry pie all over the face of Nelly Dalton.

The headline read, "Emma Gladstone Is the Talk of the Town."

So the Lord does answer prayers.

# The Pulpit Committee

I'll never forget that early spring day in 1958. It was a glorious Sunday morning and Preacher Babcock was letting us have it, and rightly so. He had titled his message, "Jesus Never Had to be Entertained and Neither Should You." His sermon was about the latest fad to hit Forbye—the television set.

For the longest time, we'd heard about television through magazines and Sears catalogs, but we lived so far back in the sticks that it was pointless to think about owning one on the account that there was no reception where we lived. That changed 'long about the late fifties, when South Creek, a town thirty miles to our south (thus the name South Creek), installed a television tower that covered nearly a fifty-mile radius. Slowly, church members started ordering the idiot box, and Preacher Babcock was fit to be tied.

He was preaching like it was his last sermon. I estimated that he pounded his fist at least fifteen to twenty times on the pulpit, each time shouting, "The devil lives inside the television screen!" He'd hoot and holler, pace back and forth, shake his fist, and totally get himself all worked up over Lucifer's newest invention.

During one particular point in the service I glanced over at Nelly Dalton. Now remember, it was early spring and the temperature inside was very comfortable. Yet there Nelly sat, fanning herself like there was no tomorrow. Why? I had it on good authority that Nelly and her husband, Fred, had just ordered a television set.

I'd never heard such brimstone fly from the preacher's mouth. *This is probably the best sermon I've ever heard,* I thought, as he unleashed an array of rhythmic rants.

"The enemies of decency are dedicated to the destruction and deception of America. Television is a portal to Satan's playground and more people will burn in the fires of hell from television than from any tavern, any prostitute, or any rock and roll music! Can I get an 'Amen'?" he shouted.

Several men obliged with a hearty, "Amen!"

Reverend Babcock continued, "Read with me, if you will, Romans chapter sixteen, verses seventeen and eighteen: 'Now I beseech you, brethren, mark them which cause divisions and offences contrary to the doctrine which ye have learned; and avoid them. For they that are such serve not our Lord Jesus Christ, but their own belly; and by good words and fair speeches deceive the hearts of the simple.'

"'The hearts of the simple.' That's you! And you're being deceived by a Soviet intrusion by way of the devil! That's right—communism! You say, 'But preacher, I get my news from the TV!'" The preacher paused, looked out over the congregation, slammed his fist, and screamed, "Well, sinner, I get my news from the Bible!"

Brother Babcock's wispy gray hair flopped about his head like cobwebs on a fence post. Each time he swung around, his coattails swung up before following him back to the pulpit. It was a sight to behold. Gauging from my watch and his cadence, I felt the sermon was about to reach its climax.

"Now it doesn't matter what this old preacher thinks, but it does matter what poison you're putting into your minds. The Way, the Truth, and the Life need no rabbit ears!" the preacher bellowed, as loud as I'd ever heard him.

"As long as I stand behind this pulpit..." Preacher Babcock stopped in mid-sentence to catch his breath. The poor man had been going at it for over an hour with the froth of a rabid dog. He pounded the pulpit one more time, leaned forward, and then his eyes froze on the congregation. We waited as he stood there, rigid, almost like the pulpit was propping him up. The church became hushed. Nobody moved, including the preacher. I don't know how long we sat there, but finally Brother Forester called from his pew, "Preacher, you okay?"

The sudden death of Preacher Babcock took us all by surprise. The man never smoked, drank, or caroused with any earthly temptations. He merely served the Lord right up till he went home. And what an exit it was: frozen in place, his fist on the pulpit. A massive coronary had killed him quicker than a bullet to the head could have.

We had a wonderful funeral conducted by the circuit riding preacher, Walter Harrison. Why, even the sheriff came out, although he was a practicing Methodist. Many town folks showed up, saints and sinners alike. Rupert Cranston, the town drunk, came sober; Ruby Duffy, the crazy woman with a house full of cats, came alone; and Melvin Bell, the town's noted hermit, came out. The *Forbye Telegraph* sent Calvin Tibbs to cover the service. He wrote up a lovely two-page pullout honoring the life and times of Thaddeus Wilson Babcock.

Preacher Babcock's wife, Mildred, held up well. Her son, Oliver, came over from Graceville to comfort her. Oliver had just finished with his studies at the Baptist Bible Institute, and I saw no reason why he couldn't just slide into his daddy's shoes right here in Forbye. But of course, that would be left up to the pulpit committee.

Church bylaws stated that two deacons and two at-large members should make up the pulpit committee. I knew one thing—Earl wasn't a deacon, so I had only two shots at getting him placed as an at-large committee member. You're probably wondering, "Why not you, Emma?" Well, this was before the woman's lib movement, and women didn't sit on pulpit committees. However, their husbands did. So, you see where I'm going with this, right? Everyone knew that when a preacher came "in view of a call" it didn't happen without a little pillow talk first.

I figured I had a week, maybe two at best, to get Earl polished up and spiritually presentable. Now, it didn't hurt that my granddaddy was a founding member of the First Baptist Church of Forbye, a fact I reminded the deacons of every so often. It also didn't hurt that Earl was a war veteran. That kind of thing always looks good on a resumé.

Without openly lobbying for Earl to get one of the chairs, I sent him down to the church whenever the doors were open. When the doors weren't open, he went down anyway—to mow the grounds, wash the windows, and even tidy up around the cemetery. I also figured that all the extra time he spent at the church would righteous him up a bit, so at worse, I'd get a better Earl.

One disconcerting thing was the apparent same idea coming from Nelly Dalton. Yes, Nelly. You may remember our history. Two years had passed since that day when we had the fight at the church social, and we were on speaking terms again. I won't say it was easy, but as Christians, we must forgive and move on. Anyway, Nelly sent her husband, Fred, down to the church just as much as I sent Earl.

If Earl mowed the grounds, Fred bagged up the clippings. If Fred scraped gum off the steps, Earl fetched a trash can to assist. They were quite a pair. Earl seemed almost eager to go down to the church each morning and work with Fred. It got to the point where I felt a little guilty putting him through such a holy workload; but true to his calling, Earl never complained.

Well, one day (I believe it was a Friday afternoon) Nelly and I went down to the church with some lunch for the boys. We made a lovely basket filled with cold fried chicken, potato salad, baked beans, rolls, sweet tea, and various types of homemade cookies. Nelly and I were actually getting along quite nicely. Maybe it was the death of Preacher Babcock or the newly formed friendship of our husbands that made us bond … I really couldn't say. But in any event we chatted like schoolgirls as we prepared the meal.

We arrived just before noon to find the church locked up tighter than a drum. We checked the front door, side door, and back doors—all of them—no luck. "That's strange," I said to Nelly. "Earl said they'd be dusting off hymnals all day."

"Well, they have to be here," Nelly replied. "They both walked to the church, so they can't be far. Maybe they're at the pastorium." So we headed over to the pastorium. On the way over, I thought of poor Sister Babcock and all she'd been through. Not only did she lose a husband, but also, she lost a home as well. The church graciously gave her all the time she needed to find a new place, but still the reality must have been awful heavy.

We arrived at the pastorium and found that it was vacant—no Earl and Fred—so the mystery continued. We checked the tool shed, the rose garden, the cemetery, and even looked up at the steeple in case they'd got the notion to give it a new coat of paint. This vanishing act seemed odd until we started connecting the dots.

"Fred seemed awful eager to leave this morning," Nelly observed.

"So did Earl. He barely finished his third cup of coffee before he ran out the back door," I recollected.

"Back door? Fred went out the back door, too. Do you find it peculiar that both our houses face the street that's closest to the church, yet our husbands chose to go out the back, then walk up beside the house and past the front door on the way to church?"

"Hey, wait a minute! Earl had on his rubbers, now that I think about it. I guess I paid no mind, figuring he'd be washing the church steps," I mused.

"Fred keeps his rubbers in our shed, by his fishing pole, which is just outside our back door." After Nelly said that, we looked at each other for a half second and then shouted at the same time, "They're fishing in the Baptismal Pond!"

It didn't take long for us to scurry past the cemetery and down the wooded path leading to the pond. It had rained the night before, so there was a trail of incriminating rubber-boot prints pointing the way. We heard the fellas before we saw them, or rather, we heard Earl holding court as usual, pontificating about war, President Eisenhower, and Korean conspiracies. We hid behind some brush and planned our next move.

"Can you see them?" Nelly whispered.

"Not yet." I carefully pulled back some overgrown vines. "Oh, dear Lord," I said.

"What? What is it?" Nelly asked.

"Look for yourself."

Before I tell you what we saw, I first must tell you about the Baptismal Pond. It's about the length of a football field. I wouldn't call the pond a rectangle, but I wouldn't call it round, either. It has a narrow end where the baptisms take place, and then it juts out to form a teardrop shape. Some say, and I agree, that God formed it with a teardrop from Jesus. This wasn't just any pond, and I'll give you some proof.

Forbye went through several droughts over the years. There was one particular dry spell back in '46 that shriveled up our lakes and a good part of Forbye's water supply. Farmers lost crops and family wells went dry. I can remember going to several special prayer meetings dedicated to just praying for rain.

Through it all, though, the Baptismal Pond never went down a drop. That's right, not a drop. In fact, it actually went up a few inches. Look it up; it made all the papers. We even had a scientist of some sort come up from the University of Florida. He brought all kinds of gadgets and gizmos for testing water depth. He'd row around in his little boat, sticking a pole here and there; he'd dive into the water, looking at who knows what; and then he'd pop up and scribble something on a notepad. The whole town found it quite amusing. The pond became more popular than the movies. It went on for weeks before Professor Einstein (that's the name we called him) made his report. To paraphrase his words, "I don't know why the pond is rising." Really now, I could've said the same thing for far less money and been more accurate by stating the obvious—God did it. Anyway, that's just one example of the pond's powers.

Of course, there are many others. For example, the Pentecostals have been known to sneak in from time to time and grab a few gallons.

Rumor had it that they used the water during their healing services. Supposedly, the water healed a crippled child and gave a blind man sight, but that's just hearsay. I'd never entered a Pentecostal church, with all their speaking in tongues and snake-handling. I do find it funny, though, Pentecostals stealing Baptist water. I wonder what Jesus would say about that?

On a more personal note, I was baptized in that pond, as was my entire family. And it's not just that the pond holds spiritual meaning to me; the town of Forbye itself considers our pond a divine institution commissioned by God. So, as far as I'm concerned, sacred water flows within its hallowed banks. Israel has the Holy Land and Forbye has the Baptismal Pond.

Well, I pulled back the overgrown vines to let Nelly take a look.

"Joseph and Mary!" Nelly gasped.

Earl and Fred were about twenty feet apart as they stood knee-deep in the pond. They had their hooks in the water, just waiting for a bite. Nothing unusual about that, right? Well, their plan to deceive us (their wives!) must have called for drastic measures, I guessed. Earl knew he couldn't come home soaking wet and smelling like fish—if he actually caught one—so it appeared they got the bright idea to strip down to their boxers and fish seminude. I mean, shirtless would've been bad enough, but those rascals had nothing on but rubber boots and cotton underpants—on church property—in the Baptismal Pond—with God's water—right in the middle of Jesus' teardrop!

I was as mad as the devil in sunshine, and Nelly wasn't too far behind. Seeing them frolic about in their undershorts wasn't an easy vision to erase. Earl, well, his belly jutted over his waistband with the ripeness of a full-term woman waiting for her water to break; he was a sight to behold. His co-conspirator, Fred, lacked definition around his hip area, which left his boxers in a constant state of retrieval. The fact that I saw Fred practically naked made me feel like some sort of concubine, and I'm sure Nelly felt the same way about Earl.

Nelly and I huddled up briefly to decide how to handle this indecent display of forbidden fishing. We had no doubt that the boys were skirting on blasphemy's edge. What if Deacon Humfinger, head of the pulpit committee, happened to wander up on this spectacle, or, heaven forbid, something even worse—a Pentecostal?

Well, we decided confronting them was out of the question. I mean, I couldn't approach a half-dressed man and demand he puts his clothes on, and neither could Nelly. We'd be red from embarrassment and stricken with shame. So we did something to teach those boys a lesson without losing our dignity.

We spotted their shirts and pants laid out on the prayer rock. Yes, sadly there is more to the story: they had put their clothes on the prayer rock. Preacher Babcock used to kneel at the rock and hold prayer before each baptismal service. However, Earl and Fred decided it would make a lovely hanger for their cumbersome clothes. I still get sick to my stomach just thinking about it. Anyway, the boys were so caught up in fishing they didn't notice us sneaking over to the rock. For the life of me, I'll never understand the fascination men have with fishing, but that's another story for another day. We crept through the bushes, moving slowly. The only sound was Earl's two-pack-a-day cough.

"Okay, we both make a run for it. You grab Fred's clothes, and I'll grab Earl's," I whispered. Nelly nodded, and we took off. We made it to the rock only to find two identical pair of dungarees and two tan shirts. What were the odds? We froze, neither of us wanting to touch another man's trousers.

"Which ones are Fred's?" I said through clenched teeth.

"You wash your husband's clothes. You tell me which ones are Earl's," Nelly whispered.

"What? You don't wash your husband's clothes?" I shot back quietly.

"Of course, I do, Emma. What kind of wife do you think I am?"

"You really want me to answer that?" I whispered. Keep in mind that Earl and Fred had their backs to us, but they were no more than fifty feet away from us.

"All I know is we wouldn't be here if Earl didn't drag my Fred into his sacrilegious fishing expedition," Nelly said through really clinched teeth.

"So this is Earl's fault, huh? Blame it on the veteran; I see how it is." My dander was up.

"Fred served, too."

Smirking, I retorted, "Yeah, I'm sure Fred killed a lot of Koreans in Nebraska."

"Well, Fred never jumped into a bottle."

"That's simply uncalled for, Nelly Dalton. You know Earl's been sober for two years." That was true; Earl cleaned up his act a couple of years back with help from the dearly departed Preacher Babcock.

We stared at each other. Finally, I picked up a pair of pants and a shirt and forced them in Nelly's arms. "Here," I said. "If they're not Fred's, I'll pray for forgiveness later. Let's get out of here."

Turns out I grabbed the right clothes; Earl's cigarette-laden garments were unmistakable once our clandestine activity diminished and our pulse rates subsided. Nelly and I cooled off as well. We agreed it wasn't the time or place to be angry at each other, since we had so much anger to reserve for our husbands. She dropped me off, and I waited for Earl to arrive.

I pretty much had things figured out. The fellas would notice their clothes missing and immediately be hit with shame. They'd probably think some high school kids were out doing monkeyshines and stole their clothes. Eventually they'd come to the realization that the only way home was to sneak through cow pastures and backyards. I decided to sit in my usual chair and pretend to be doing crossword puzzles when Earl walked through the backdoor.

Anticipation ate me up with each passing hour. I paced, I peeked out the backdoor, I straightened the pillows on the couch, and I did it over and over. I wore a path between the front and back doors just looking for any sign of Earl. The later it got, the madder I became.

Then I saw him. He wasn't sneaking through the back way as any man who was trying to hide his nakedness would do. No, sir: Earl Gladstone was walking right down the middle of the street with all the decorum of a tomcat. I even saw him wave to Mrs. Ryan as he came marching up the sidewalk. If I didn't see it with my own eyes, I wouldn't have believed it: Earl, fishing pole in hand, rubber boots on his feet, and military issued boxers covering up only about twelve inches of his midsection. There he pranced for all of Forbye and Mrs. Ryan to see.

I ran to my chair and acted busy with my crosswords. What would the excuse be? Some wild animal stripped him and he barely made it out alive? Maybe he gave his clothes to a hobo who was passing through town? Throughout the years, Earl had told some wild ones, but I thought this might be an Academy Award winner.

The front door swung open. I buried my head in the crosswords. *I'll let him get almost to the kitchen before I tilt my head up,* I thought. Instead, Earl shut the door and stood there. I felt him waiting for me to look up. I didn't oblige him, though, and tried to think of a four-letter word for sin. *Oh, there it is: E-A-R-L.*

Finally Earl spoke. "Emma, why did you and Nelly take off with our clothes?"

We'd been compromised. I had two choices—admit what we had done or turn it back on Earl. I'll give you a brief second to figure out which option I chose.

"Earl Gladstone, what on earth were you thinking? The sight of you two! You know, Nelly saw you shirtless and in your underpants! And think about this, Mister—I saw Fred as well," I huffed.

"Emma, please. My bathing trunks are shorter than this," Earl replied as he tugged on his boxers.

"So I guess you wouldn't mind if I went down to the store in just my girdle and underthings?" I shot back.

"Suit yourself. I'm taking a shower," he said.

"Oh, no, you're not. You're gonna stand there and listen to me. What would Jesus say if he saw you half-naked? Huh, Earl, huh?"

"I got news for you, Emma. He's seen me all the way naked," he said. "And I'll tell ya something else. He's seen you naked, too."

"Shut your mouth, Earl! Jesus doesn't look at nude women."

"I'm just saying—"

I didn't let him finish. "Well, you say it to yourself. I'm not having your nasty thoughts run around in this house," I said. "Besides, what if Deacon Humfinger saw you two out there fishing in sin?"

"You mean Hiram?"

"Yes, Earl. Hiram Humfinger, the deacon who heads up the pulpit committee."

"He did," Earl said.

"No! Don't tell me that Earl. No, he didn't," I gasped.

"Yeah, Hiram stopped by," Earl shrugged, without emotion.

"What? Hiram stopped by?" I glanced at the flower vase sitting on the coffee table. It took all I could muster to keep from grabbing it and smashing him over the head. Pardon my French, but I said, "Your fanny is in trouble now and you can kiss the pulpit committee good-bye."

"Huh," Earl grunted, "that's not what Hiram said."

"Wait. What happened, Earl? And leave nothing out. Honesty works best when it's the truth," I reminded him.

"Before we saw you and Nelly steal our clothes or after?"

"Forget me and Nelly and start with Hiram stopping by," I said.

"Yeah, but you and Nelly were so funny. I bet elephants tromp through the jungle in a more nimble state."

"So I'm an elephant, huh?"

"Didn't say that."

"Forget it. Just move on," I demanded.

"Then you two were arguing over which clothes were mine. I had to pretend to cough just so I wouldn't laugh."

"Earl, I said forget it."

Failing to choke back his laugh, Earl snorted, "Yeah, but this is funny! I glanced at Fred and his belly was shaking. I almost lost it!"

I closed my lips tight and narrowed my eyes right on him. Had that vase been in my hand, I'd be a widow writing this from prison. Earl understood the look and gathered himself.

"So Hiram came up while we were fishing," he continued. "He asked if we had any bites—you know, small talk, the weather and so forth. Just the stuff three guys talk about when they're fishing."

"Wait. Hiram fished too?"

"Yeah. Why else would he be at the pond?"

"So he fished in waders, or did he just stay on the bank?"

"Nope," Earl said.

"Earl, don't tell me Hiram stripped down to his boxers,"

"No, he didn't."

"See, Earl? That's why Hiram is a deacon and you're not," I stated.

"He stripped down to his briefs. You know, those newfangled things. I think they're called Jockeys. You need to get me a pair."

"You're lying to me, Earl. And you can go to hell for lying. You know that, right? And you've gone completely batty if you think I'm buying you a pair of those things."

"Emma, I'm not lying," Earl insisted. "I guess since you had to stick your nose where it didn't belong, I may as well tell you the rest."

"What do you mean, the rest?"

"Just listen. First of all, the pond is on private church property. It's not visible to the road, and you have to walk through heavy brush to find it. And secondly, the men of the church fish there in total relaxation."

"Men of the church? Total relaxation? What are you getting at, Earl Gladstone?"

"What you saw is how we fish."

My eyes sprang open wider than manhole covers. My mind whirled with so many thoughts, my mouth couldn't move. Then all at once, I lashed out with a series of questions.

"Earl! What kind of perverted secret society are you involved in? Who knows about this? You're telling me that all the men of the First Baptist Church of Forbye fish naked?"

"Not naked," Earl interrupted, but I was on a roll and kept going.

"Do you know children have been baptized in that water? How

long has this been going on? Who started this warped form of fishing? And what about Preacher Babcock? What would he think about all the men …men he thought were righteous and upstanding frolicking around without their britches?" I ran out of breath.

"You're making more out of this than there really is, which is exactly why we agreed to never tell our wives."

"Well, did you tell Preacher Babcock?" I huffed.

Earl hung his head. *Uh-huh, that's it; he finally feels shame,* I thought.

"It was the preacher's idea," Earl mumbled.

"Get out of the way, Earl. You're either crazy or perverted, maybe both. I've heard enough. I need to use the phone." I went to push my way past him.

"But I'm not finished with—"

"Yes, you are, Buster," I snapped. "Now out of the way!"

"At least let me tell you about Hiram. Don't you want to hear the news?"

"I said I've heard quite enough!" I picked up the phone. The women of Forbye were about to get an earful.

"Huh. Thought you'd wanna know I'm on the pulpit committee," muttered Earl.

I dropped the phone onto the receiver. Two conflicting emotions ran through me. On one hand, it seemed the devil himself had possessed every man in Forbye, but on the other hand, as queer as it sounded, the news might work to the ladies' advantage. Think about it. With Earl and every other man in the doghouse, the women would decide who the next minister of Forbye Baptist Church would be. I spent the next three hours on the phone.

Sunday morning rolled around, and I think it was safe to say the word had gotten out. When interim preacher Henry Donavan looked out at the congregation, he was met with a telling sight. All the women were seated on the left side of the church, and all the men were seated on the right, no exceptions.

The preacher opened up his remarks by saying, "I don't know what you fellas did, but today's message is on forgiveness."

I found the sermon quite boring. He didn't mention Hell, eternal damnation, or Satan one time. In fact, he didn't say anything to make the men squirm in their seats. It was funny though, because most of the men kept rubbing their necks; I supposed Earl wasn't the only one sleeping on the couch.

After service, the pulpit committee and their wives had a rather cool meeting in the fellowship hall. The men went over resumés and whittled the candidate list down to a select few. It was decided that we would spend the next four weeks on the road looking for a new preacher. Our first trip would be in the city of Ocala, which meant an overnight stay and plenty of bright lights. Hopefully, the boys could keep their pants on.

I spent most of the next week giving Earl the silent treatment. He'd come in from the farm to a cold supper and a colder shoulder. I made none of his favorites and stuck my nose in crossword puzzles the minute he walked in the door. I'm telling you, for the life of me, I could not understand men. Preacher Babcock! Of all people! There had to be a reasonable explanation, but I suwannee—men are strange creatures indeed.

One evening I saw Earl walk up the steps and I plunked down to do my crosswords. Cold tuna casserole waited for him; I planned to ignore him. However, Earl had other things on his mind when he opened the door.

"Emma, this has gone on long enough. You've made your point. How long are you going to ignore me?" he asked. "I tried to tell you the whole story last Friday, but you kept cutting me off."

I said nothing as I wrote a seven-letter word for crazy: b-e-r-s-e-r-k.

"Still not talking huh? Okay fine. I don't want you to talk. I want you to listen. This sin you and all the women think us men committed is ridiculous. You wanted to know how it started. Okay, I'll tell ya. You know my past struggles with the bottle, and you also know I haven't touched a drop in two years. Well, it's because of Preacher Babcock. He called me down one day to go fishing. Did we plan to fish in just our underwear? No. But it was a particular hot day and the preacher wanted to wade out a bit to cool off. So, we pulled off our shirts and pants and went out into the water. It was no big deal, really; we did it all the time in Korea ...but you know what? There was something about it I can't describe. The peaceful water, the calmness of the day, the soundless atmosphere ... It was like nature blending with spirituality."

I quit doing my crosswords and looked up at Earl. He didn't notice. His mind was in another place.

"So, as we stood there in the pond talking, I poured my heart out to the preacher. The demons, the drinks, the war, the gunfire, the deaths, all that stuff, well, it all came out and then disappeared. I tell you Emma, it was like that pond somehow swallowed up each trial and tribulation I'd ever faced deep into its watery soul. I wasn't giving a confession, you see. It was more like I was—was receiving an understanding or an acceptance—an acceptance that I can't change the past, with an understanding that good men fail...yeah, good men fail. I guess I never considered myself a good man. I mean, I knew God forgave, but I couldn't forgive myself...not until that day at the pond, and then everything just sort of washed away. I finally got it.

"The preacher looked at me and said, 'You know, Earl, this is how God wants to see you. You're standing before Him with nothing to hide, like Adam before his first sin.' Now I know, Emma, you women think this is silly, but the preacher went on to say he felt closest to God when he stood before Him undressed, hiding nothing from the King. So the next Sunday during the men's prayer breakfast, the preacher shared that experience with the men. And before you knew it, the pond became a spiritual gathering place. Not by appointment, but just whenever a fella needed to listen to God. I'll tell ya something else. If ever I get the urge to jump into the bottle, and I do get that urge, I just grab my fishing pole and head down to the pond. If that's a sin in your eyes, Emma, I'm sorry; but what would you rather me do, go to some bar and drink the night away? Or fish in my underwear?"

I still wasn't talking to Earl, not because I was mad, but because I was speechless. I'd never heard him utter such words, such poetic emotion from a simple farmer. Perhaps fishing in underwear was an unorthodox measure in finding spiritual bliss, but Earl was right, I would take it any day if it kept him sober.

I finally spoke, and it was the words he'd been waiting to hear: "Come on, Earl. Let's go to the kitchen, and I'll fry you up a hamburger."

That Saturday afternoon, the pulpit committee drove down to the wonderful city of Ocala, Florida. Earl and I rode with Hiram and Doris Humfinger, while Fred and Nelly went with Duncan and Martha Bennett. The trip was about one hundred and fifty miles south of Forbye, so a night's stay was required in order for the committee to look fresh and presentable to a possibly hostile congregation. Oh, don't get that look; yes, I meant hostile. Normally, churches don't take a shine to, for lack of a better phrase, "preacher stealing." I can recall several pulpit committees that we ran off in Forbye when they came calling on Preacher Babcock. I know that sounds awful, but when you have a good preacher, you want to hold on to him. If the Lord wants him to leave, he'll leave, but think about this: sometimes the Lord may want us to fight for our preacher. Remember, we Christians aren't perfect—just forgiven.

The preacher we were going to see was Alistair Colgate. He was from England, "across the pond" as they say, but he had preached in the states for ten years. According to his resumé, God called him to serve when he was a pilot flying in the Queen's Army. He wrote a brief testimony, which included a breathtaking story about surviving a dogfight over London. Of course, he gave a full account of his education level and preaching degrees, but it was his war record that grabbed the men's attention. The trip called for us to drop by his church on Saturday afternoon for a brief, informal meeting, and then follow up the next morning to hear him preach.

We drove down Fort King Street until we saw a sign that read "Union Hill Baptist Church." Pulling into the parking lot, we couldn't help but notice the church was larger than our little Forbye Baptist. I think we all had the same thought: *Is he here to sell us, or are we here to sell him?*

We parked and had barely got out of the car when a man (I assumed it was Alistair Colgate) stuck his head out the door and hollered, "Good afternoon, brothers and sisters! So kind of you to include me on your schedule. Please stride up the steps and come inside."

"What's a shed-jool?" I whispered to the group as we walked.

"It's English for schedule," Nelly said.

"Oh, schedule. Fancy those Brits. Should we curtsey?" I muttered.

Alistair Colgate met us at the door. "Come in! I hope you found the drive comfortable," he enthused. He then went to us one by one, shook our hands, and formally introduced himself. I was toward the end of the line, so it gave me the opportunity to give the preacher the once over. I first noticed his shoes could use a better shine, and his pants were a little tight for a man of the cloth. Moving up for a closer study, I detected a pencil-thin mustache that grew below a sloped nose, while randomly placed freckles dotted his narrow face. Finally, he presented himself to me.

"Good afternoon, Sister. Pleased to make your acquaintance," he said with a somewhat squishy handshake. "I'm Reverend Colgate."

"Emma Gladstone," I smiled. "And it's absolutely wonderful to meet you, Preacher Colgate."

"Pardon my directness, Mrs. Gladstone, but I prefer to be addressed as Reverend or Minister. I'll even accept Rector, if you please. I find the word 'preacher' gives a certain connotation of a traveling tent show. A preacher barks orders, whereas a studied man ministers to his flock. Don't you see?" he said.

I let go of his limp handshake. I felt my face redden with embarrassment. Mr. Alistair Colgate had one chance to make a first impression, and he chose to dress me down? Well, I had several names in mind to call him, but thought better of it. Instead I replied, "How about Mr. Colgate, for now? We wouldn't want to get ahead of ourselves, now, would we?"

Hiram Humfinger sensed my agitation and quickly moved the conversation along.

"Can we sit for a brief informal chat?" Hiram asked.

"Why, certainly. By all means, please help yourselves to a pew," Mr. Colgate answered. We all took a seat, like a jury awaiting testimony.

"First, please permit me to say," Mr. Colgate began, "that it was the most unpleasant news to hear of Reverend Babcock. I pray daily for your church in dealing with these unfortunate circumstances."

"Thanks for your concern. We're getting along as well as expected," Hiram replied. "We just have a few questions. We know you're schooled in Baptist teachings, top of your class. So, if you are called, would Forbye just be a stepping stone to a more lucrative church?"

Mr. Colgate let go a loud laugh. "Forgive my laugh, sir, but I'm sure you'll agree that 'lucrative church' is a bit of an oxymoron. However, to be forthright, I couldn't find Forbye on a map. So, if called, I'd probably reside in your quaint little town until the Lord came back, just for the mere fact that nobody could find me."

*Or we ran you off,* I thought. Perhaps it was me, but I gathered the preacher wasn't earning points.

"Okay then," Duncan Bennett said. "Tell us about your style."

"Oh, you mean the ol' fire and brimstone, that type of thing? Well, shouting at the congregation isn't my cup of tea. However, from the pulpit, I've never run away from the opportunity to give the devil a good thrashing. You know, box Beelzebub's ears," Mr. Colgate replied.

I piped up to ask, "What about men shouting 'amen' from the pews?"

"If I entertained any preference in the matter, I believe a congregation shouldn't allow themselves to be disruptive. If I'm properly genned up on the gospel, which I am, then why should I place great emphasis on members shouting approval? If I had my druthers, I'd rather forgo obstacles that would yield an unproductive harvest. Allow me to illustrate. Say from the pulpit I stated, 'Now shove off, Satan, back to the pits of hell!' and some gentleman shouted, 'Amen!' What am I to assume by his outburst? That he agrees with me? All right then. But now what about the other men in the congregation who said nothing; are they not in favor of Satan burning in the pits of hell? Of course not. I find it a slippery slope which ultimately reduces a sermon to a contest. A rudimentary behavior, if you will, that lowers the congregation to nothing more than a series of holy grunts—or maybe a sanctified growl. It reminds me of back home, and our parliament sessions where all the politicians shouted, 'Bully, bully!'" He looked at each of us before he continued, "Having said that, I appreciate the way you colonists pull yourselves into a minister's sermon. So, if I'm called as your reverend, I'll view the amen section as a welcomed nuisance and think little of it."

I think we were insulted, but we were not quite sure because we were divided by a common language—English. Mr. Colgate went on to tell other facts about himself, but honestly, I had a hard time picturing him filling Preacher Babcock's shoes. Yes, I said "Preacher."

We said gracious good-byes and left with a mixed impression. *Tomorrow's service will be interesting indeed,* I thought as we drove away.

We checked into the Ocala Motor Lodge just off Route 41. The boys, tired from driving, passed on going out for supper and decided to stay in the room and play pinochle instead. We girls really didn't mind; it gave us a chance to compare our thoughts on Mr. Colgate. Before we left, I had to give Earl a lecture about his card game. Without a godly woman in the room, sometimes his pinochle turned into poker, and we all know how the Lord feels about gambling. I kissed him on the forehead and said, "No drinking and gambling, boys," and then I left with the girls in tow.

We found a little place within walking distance from the motor lodge. Doris, Martha, Nelly, and I went inside Mamma's Italian Cuisine. While we waited to be seated, we noticed that the room was fairly busy. We talked over the sound of clinking glasses and background chatter in the smoke-filled room.

"Was it me, or did Mr. Colgate seem a little standoffish?" Doris asked.

"It wasn't you," I said. "Seemed uppity, too."

"Oh, come on ladies. He's British. That's how they are," Nelly replied, in the minister's defense.

"Right this way, ladies," announced the maître d', leading us to a large table.

I could tell right away by the red-and-white checkered tablecloths that this was an authentic Italian restaurant. Each table had a candle and a flower arrangement that created a lovely touch of ambiance. The waiter came up to announce specials and to place drink orders. Since for all practical purposes we were on a mission for the Lord, I suggested we drink grape juice to put us in the right frame of mind, an informal Lord's Supper. All the ladies agreed. "A round of grape juice," I said.

"I'm sorry, ladies, but grape juice is not on our menu," the waiter replied. "Of course, we do have a very nice selection of wine."

"Oh, no, I'm afraid wine is out of the question. Do you have anything fruity, besides wine, of course?" I asked.

"Well, our Planter's Punch has pineapple juice in it."

"Pineapple juice, how exotic," Nelly said. "How about it, girls?"

"You can never go wrong with punch," Doris chimed in. So, it was Planter's Punch for everyone.

Dear reader, I feel I must stop this story briefly. I know what you're thinking. But just to let you know, we had no intention of ordering an alcohol-laced drink consisting mostly of rum with a little sugar and juice to cover up its potency. The fact that just a few sentences above, you clearly read my statement to the waiter—when I said, "Oh, no, I'm afraid wine is out of the question"—should support my conviction to sobriety.

The waiter sat the drinks down before us, and we proceeded to order. Everyone wanted spaghetti and meatballs except Nelly. She had to have the lasagna. There's one in every crowd.

"Whew, this punch is on the sour side," Martha said. "You think the pineapple juice has gone bad?"

"It tastes sweet to me, but I don't drink pineapple juice that often," Doris responded.

"The first sip tasted funny, but it gets better the more you drink," I added.

"I'll have another one," Nelly said holding up an empty glass.

"Why, Nelly, the waiter just set the drink down," I said.

"Well, when in Rome," Nelly kind of slurred as she licked the tiny straw. Truth be known, I felt a little lightheaded. I blamed the long car ride and the peculiar encounter with Mr. Colgate.

"Nelly, listen. Listen... is it hot in here to you?" I asked.

"What?" Nelly asked. "Hey wait, Mr. Waiter!" she shouted to the waiter passing by. "Another one of them punches, but less ice." Other than feeling hot, everyone at the table was in a great mood. I reckoned the pressures of the pulpit committee had finally driven us to a silly mood.

"Have you ever heard of a preacher who didn't want to be called Preacher?" I asked anyone at the table.

"The only one I can think of is Preacher Tight Pants," Doris said and then she put her hand to her mouth like the words just slipped out. We all fell silent and then all at once let go with a multitude of giggles.

Nelly, trying to use a British accent, said, "I find the word preacher as distasteful as my mum's blood pudding."

"Bully," Martha slammed her fist on the table, and then we all followed saying, "Bully, bully, bully!"

The food arrived. "More punch, please," we all chorused.

"I must talk to the chef about his drink recipe," Nelly mused aloud. "It would make a delightful beverage for the ladies' Bible study."

"Well, Nelly, it certainly wouldn't be the first time you stole a recipe," I stated, and the table fell silent again.

After a slight uncomfortable pause, Nelly admitted, "You're right, Emma," and we all broke out in laughter. We were having such a great time.

More punch was placed on the table. Nelly grabbed her glass, held it up in the air, and said, "To Jesus." We all lifted our glasses, "To Jesus," we chimed together.

The punch flowed steadily while lips told of gossip, preachers, and men fishing naked. About halfway through our meal, we heard a drum roll, and a spotlight directed our attention to a small stage located near our table.

A gentleman stepped up to a microphone. "And now, ladies and gentleman, all the way from Miami Beach, please give a warm welcome to Dean Martini and the Ice Cubes," he announced.

A man walked out who was the spitting image of Dean Martin. In fact, Nelly yelled, "It's Dean Martin!" Of course it wasn't. But why spoil it for her? He sang all of Dean Martin's hits, and I found him to be quite entertaining. I lost track of how many punches we all consumed, but by the time the next one arrived, Nelly was ready to dance with Dean.

"I see there's a table full of beautiful ladies here tonight," Dean said as the spotlight hit our table. "I can't believe you gals couldn't find dates for the evening."

I felt flushed.

"They're at the motel playing cards!" shouted Nelly.

"Shh," I hissed. "Don't engage him."

"Playing cards instead of knocking around town with a pretty young thing like you?" Dean asked. "What kind of men do they grow in Ocala?" The audience laughed. "They're stuck in a motel looking for queens and I got four of them right here." More laughter. "What's your name, sweetheart?"

"No, Nelly. Don't," I whispered.

"Nelly," she said.

"I once knew a gal named Nelly who loved to dance. She danced so hard I lost my pants," Dean said to the room, which roared with laughter. Nelly stood up and started dancing without music. "She's ahead of us, boys," Dean said. "Hit it." And the band started playing "Mambo Italiano." Nelly grabbed a flower from the centerpiece, stuck it sideways in her mouth, and then moved somewhat suggestively around Dean Martini and the Ice Cubes. Frankly, I couldn't imagine what had come over her.

Just then, another round of punch appeared at our table.

"I didn't order this," I shouted to the waiter over a loud mambo beat.

"I know. It's from the two gentlemen over there at the bar," the waiter explained, pointing. I looked through the dimly lit dining room and observed two men. My eyes could not fully adjust to their appearance, but I did notice they were smiling. They raised their glasses as a salute. "They'd like for you and the dame up there dancing to join them," the waiter said.

I looked at Doris—she was keeping time with her fork. I looked at Martha—she was playing drums with her with breadsticks. And then I looked on stage—Nelly was on top of the piano leading the band. *I hate to be a party pooper, but we have to get out of here,* I thought. I stood up and the room suddenly went wobbly.

"Doris, I think we better leave," I managed to say.

"But the band is—"

"Doris, we have to leave now! I'll get Nelly off the piano. You and Martha pay the bill. We'll settle up later," I insisted. "Meet us outside. Just do it!"

"Emma, what's the rush?" Martha wanted to know.

"The two devils at the bar, that's the rush. They just bought us drinks, and I think they got another kind of mambo on their mind," I said.

Doris and Martha quickly understood that all the merriment involved in the night sure wasn't enough to draw us into a sordid encounter with strange men. "Oh. Yes, I see them," Doris nodded. "Okay, we'll pay the check; you get Nelly off the piano."

I moved carefully to the stage. Some who witnessed might call it a stagger, but in any event I made it onto the stage. Nelly was into the second verse of "That's Amore."

"Nelly, come down, it's time to go," I commanded. Suddenly, Dean tapped me on the shoulder. I whipped around and started swinging my big purse around in circles. Dean raised his hands up and backed away.

"We got a live one, folks!" he laughed.

Still swinging the purse, I didn't realize how close I was to the piano. Apparently Nelly was behind me trying to climb down when all of the sudden my purse stopped right on the side of her face. *Thump*! Down went Nelly—right in the middle of the horn section. The audience roared like it was part of the show, while Dean doubled over with laughter because he knew it wasn't. The band looked confused, and I was confused. I grabbed Nelly to make a somewhat dignified getaway. I'm not sure how graceful it looked, but I managed, with a wobble, to get Nelly outside to where Doris and Martha were waiting for us.

"Oh, my eye," Nelly moaned. "What happened?"

"You ran into something, dear," I said. Theoretically, I had told her the truth.

"Good heavens, Nelly! It's swollen!" Martha exclaimed.

"Let's get her back to the motel. She needs some ice," I said.

I turned Nelly around and started to head west toward our motel. Doris and Martha started to head east. "It's this way, girls," I said.

"No, Emma, it's this way," Doris corrected.

I gave a half-hearted, "Are you sure?" because to be honest I really didn't have a clue.

"Yes, this way," Martha agreed, so we all headed east. It was a very lovely evening as we ambled down the sidewalk. Okay, maybe it wasn't really ambling, because for some reason one of us would stumble every so often. But it was a lovely evening indeed. Even Nelly, with her ever-increasing shiner, seemed to be having a good time. We sang "When the Roll Is Called up Yonder" as we walked under the Ocala night sky. We were happy, we were silly, and we were the ladies of the pulpit committee rejoicing in God's love.

*Crash*! Doris ran into a lamppost.

"Doris, are you okay?" somebody asked.

"I think so, but my face is numb," she answered.

"My face is numb, too, but I didn't hit a lamppost," shrugged Martha.

"Now that you mention it, my face is numb too," I said. "Here, Doris. Let me take a look." Doris tipped her head up to the light and smiled. "Oh, honey, you've lost a tooth," I told her.

"Really," Doris said, "I did feel something sharp when I swallowed."

"You swallowed your tooth?" Nelly chimed in.

"Well, to be honest girls, I'm not feeling any pain. Hey! Can we go back and get some more punch? I need to wash my tooth down," Doris said.

"No, Doris. That punch was ninety-five cents a glass," Martha complained. "Highway robbery, if you ask me. Ninety-five cents for some sugar water and pineapple juice!"

"But it was good punch," Nelly said.

"Yes, it was good punch," I agreed.

"Yeah, good punch," Doris said.

"I know, but ninety-five cents a glass?"

"Forget the ninety-five cents, Martha. Shouldn't we be at the motel by now?" I asked. "We've been walking for blocks."

"I dunno. Where's the main road?" Martha wanted to know.

"What main road?"

We looked around and nothing seemed familiar. Perhaps we were having such a good time we passed right by our motel, or we made a wrong turn. Either way, we were lost.

"Where are we?" I asked no one in particular.

"Ocala," Nelly replied.

"Thanks, Nelly," I said.

"We musta made a wrong turn," allowed Doris.

"I don't remember making a turn," I said.

"Do you remember where our motel is?" she replied.

"No," I admitted.

"Well, okay then. So you don't remember everything, now do you?"

"You don't need to snap at me, Doris."

We started backtracking, yet the roads became even less familiar. Without knowing it, we were walking deeper into Ocala and further away from our motel. City lights that once paved the way were now absent as we toddled along in near darkness. Strange neighborhoods and barking dogs became our surroundings, and fear replaced the joy we had felt just a few moments earlier. The night seemed to wear on. *Are we destined to wander in the wilderness all night? What about those two men at the bar? Are they following us? Will our husbands find us dead in a ditch?* Those were my thoughts as the night became cold, damp, and frightening. Finally, Nelly and Doris plopped down on the wet grass. Pain had set in on their injuries and they started crying.

"We'll never make it back to the boys, and I can barely see out of my right eye," Nelly moaned. "Poor Fred, he must be worried sick."

"My mouth is killing me, and that tooth I swallowed is making me nauseous," Doris said.

"Come on girls, we need to keep moving," I said. "How about it Martha? Martha? Martha, watch out!" Martha either passed out or fell asleep; she tumbled face first onto the sidewalk.

"Oooh nooo," she groaned as she rolled over. "I think I broke my nose." Her whimpering grew louder. Although all I had was the light of the moon to assess her injury, I felt she might be right. Blood poured from her nose onto the concrete. I fumbled through my purse for a handkerchief.

I bent down. "Here dear," I said as I cradled her head and gently placed the cloth to her nose.

"Ouch!" Martha yelled.

"I'm sorry, dear, but we must stop the bleeding," I said.

So there we sat in the dark: lost, cold, and lonely. The wounded huddled around me. A black eye, a missing tooth, and a broken nose comprised the casualty list. I got the sense of how Earl must have felt in Korea—scared and longing for home. The night got deathly quiet. The dogs quit barking and the wind became still. I didn't notice at first, but through the sobs of the girls, I thought I heard something.

"Shh," I said. "Listen."

"What is it, Emma?" Nelly asked.

"It's music and singing," I replied. "Do you hear it?"

The girls managed to stop crying, and sure enough, we all heard singing. I stood up carefully in an effort not to spill Martha's head. "I see a light just up the road. I bet that's where it's coming from," I announced.

"Are you sure?" Doris asked.

"Yes! Come on, girls," I urged.

I gathered up the troops like the war hero Audie Murphy did in one of his motion picture shows, and we hobbled towards the light. I must say, with all the events that had taken place, I felt my stomach starting to sour. As a cold sweat broke out over my head, a queasy jolt rattled through my insides. *This is a heck of a time to be coming down with the flu,* I thought. Strangely though, the girls suddenly felt the same symptoms.

"I'm gonna be sick," Doris said.

"I don't know which feels worse, my nose or my stomach," Martha told us.

"I'm afraid to say it, but we all had the spaghetti and meatballs. We got a case of food poisoning," I said. "Luckily, Nelly had the lasagna."

To my left I heard a loud guttural heave. "What was that?" I asked.

"Nelly just threw up her lasagna," Martha said.

"Then it's the tomato sauce! Don't look at it, girls! Just keep moving."

As we drew closer, the music became clearer and its source became obvious. The sound was sweet gospel music coming from a church. I guessed by all the singing and shouting going on, there must be some sort of revival inside. All I knew was the Lord just threw us a lifeboat. All we had to do was negotiate our way down a small hill and make it to the front door.

"Praise God," I said with relief. "It's a church, and they'll help us home."

Caught up in the emotion, I stepped too quickly and lost my balance on the loose gravel. Before I knew it, I was sliding head first down a pitched road. Okay, maybe it was more than a small hill, because I flipped, rolled, went sideways, and then end over end. When I finally came to rest, my cheeks were covered in blood and small pieces of gravel were embedded all over my face. And then I lost my spaghetti and meatballs.

I just lay there, catching my breath, holding my stomach, and whimpering in pain. *Where did the night go wrong*? I asked myself. What a short journey it was from sipping punch and toasting Jesus to lying on the roadside and eating gravel. The girls made it down the hill and arrived at my side.

"Emma dear, are you okay?" Nelly asked. "You took a nasty spill."

"Oh, nothing that a little soap, water, and prayer won't cure," I answered. To be honest, I was in great pain, but if we were going to see this thing home, I had to be strong. "Just help me up and I'll be fine."

Back on my feet, I noticed my nylons were ripped and one of my heels had broken off during the fall. I let out a sigh and started walking unevenly towards the church.

Even in our condition, the music flowing from the church sounded absolutely beautiful. We were close enough to hear the choir singing, "What a Friend We Have in Jesus," and by the rhythm and celebration, we knew there was some serious worshipping going on.

After a short conference, we decided that Doris, as long as she didn't flash a smile, looked the most presentable. The plan was for her to slide into the back pew, unnoticed, until she could find a deacon to help us out. Hopefully it wouldn't take long.

We watched as Doris went up the church steps and pulled on the door.

"It won't open," Doris reported.

"Is it locked?" I asked.

"I don't believe so. I think it's just stuck," she said.

Inside, the church was on fire for Jesus. The windows rattled, and the building shook with praises to the King. I heard the preacher shouting over the gospel choir in a cadence like nothing I'd ever heard before. *Now this is the preacher our pulpit committee should be coming to see,* I thought as his voice kept tempo with the choir. I guessed the worship was so loud inside that no one could hear Doris pulling at the door.

"Come help me," Doris called. "I can't pull any harder."

Martha went up the steps to help. They both pulled, but no luck.

"Are you sure it's not locked?" I asked.

"Pretty sure. See, I can turn the handle, but it won't open," Doris said.

"Those two couldn't open a jar of pickles," Nelly said. "I'll go open it."

So now, Doris, Martha, and Nelly were at the church door pulling with all their might, but still it wouldn't budge.

"The door is not locked, Emma. It just won't open!" Nelly said in desperation.

"Jar of pickles," I said under my breath, as I hobbled up the steps and to the door.

The sound emanating from the chapel was bone-jarring. Jesus was praised at an unimaginable volume. I felt a bass beat course through my chest while the shouts of joy rang inside my head. I couldn't help but get the feeling that my people were on the other side of the door.

I approached the door. The music was so loud I had to shout in order to be heard.

"The door has to open," I insisted. The girls gathered around me, all pressing on the door. "Oh, you silly girls, you don't pull on it—you push on it!" So I did, and we all tumbled inside. The music stopped before we hit the floor.

I'm not very good at judging crowd size, but I'd estimate at least one hundred black folks stared with curiosity at the white women piled up on their floor. While the church remained silent, we unfurled ourselves and slowly came to our feet.

"Is there a deacon in the house?" Doris inquired, completing her mission. The shock of our interrupting their service must have worn off, because all at once several members came to our aid.

"I'm Luther Jenkins, and I'm a deacon here. Are you ladies all right?" he asked.

Another man yelled, "Somebody just gave these women a beatin'. Eddie, fetch some towels and ice!"

I tried to reassure them. "No, sir, we weren't beat up. We just need to get back to our motel; I think we made a wrong turn."

"I know that's right," someone from the congregation agreed.

A lady, nicely dressed and a little on the heavy side, looked us up and down. "My, my, my, looks like you ladies had quite an evening," she said.

"Oh dear, you don't know the half of it," Nelly replied.

"So what motel are you tryin' to find?" Mr. Jenkins asked.

"The Ocala Motor Lodge," I said.

"Oh Lordy, you gals are lost! It's a fair piece down the road, maybe eight, nine miles from here," he said.

Eddie came back with some towels and ice. We cleaned up a bit while briefly telling them our story. They seemed amused and kept asking us to repeat ourselves because they said we were incoherent. Anyway, gratefully, Mr. Jenkins said he had a pickup truck and if we didn't mind riding in the back, he wouldn't mind driving us back to our motel. Finally our prayers were answered, and we were headed for our loved ones.

The cool night and the open air refreshed me as we sat in back of Mr. Jenkins' Chevy pickup. I worried about Nelly though. Her right eye was the size of a turnip and I feared she had a concussion because she kept slurring her words. I brought it to Doris' attention. "Nelly might better go to the hospital and get checked out. Do you notice her words are slurring?"

"I was thinking the same thing about you, Emma. Your words are slurring too," she informed me.

"My words? You're batty, Doris. I'm not wording my slurs," I said.

"See, you just said, 'wording my slurs,'" Doris replied.

"Huh?"

"You've both been slurring words all night," Martha joined in, "but I didn't say anything because I thought I was hearing things since I broke my nose and all."

"Martha, I didn't understand one word you just said. It sounded like, 'youuuvv bofh bin slurping woods alllrightt, and my nooose ate it all,'" I said.

"You're swilly, Emma," Martha said.

"What? Swilly? What on earth is swilly?" I asked.

"I think she combined swell and silly. You know, swilly," Doris explained.

Mr. Jenkins pulled his pick up into the Ocala Motor Lodge parking lot. When he stopped his truck, we strangely felt like we were still moving. "Where can I find your husbands?" Mr. Jenkins asked as he walked to the back of the truck.

"Go to room number one hundred and twenty eight," I said. "Ask for Sergeant Gladstone. Tell him the troops came under enemy fire. He'll know what to do."

Mr. Jenkins shook his head and mumbled something about a crazy drunk white woman, and then left in pursuit of our husbands. I guess we caught our second wind because we decided to break out in song. I think Martha started, but soon we were all singing,

*Shall we gather at the river,*
*where bright angel feet have trod,*
*with its crystal tide forever*
*flowing by the throne of God?*

"Here come the boys. Sing the chorus louder," I urged, and we continued,

*Yes, we'll gather at the river,*
*the beautiful, the beautiful river;*
*gather with the saints at the river*
*that flows by the throne of God.*

"Emma, where have you been? And what happened to your face?" Earl demanded.

"Oh Earl, it was a dreadful set of circumstances—"

"Emma, stop," Earl interrupted. "You're gassed!"

"Huh, what?" I said.

"Doris, where's your tooth?" Hiram asked.

"In my stomach," Doris said right before she passed out.

Hiram turned to the men. "They're in no condition to explain what happened. It'll wait till morning. I'll haul Doris to the room and put on a pot of coffee." About that time, Nelly let go with the rest of her lasagna.

"Oh yeah, Earl, we all have food poisoning," I explained. "We keep having bouts with a sour stomach."

"Food poisoning, huh? A lot of that went around in Korea, but it came from a bottle," Earl said. "Now let's get you to the room and dry you out."

"Yeah, we better get 'em inside before they wake up the other guests," Fred said.

"Wait. Wait! Let's not see that English fella tomorrow. Instead I want the committee to go see Mr. Jenkins' preacher. Oh, how I'd love to call their preacher to Forbye."

"Come on, Emma. Let's go," Earl said. The last thing I remembered was Earl throwing me over his shoulder like a sack of potatoes.

At some point on Sunday, daylight hit my eyes after Earl yanked open the motel curtains. The first of several pains I felt was in my face. It burned like the devil's backyard. My foggy and pounding head tried to deduce why my face hurt. I've always been good with memory, hence this story, but at the time I was clueless. Earl sat a cup of coffee on the nightstand. Then I realized. "Oh, the committee...we got to go see Mr. Colgate preach," I said and went to get up—and then fell back down. The room spun.

"Don't think so," Earl said. "Too late, we already went."

"We?"

"Well, the sober ones—me, Fred, Hiram, and Duncan," he said. "You gals got drunk last night."

"Earl, don't be ridiculous. I remember now. It was food poisoning. Oh, my face, it's killing me."

"Still playing that card, huh?" Earl laughed. "Let me see. Do you remember how you scratched your face?"

"Well, no," I said.

"How about Nelly's black eye, Martha's bloody nose, and Doris' missing tooth? Do you remember any of that?"

"Doris is missing a tooth?"

"I hate to break the news, dear, but that bull you're feeling right now, the one that's stomping through your head? It's called a hangover."

"Earl, good heavens, no!"

"Oh yes, I've had my share of 'em," he said, struggling hard to hold back his laughter.

"All we drank was pineapple punch," I said.

"Nelly told Fred it was Planter's Punch," he replied.

"Yes, that's right, Planter's Punch."

"Oh, my little girl is not in Forbye anymore," he grinned.

"What's so funny, Earl? Can't you see I'm in pain?"

"Certainly. I know you're in pain. I've been there. But I was just thinking—oh, never mind," he said.

"Earl, you better tell me what amuses you about this situation," I demanded.

"I was just thinking, maybe when we get back to Forbye, you and the girls might need to go fishing in the baptismal pond."

"Funny, mister, real funny," I said. "Oh, my head hurts! Quit laughing!"

Earl packed the car while I drank coffee. I hadn't seen the girls since our—I hate to say it—since our bender. Most of last night was coming back to me. Oh, dear, it came back in droves: Dean Martini, the men at the bar, my handbag hitting Nelly. All of it ran through my head, which was killing me, by the way. At least I wasn't alone. I had the comfort in knowing that three other women felt the same way.

I cracked open the motel door, and the sun became my enemy. I reached for my sunglasses and tried to move toward the car, but each step brought a temple-piercing throb. Earl saw my discomfort and guided me across the parking lot. Doris, already in the backseat, sat motionless with her head resting on the palm of her left hand. I managed to slide in beside her, but said nothing. Earl got in the front passenger side and slammed the door. It felt like a bomb went off at the base of my skull. I softly placed my head against the window, and Hiram started the car. I glanced out the window to find Nelly and Martha sitting in the other car. Though we all wore sunglasses, I felt my eyes meet Nelly's. We stared at each other until Hiram plunked the gearshift down, and we drove away.

The next few days I hid from embarrassment and prayed for forgiveness. How could I have been part of a drunken stupor? As part of the pulpit committee, no less! Was it a sin? I hoped ignorance of the intoxicating punch would excuse me from such a transgression, yet I was troubled by one particular Bible verse on the topic: *Envyings, murders, drunkenness, revelings, and such like: of the which I tell you before, as I have also told you in time past, that they which do such things shall not inherit the kingdom of God. (Galations chapter 5 verse 21)*

Paul stated very clearly that drunkenness is no better than murder. When I first read that, I thought, *Oh, Lord, what have I done?* And then I noticed the other sins: envy and reveling. For some reason, Nelly Dalton came to mind—*envy and reveling.* Maybe committing just one out of the four sins mentioned wasn't so bad after all. I also knew Earl had been forgiven for countless nights filled with drunken debauchery, so I was pretty confident that one mishap by an otherwise godly woman would be forgiven and I would still be granted entrance into the kingdom of God.

After many hours of deep reflection and soul searching, I decided to rededicate my life to God by serving Him through the pulpit committee. Who knows; maybe I needed the fuzzy haze from a drunkard's view before my eyes could see clearly.

The pulpit committee met on Friday. This was the first time we were all together since that evil trip to Ocala. The meeting was held at Doris Humfinger's house, and I must say, I was a tad uneasy facing everyone. My wounds had practically healed; just a few scabs were left on my cheeks, so I looked mostly presentable when Earl and I knocked on the Humfinger's door. Doris greeted us with the biggest smile on her face.

"Well, what ya think, Emma?" Doris asked and then grinned to show her teeth.

"Why, Doris, they look lovely," I said.

"You think so? The dentist figured it was easier to pull out all my teeth than to put one back in, so I got a new set of choppers. I didn't even have to order them. The doc had these stuck back in his desk. They were made for Tess Jacobs, rest her soul, but she had that combine accident the day before her fitting," Doris said.

"Oh, yes, poor Tess. You know I told her not to run that combine with her apron on. I can't believe it's been a year," I replied. "Are we the first to arrive?" I looked into an empty room.

"So far. Have a seat, and I'll go fetch Hiram," Doris said.

As Doris left the room, Earl whispered to me, "I've seen smaller teeth on a horse."

"Hush, Earl, or you'll need a trip to the dentist," I whispered back. "But you're right."

"I'm just saying, I hope she doesn't walk by a glue factory, 'cause they might try to lasso her in."

"Okay, Earl. I get it. Her dentures are big," I said with a slight chuckle.

Nelly and Fred Dalton knocked on the door, with Martha and Duncan Bennett right behind them. Nelly's black eye was now yellowish gray and a little bloodshot. When Martha stepped inside, I noticed her nose pointed a bit off kilter, but otherwise appeared normal. Few words were spoken between pregnant pauses and uncomfortable forced smiles. Luckily, Hiram came into the room and took control. He led off with a prayer and then cleared the air.

"Does anyone outside this committee know what happened in Ocala?" Hiram asked.

All the women shook their heads no. Men, of course, are tightlipped by nature, so I'm sure the question was directed to the wives.

"Okay then. I've come to the conclusion that the Ocala trip should be forgotten. It doesn't serve the First Baptist Church of Forbye to let this get out and fester in our congregation. What's done is done. We go forward and never speak of Ocala again," Hiram said.

It felt like a blast of spring air went into the room. All week I had carried the burden of being church gossip. I had worried that Hiram was calling us there to say he would bring our sins before the church. And let me tell you, there was no telling what Rose Carter would do if she had that information. If Rose knew, then not only would the whole town of Forbye know, but the whole northern border of Florida would know. I doubt I could find a place to worship without humiliation until I reached Valdosta, Georgia—Rose was that connected. Since Hiram decided to keep our little secret mum, I finally let a week's worth of air out of my lungs. *Our secret.* It sounds so shady, doesn't it?

Hiram went over the itinerary for Sunday. We would drive over to Lake City and hear Preacher Gavin McGreevy. After the service, the committee would take the preacher out to lunch, probably a fried chicken place, as a get-to-know-you dinner. Thankfully, an overnight stay wasn't in order, and we could rest comfortably and *sober* in our own beds. (I can't believe that I, Emma Gladstone, just wrote that last sentence!) The meeting adjourned, and we all left feeling much better than when we arrived.

The next evening, instead of doing my usual crossword puzzles, I came up with the idea of a Preacher scorecard; and if you, dear reader, ever find yourself on a pulpit committee, might I suggest you do the same. It will come in handy when stacking preachers up against each other. For instance, I grade a preacher on fire, brimstone, and Heaven-to-Hell ratio. I'll explain because it's really not all that complicated. Below, you will find my scorecard on Jeremiah Carmichael. Though you haven't met him yet, you soon will. Take your time to study it, and then I'll explain the grading system.

Jeremiah Carmichael's Preacher Scorecard

Pounded the pulpit ☑ ☑ ☑ ☑ ☑
Raised voice for effect ☑ ☑ ☑ ☑ ☑
Shook his Bible ☑ ☑ ☑ ☑
Amens from the congregation ☑ ☑ ☑ ☑ ☑ ☑ ☑ ☑ ☑ ☑ ☑ ☑ ☑ ☑
☑ ☑ ☑ ☑
Read from the book of Revelations ☑
Told the congregation we were going to hell ☑
Referenced eternal damnation ☑ ☑ ☑
Referenced the devil, Lucifer, or Satan ☑ ☑ ☑ ☑ ☑
Referenced sins of the flesh ☑ ☑
------- Heaven/Hell ratio----------
Said the word Heaven ☑ ☑ ☑
Said the word Hell ☑ ☑ ☑ ☑ ☑ ☑ ☑ ☑ ☑ ☑ ☑ ☑ ☑ ☑ ☑ ☑ ☑ ☑
☑ ☑ ☑ ☑ ☑

I rate fire and brimstone on a point system. Each check mark is worth ten points, with the exception of reading from the Book of Revelations—that's worth thirty points. So, simply add up Preacher Carmichael's points, and you'll find he scored four hundred sixty points on his fire and brimstone portion of the scorecard.

Now, the ratio portion is a bit more complicated. A perfect score would be at least five mentions of Heaven with matching references to the other place. So, if a preacher said "heaven" six times and "hell" six times, he met the quota of at least five each and matched an equal number. This would earn the preacher one hundred additional points. Simple, right? However, as we know, not all preachers are perfect, so we must deduct from one hundred. Look up to Jeremiah Carmichael's scorecard, and you'll find he did not meet the five "heaven" mentions quota. The penalty is minus twenty points. You'll also find that Preacher Carmichael did not reference the two equally. Simple math deduces he was overdrawn by twenty in the inferno department. For each debt, the preacher will be deducted two points. So, for his ratio, Jeremiah Carmichael had to have forty points deducted.

Heaven/Hell ratio: 100
Quota penalty: -20
Debts: -40
Total points: 40

From the example above, take the forty point total and add it to the fire and brimstone total.

Fire and brimstone: 460
Heaven/Hell ratio: + 40
Total Preacher points: 500

Now you're up to speed, so later in the story when I reference a preacher's grade, you'll know exactly how I reached this conclusion.

Sunday came faster than expected, and we had a lovely morning drive over to Lake City. Earl drove this time, and Hiram and Doris rode with us. The feeling of renewal occupied the air, leaving us all giddy with the spirit. Duncan, Martha, Fred, and Nelly went in the other car, and I'm sure they felt the same way. Our little convoy motored down Highway 47 like two chariots of fire guided by God. Now all we had to do was find Elijah. After a couple of lefts and a few rights, we found the church. The sign out front read "Gwen Lake Baptist Church," and Earl pulled the old Dodge into the parking space. The building looked about the same size as ours, nothing intimidating. I just hoped the preacher liked to be called "Preacher."

As we walked into the chapel I felt the room drop twenty degrees. Instead of the normal warm reception a church member bestowed upon a visitor, we were greeted with icy stares and old ladies poking their husbands' ribs. Clearly word was out: we were the pulpit committee. To make matters worse, the only vacant pew was right up front, which made for an awkward parade down the middle of the aisle. We tried to slide into the pew like it was just a normal Sunday service, but I knew we were among lions. I prayed for the courage of Daniel and said under my breath, *"Thy God whom thou servest continually, he will deliver thee." (Daniel chapter 6 verse 16)*

We waited as the pianist played softly. Two gentlemen sat side by side on a small pew just behind the pulpit. Having never met Preacher McGreevy, I assumed he was one of the two men, but which one? Both men were relatively the same age, mid-thirties I guessed. However, their looks went in different directions. The first man was plain, with black-framed glasses, nothing odd or peculiar about him. He seemed to look the part of a preacher—full head of hair, adequately dressed. However, sitting next to the other fella he appeared disheveled, almost unappealing. Glancing back to that other man, I found him too good-looking for a preacher. Call me old-fashioned, but preachers need a touch of ugliness to remain humble. This man belonged on the silver screen, not behind a pulpit. His face carried exquisite features—striking blue eyes, sparkling white teeth, and a jaw line that could have been lifted from a quarry. I'm sure most women followed his lightly tanned skin as it slipped underneath a finely pressed collar. His flawless suit may have tried, but it could not contain an icebox chest and shoulders so wide they seemed like they were in different time zones. I imagined his sermons would be a hard listen because your eyes would use up all your senses.

*Please, Lord. Don't let the good-looking man be the preacher,* I prayed silently. Nelly turned to me and whispered, "I hope the good-looking one is the preacher."

The mystery was soon solved when the fella in black-framed glasses approached the pulpit and led the congregation in "Are You Washed in the Blood?" I'd never heard Nelly sing louder nor smile brighter as she gazed upon the newly revealed Preacher McGreevy.

We sung two more hymns, and when the ushers took up offerings, Earl placed fifty cents in the plate before we all settled in to hear the sermon. I pulled out my scorecard and placed a mint in my mouth.

"What's that?" Nelly whispered.

"A mint. You want one?"

"No, the paper. What are you doing?"

"Oh, it's my scorecard," I explained.

"Scorecard?"

"Good morning! It's so nice to see all of your smiling faces," the handsome preacher said.

I whispered to Nelly, "I'll tell ya later," but she was already in a trance. Refusing to let appearances persuade me, I carried out my due diligence by keeping my head down and eyes fixed on my scorecard. I purposely wouldn't look at the preacher. This wasn't a beauty contest; preaching was and always will be a soul-winning contest.

I kept fairly busy checking off my card. It was amazing what I picked up on without a view. I heard pages flop, so I gave him a check for a Bible shake. Detecting fist pounding was much easier, and I didn't miss one. There were four, to be exact. I was in total tune with the message by using only my ears as receptacles. On the other hand, Nelly had that same fixed stare throughout the service, but I doubt she heard a word.

It was quite a sermon! That good-looking fella did know how to preach, but my fear remained tethered to my intuition. *No one looks that good and speaks that well. There has to be an unforeseen fault somewhere between his thick, dark locks and golden tongue,* I thought. After the last "amen," I did a quick tally of the numbers and scribbled a few notes on my scorecard while Nelly dabbed at her forehead with a dime-store kerchief.

Hiram went up to say a brief word to the preacher, while the rest of the committee tried to slip out the side door. We'd have plenty of time to socialize at the restaurant; avoiding a confrontation was first and foremost on our minds. Well, Nelly forgot her pocketbook on the pew. Imagine that—Nelly unable to concentrate on her belongings because of a mesmerizing spell induced by a handsome preacher! Anyway, I returned with Nelly to scoop up her purse when a frumpy old lady accosted us between the pews.

"Where are you from, dear?" she asked me.

"Forbye."

"Forbye? Never heard of it," she stated. "Looking to change your membership, are you?"

"Oh, no. Just came over for service," I said.

"You're part of that pulpit committee, aren't you?"

"Well—"

"Forbye, huh? And you think you can waltz right in here and steal our preacher to a hayseed town that's not on a map? I mean, Miami, maybe even Tampa, but Forbye?"

Careful not to speak unkindly, I said, "First off, God doesn't steal. And for your information, I wouldn't live in any other town. On the way to your church we passed by three bars and one kit-cat club, something you'd never find in Forbye! Let's go, Nelly. I'm allergic to pompousness, and I feel a sneeze coming on!" We left without looking back. The woman kept yapping about Lake City like it was Ocala. Please. I've tasted those lights, and Lake City was no Ocala.

We waited in our cars until Hiram came out. Most of the committee was impressed with Preacher McGreevy. Nelly wanted to call him on the spot, even though we hadn't officially met with him. I sensed Duncan liked him, too. And who could tell about Earl. But as for the other two ladies, you'd think John the Baptist just preached a sermon.

"He wants to go to a Chinese place up the road," Hiram said as he approached the cars.

"Chinese? On a Sunday?" I questioned.

"Oh, how lovely," Nelly said. Of course, the preacher could've asked for a Spam sandwich with a side of dirt, and Nelly would have said, "Oh, how lovely."

"Well, the preacher doesn't want to eat in town. Too many parishioners eat at the fried chicken joint, and it wouldn't look right," Hiram told us.

"I suppose so," I conceded, going to the car door.

Just then, Earl pulled me aside. "Chinese—I don't know if I can do it, Emma," he worried.

"Oh, honey, it'll be fine. They're not Korean."

"Well, I don't like it. Plus, I had my heart set on chicken," he said.

"Tell ya what. Be a good boy, and I'll fry you some chicken when we get home," I soothed.

Earl said nothing and continued to say nothing all the way to the restaurant. We parked right behind Fred's car. I don't think our vehicle came to a complete stop before Nelly pulled open our passenger side door.

"Hiram! I just thought about it. Brooksville needs a preacher as well. We can't lose him. Don't wait for the main course. Make him an offer over eggrolls!" Nelly commanded.

"You know it doesn't work that way, Nelly," Hiram said as the preacher pulled his car into a space beside us.

Gavin McGreevy slid out from behind the wheel and, mercy me, what a good-looking man! I know I've already told you that, but my heavens, up close this man was breathtaking. Think of Ronald Reagan, but better looking. And he was Irish, too. *My goodness, I sound like Nelly*, I thought. *Forgive me, Lord.*

Preacher McGreevy approached the men as they stood huddled in a semicircle. He stuck his hand out to Fred, and just before their hands made contact, Nelly slid in between them and intercepted the preacher's hand. "What a fabulous sermon, Reverend McGreevy. I'm Nelly Dalton."

"Ah, pleased to meet you, Sister Dalton. This is my wife, Ju—"

"You will absolutely love Forbye," Nelly interrupted. "We're only a few hours from Atlanta. Is that where you bought this suit?" Nelly brushed her hand down his coat sleeve.

"Well, ah, my wife Ju—"

"You know the railway runs right through Forbye," Nelly interrupted again, "so we get daily mail service."

The beautiful and patient woman to the preacher's left had heard enough. She stepped in. "I'm June McGreevy, Reverend McGreevy's wife." She stepped closer to Nelly and grabbed her hand; it was white glove on white glove, eye to eye. "I order the Pastor's suits from JC Penney's, and it doesn't matter if we like Forbye or not because wherever *He* leads, *we'll* go."

"So, everyone ready for some Chinese?" Hiram blurted out, with a quick change of subject.

On the way in, the rest of us introduced ourselves, although Earl just sort of grunted when he shook the preacher's hand. It wasn't out of rudeness, mind you, but from distraction. Earl was nervous about the restaurant.

"Table for ten," Hiram said to the man just inside the door.

"Ah, yes, very good. One moment please," the man said, and then barked out orders in Chinese to another man. The restaurant was half full and we were the only guests waiting in the reception area.

After a short wait, the man came back and led us to our table. I must be honest with you—I had never experienced Chinese food. I'm a grits and gravy gal. Line me up a plate of turnip greens and cornbread and I'll sing for my supper, but as we walked through the dining room I didn't see anything that resembled my momma's cooking. I saw noodles mixed with odd-looking vegetables on someone's plate. Another plate had orange goo smothering something brown with eyes. Suddenly, I felt Earl's pain.

We all circled around three tables that had been pushed together. Preacher McGreevy and his wife sat down. Nelly went right to the preacher's other side and grabbed the chair.

"Hold on, Nelly," Fred ordered and then grabbed his wife by her shoulders and led her to the other end of the table. "Sit down here with the rest of the gals; let the committee sit by the McGreevys." Nelly pouted for a good ten minutes.

A Chinese fella dressed in a white smock came to our table. Without asking he started filling up a small cup that was in front of me. "Hold on," I said. "Is there any alcohol in that stuff?"

"No, just tea, hot tea," he answered.

The McGreevys gave me a quizzical look. They were probably thinking I was the church lush. The committee, however, knew my concern—I didn't want another Planter's Punch surprise, Chinese style. Anyway, the waiter continued and then went to each place setting, smiling and pouring his concoction into our cups. I glanced across the table at Earl. His head was down, avoiding eye contact with the Chinese waiter. About the time Earl had his cup filled, he lifted his head and said rather loudly, "Ballee, tung shuden ta' pal!"

Everyone looked at Earl, including the waiter.

"Ballee, tung shuden ta' pal!" Earl shouted louder.

"Sorry, I not understand," the smiling waiter said.

"Forget it," Earl mumbled.

Within the span of about thirty-seconds, I'm sure the McGreevys thought the Gladstones and the town of Forbye were completely off our rockers and nuttier than Christmas fruitcake. Throw in Nelly and her wild imitation of Mae West, and Doris, who had a face more suited for the fifth race at Churchill Downs, and it was a wonder the McGreevys didn't run out of that restaurant as fast as they could. But to the contrary, they didn't. In fact, they were at ease talking to us during a nearly two-hour lunch. We stayed there so long, gabbing, sharing testimony, and laughing, that I was hungry again by the time we left.

The committee found out that the preacher was truly a servant of God. Forbye, Lake City, or Salt Lake City, as far as he was concerned, didn't matter to him. He prayed and the Spirit led, pure and simple.

We left the restaurant, and while we were walking to our cars, the preacher said he wanted to tell us one more thing. Naturally, that gave Earl a chance to light a cigarette. (The man never missed an opportunity to prop his foot on a bumper and enjoy his favorite pastime.) We gathered around our dusty cars and listened to the preacher. "I would like to share with you something that happened the day Reverend Babcock passed away. I'm not telling you this to persuade you into calling me as your pastor. I'm telling you this because I'm willing and ready to follow the Lord," he said, and then drew his wife close to him. "I should say, *we're* ready," he continued. "That morning I was praying in my study when an overwhelming emotion came to me. Now, I'm not certain enough to say it was a vision, and yet, I believe that's what I had. At first, I felt a strong spirit in the room, and then a subtle but clear voice telling me to prepare for a new calling. I wanted to deny it. I mean, leaving Lake City was the last thing on my mind. I'm happy here. My wife and children love this place. I guess you could say I knew better than God when it comes to serving Him."

We all let out an uncomfortable chuckle. "However," the preacher continued, "I went on and delivered the sermon without any thought of my morning prayer. Suddenly, right before the Invitation, my soul felt pain and grief for a distant congregation. Somewhere in my mind I knew a flock just lost a minister."

"That's about the time Preacher Babcock passed," Hiram said.

"I figured that out, Hiram, when we spoke a few days later," Preacher McGreevy said.

Okay, as visions go, that was pretty impressive. I'm not saying the preacher was lying; in fact, I believed him. Still, this was all too perfect in what was now a spooky way. For the record, the devil has been known to swindle the most righteous men. Of course, in Nelly's mind it confirmed her belief that God wanted her to have a good-looking preacher.

We said our good-byes and Hiram told the preacher we would be in touch. Something had been bothering me since lunch, and once I knew the McGreevys were out of earshot I turned to Earl. "What on earth was that gibberish you shouted at the waiter?" I asked.

"You mean 'Ballee, tung shuden ta' pal'?"

"No, I mean, 'How much for eggrolls?' Of course, I mean ballee tung whatever you said," I huffed.

"Oh, that's Korean for 'Quick, look behind you!'"

What a day it was: the perfect preacher giving a perfect sermon to Earl—the perfect idiot.

The next week the committee went to Jasper, Florida. It was just a short drive, maybe two hours, out on Route 6. The preacher's name was Jeremiah Carmichael, and he preached at Grace Baptist Church. Having learned our lesson from the previous week, we decided that each couple would enter the church separately, at five-minute intervals, in hopes of looking like average visitors. Anyway, that was the plan.

Our two cars pulled into a sandy, half-filled parking lot. A short, round man stood on the edge of the driveway, smiling and waving us over.

"Well, so much for going unnoticed," Hiram said as he drove over to the man.

Hiram rolled down the window and the man stuck his head inside. "I didn't recognize the car, so y'all must be from the pulpit committee," he said.

"Well, ah, we're from Forbye," Hiram stammered.

The man grinned, "What about the other car? They with you?"

"Yes, they're with us," admitted Hiram.

"Good, good. I'm Homer Vaughan; I'm in charge of the reception. Looks like your committee has, what, eight members?" he said as he counted heads.

*In charge of the reception?* I thought.

"That's right," Hiram confirmed as we poured out of the two cars.

"Hey, Larry, we got eight of 'em," Homer shouted to a man by the door. "Rope off a pew!"

Larry nodded and went inside. "We got coffee and doughnuts for y'all in the fellowship hall and a place for you ladies to freshen up. Come with me." Homer beckoned and, somewhat dazed, we followed. I'd never heard of a committee to welcome a pulpit committee, yet that appeared to be the case.

"Too bad 'bout your preacher, but I tell ya this, there ain't a better man than Jeremiah Carmichael. He'd make a right fine preacher for y'all over at Forbye."

"If we call him," Hiram said.

"Right, right, if you call him." It seemed almost an afterthought.

Nelly piped up and said, "We heard a wonderful sermon last week from Preacher McGreevy."

You'd thought Homer had run into a wall because he stopped while we all kept walking. "You know about McGreevy, do ya?"

"Sure do," Nelly said. "Delightful man; delightful indeed."

The blood left Homer's face; he nervously tugged at his necktie. His casual and friendly demeanor suddenly turned into a hurried and gruff behavior. "Go right inside," he barked, pointing to a door. "Help yourselves to coffee, and I'll go get Preacher Carmichael." Then he was gone.

We found ourselves in a small room with metal folding chairs, a pot of coffee, and a table full of doughnuts.

"You see what's going on," Nelly said. "They want Preacher McGreevy!"

"Just hold on, Nelly," Hiram said. "Whatever their interest, it isn't our concern."

"Hiram," Nelly interrupted, "we need to get out of here, right now—right now, I'm telling you—and bring Preacher McGreevy in view of a call."

"Fred."

See, in those days an out of control wife was neutralized by her husband. Hiram had been getting an earful from Nelly since she first laid eyes on the handsome Preacher McGreevy, and he'd finally heard enough. Fred took his cue.

"Nelly," Fred stated firmly, "we are here to listen to Preacher Carmichael. If you'd rather go sit in the car, fine, but not another word 'bout Preacher McGreevy. Forbye needs a preacher and the committee will decide—a committee of four: Hiram, Duncan, Earl, and me. Understood?"

"I suppose so," Nelly grumbled, and then clicked her tongue against her teeth.

"Look, we have a serious job to do here. Not that I don't appreciate the input you ladies give us, but we can't allow ourselves to draw any conclusions that would undermine our purpose or impugn the integrity of this committee. We stick to the plan, and God will give us the preacher we *need,* not the preacher we *want*. And believe me there is a difference," Hiram said.

"I got a question," Earl chimed in.

"Shoot, Earl," Hiram said.

"Can I get a doughnut?" God bless my Earl. He'd been thinking about those doughnuts since Homer said the word. Well, just about the time Earl bit into a cruller, a man opened the door and bounded through it like it was an obstacle that was merely a nuisance. He strutted to us, attacking each step as if to leave behind a trembling wake.

"Carmichael, Jeremiah Carmichael," he boomed. "Which one of you fellas is Hiram?"

Preacher Jeremiah Carmichael was built like an English bulldog. His flat nose commanded a wide face. Bushy eyebrows jutted over his droopy eyelids, which barely exposed dark, round pupils that looked wild and menacing. His shoulders pressed forward as an imposing gesture even when he stood at ease. And the man's voice—I suwannee, I'd never heard a deeper tone travel through vocal cords.

Hiram stepped forward. "I'm Hiram Humfinger, head of the pulpit committee."

"Good to meet ya, Hiram," said the preacher, slapping Hiram on the shoulder. Hiram went sideways.

"Who else we got here?" Preacher Carmichael looked at us and then proceeded to shake the living daylights out of all our arms. It started with a hard squeeze to the hand, and ended with a violent vibration up to the shoulder; nothing was gentle. After the physical assault he went verbal at about ninety miles an hour.

"I only got ten minutes before my preaching starts, so I'll be brief. How many does Forbye run in Sunday school?"

"Well, ah, about seventy, maybe seventy-five," Hiram said while rubbing his shoulder.

"Before the first year is out, I'll double it," Preacher Carmichael said. "What's your annual budget?"

"Ah, well ..." Hiram hedged.

"Forget it," Preacher Carmichael waved him off. "I'll double that too. I have a reputation for filling the seats and stuffing the plate. Take the Catholics, for example. Most of them are going to hell because they don't fear God. Christ is an afterthought in their religion. They pray to Mary, have a saint for this and a saint for that, sprinkle some water, and eat a wafer—I challenge you to find one of them that is saved! And none of them feel guilty about anything as they drink their wine and bingo their brains out. Well, Brother, I'm here to put the guilt back into Christianity. I mean, what's the point in going to church if you don't feel guilty? Baptist preachers have had it too easy for too long as far as I'm concerned. We've become nothing more than Catholic priests with wives. Love and forgiveness is all fine and well for some people, but you see, I use God as a weapon; nothing empties a sinner's wallet better than the wrath of God. I supply that wrath. God gave me a gift; I can make a sweet little old lady feel guilty about an overdue library book. And trust me, my brethren—hell is filled with sweet little old ladies."

Right then and there it hit me: Homer and the congregation of Grace Baptist Church were frightened to death of Jeremiah Carmichael. They were running him out of town by letting him believe he was leading a parade.

Preacher Carmichael stood over us. His abrasive behavior made sandpaper feel smooth. The only one not cowering in his seat was Earl as he chomped on another doughnut. "Well, I must go prepare for my sermon, and y'all will stay for dinner on the grounds." He slapped Hiram on the shoulder and stomped out the door like a bulldog sniffing out gravy.

We gathered ourselves and walked over to the church. Along the way we passed several congregants, and I noticed one odd thing—they all had a strange glaze in their eyes. "These people are brainwashed," Earl commented. "We freed a prison camp in Korea one time, and all our boys had this look. For two weeks, we had to feed 'em hot dogs and tell 'em ball scores from home just to get the color back into their eyes."

"I bet Preacher Carmichael's got them hypnotized," Nelly said.

"Oh, Nelly, you've been listing to 'Beyond Midnight' on the radio again, haven't you?" I chided. But to tell you the truth, God did place an uneasy feeling in my heart. Something just wasn't right.

"Well, we have to hear the preacher. That's why we came, but we'll slip out as soon as the last amen is said," Hiram promised.

Homer, apparently recovered from the McGreevy incident, greeted us at the front door, all smiles. "We have a pew reserved for y'all. Larry will usher ya in."

Several members were in the vestibule and formed what would best be described as a reception line. We shook hands and said pleasantries, but it was odd, to say the least. Nothing made sense: a pouncing preacher who liked to threaten members, a church all too eager to welcome a pulpit committee, and the zombie-like look on every member's face. I wasn't sure if we were in Jasper or on Jupiter. Larry ushered us down to the front row, but not before we waved, smiled, and gestured to each church member. Honestly, I felt like the newly crowned queen of Forbye's annual Watermelon Festival.

Dear reader, I will not trouble you with Preacher Carmichael's sermon. For details you can refer back to his scorecard I gave as an example. However, I will throw in this caveat—I felt his "amens" were forced by a willing congregation, which obviously skewed his overall score. In addendum, three people went forward during the invitation. Normally I would say, "Praise God," but under the circumstances, I concluded that they were plants, merely for show.

When someone who went by the name of Brother Harris said the last amen, the church suddenly became an obstacle course to the parking lot.

"Y'all will stay for dinner?" an elderly woman asked us. She seemed sweet, little, and old. I wondered if Preacher Carmichael thought she was going to Hell.

"Why sure they're staying," Homer assured her, seeming to appear from out of nowhere. The man had an odd talent to appear and disappear at the drop of a hat. Spooky.

"Well, it's a long drive back to Forbye," Hiram said. "I think we better get going."

"Get going? Not until ya hear the tribute we got planned for Preacher

Carmichael, and maybe we can close this deal before Ruth Johnson's peach cobbler gets cold. What d'ya say?" Homer persisted.

"We really need to get on back to Forbye," Hiram insisted.

"Oh, don't be ridiculous. We can't let ya leave on an empty stomach," Homer countered. "The deacons here will escort y'all to the fellowship hall."

"But—" Hiram said.

"Now look," Homer spat, as his eyes went spirally. "You will break bread with Preacher Carmichael. It's your duty as pulpit committee members!" Then five men surrounded our pew. One of them, who answered to the name Junior, (I'd hate to see how big Senior was) pointed to a side door as they moved us along. The men didn't speak, but they gave the look that clearly announced, "Follow us and nobody gets hurt." No longer was I the Watermelon Queen waving to my subjects; now I was the subject apparently waiving my rights as a free individual. Hostages! That's right; I felt we were being held hostage until we agreed to take Preacher Carmichael with us. Well, I was fairly sure Earl could take on one of them, maybe even two. But that left three for Hiram, Duncan, and Fred, and I'm afraid to say that would not have been pretty, being our boys were on the doughy side and probably didn't have one spine between them.

We all pressed together and moved slowly down the aisle. Nelly, whiter than linen sheets, seemed faint. The whole group, with the exception of Earl, was in a panic. Thanks to the Koreans, this wasn't Earl's first prison march. "Play along with me," Earl whispered. God bless the army—Earl had a plan.

"Hey, fellas," Earl said to the men, "the committee needs to go over some notes before we forget what excellent points Preacher Carmichael made during his sermon. You got a quiet room we can borrow?"

"Yes," I agreed. "It was a lovely sermon. My husband is right, I want to make sure the group is ready to call Preacher Carmichael or I'm not leaving."

"Call Preacher Car—" Nelly said right before I jabbed her in the ribs.

"Well," Junior said as he looked around, "Brother Homer did want y'all to come directly to the fellowship hall, but if you're this close to calling Preacher Carmichael, I guess a few minutes won't hurt." Junior opened up a door just off the main sanctuary. We went through it and then the door locked behind us. Yes, the door locked behind us.

Chaos consumed the room—everyone talked at once. "What are we going to do? I'm scared. We're trapped. This is weird. I can't breathe," we muttered collectively until Earl brought order.

"Quiet," he said. "Stay calm, and we'll get through this. Hiram, you ever hit a man?" Hiram shook his head no. Earl looked at the other men. "Fred? Duncan? How 'bout it? Ever been in a fight?" Both men shook their heads no.

"I have. Remember the church social?" Nelly offered.

"Not now, Nelly. This isn't a picnic. It might get ugly if we don't play it right," Earl murmured as he looked out a nearby window. "Just as I figured—they got a guy guarding our cars. Okay, we can't fight our way out of this. That means we need a diversion."

Watching Earl in control reminded me why I married the man. While the other husbands were scared of their shadows, Earl was cool, calm, and handsome. He went to the back of the room and found a small window overlooking an alley. "It'll be a tight fit, but I think it will work," he said after sizing it up. "Nelly, you, Fred and me are gonna climb out the window, and here's what we're going to do."

"I'm not going through that little window," Nelly said.

"Do you want our church to call Preacher Carmichael so you can get hypnotized?" Earl asked.

"Okay. I get it. I'll go."

"Now," Earl continued, "take off your hat, let your hair down, and loosen up a few buttons on that blouse."

"Earl Gladstone, I'm a married woman, and it's Sunday!"

"You're just gonna love Preacher Carmichael," Earl reminded her.

"Oh, alright, fine," Nelly sighed as she flipped off her hat and shook her hair out until it fell on her shoulders. "But what does this have to do with your plan?"

"Here, take a cigarette, and put on sunglasses. You gotta look unfamiliar to the man guarding our cars," Earl told her.

"Why?" she asked.

"Because you're gonna flirt with him while Fred and me jump into our cars."

"Flirt with him? I don't know how to flirt," Nelly blushed. In unison, the rest of us cleared our throats.

"Right, I got it. I know. Preacher Carmichael will hypnotize me," she said. "Fine."

"Now quick, men take off your neckties and tie them together making a long rope. Doris and Martha, I need ya to stand in the back of the room by this window. Hiram and Duncan, y'all lay the rope across the doorway, And, Emma, you look out the other window. As soon as you see Fred and me start up the cars, signal Doris and Martha to scream—and girls, you scream as loud as you can, 'They've escaped!' The men will come rushing through the door. When they do, Hiram and Duncan, y'all yank up on the rope and trip 'em right then and there. Got it?"

We all nodded. "Better pull off your shoes because you can't run in heels. As soon as those rascals hit the floor, make a beeline to the front door of the church. I'm gonna drive through the grass and right up to the front steps. Fred, you stay on my tail. I'll slam the car in park, swing the car doors open, and y'all dive in. Any questions?"

"You think I should slip out my teeth in order to give a good holler?" Doris asked.

"Might be a good idea; we wouldn't have time to look for those things if they flew out," Earl replied. "Okay, does everybody know what to do?" Our hearts were pumping too fast to say anything. "Good," he said. "Hiram, I need your keys. How's the clutch on that thing?"

"Smooth as silk," Hiram smiled, tossing Earl the keys.

"Great. Let's go."

Fred climbed out the window first, and then with a boost from Earl, Nelly went through. Earl looked back at me, winked, and then shinnied up the wall and disappeared to the other side. I went to the window and waited. I was nervous. This church was so weird that for all I knew, if we didn't take Preacher Carmichael with us, we would be dinner on the grounds—the main course!

"What do you see?" toothless Doris asked.

"Nothing yet. Oh wait, there's Nelly. She's walking to the car, kinda moving her hips funny. Ooh, now she's pretended to drop something and the man just noticed her. Nelly is bending down to accentuate her plunging neckline. Now she's lifting up her skirt checking her nylons for a run. The man seems interested. He's walking toward her. I think she's asking for a light. She's laughing. Ooh, she just touched the man's biceps." I snorted. "'I don't know how to flirt'—puh-lease. Wait, there's Earl and Fred ducking behind a Buick. They're waiting for Nelly to turn the man around. Come on, Nelly, do your thing. There she goes, back to the trunk. Now the man can't see Earl and Fred. There they go. Get ready, Doris. Oh, wait! Oh no, the man sees them ... He's confronting Earl ... Oh, my, he's taking a swing at him! Earl just ducked and returned with a right of his own. The man is knocked out cold, girls! I see Nelly and Fred jump into their car. Earl gets into your car. Now, girls! Scream now!"

"Help, they've escaped!" Doris and Martha cut loose.

I heard keys jingle. Hiram and Duncan nodded at each other as the door flew open.

"What's goin'—Hey!" exclaimed the first man before the five of them tumbled over each other.

"Come on, girls!" Hiram yelled as he dropped the rope.

I hurdled over Junior and his outstretched hand. Another man took a swipe at Martha's feet, but it was pointless. We scattered like a herd of cats. Doris and I went up the side aisle while Hiram, Duncan, and Martha sped up the center aisle. Duncan ripped open the front door and waited for us to pass through. Daylight, glorious daylight, hit my eyes, and when I could see again, there stood Earl by the car door, waving us in.

"Come on! Hurry, hurry!" he shouted.

My feet left the ground five steps before I reached the car. *Thump*! I hit the backseat. Doris, right behind me, landed on my back. Earl slammed the door. I quickly looked up to see Homer charging at Earl. The reappearance of Homer—imagine that! Well, Earl bent down and somehow, I have no idea how, catapulted Homer over his shoulder a good six feet into the air. Sir Isaac Newton was correct: universal gravitation brought Homer down—right on the hood of Hiram's Dodge. Other men came running. Earl jumped into the car and took off with Homer sprawled out from the ornament to the windshield. Tires spun, dust flew, and we all said a little prayer. Homer kept pounding on the windshield. We could hear him through the glass saying, "Please, take Preacher Carmichael. I'm begging you as a Christian! Please!"

Earl drove around the parking lot looking for a soft place to dump Homer. Suddenly, Homer had another thought. "Okay, take me with you! I'll join your church!" he screamed at the windshield. "Does Forbye need a plumber? I have reasonable rates!"

Earl found a clump of brush and slammed on the brakes. Homer shot off the hood with the velocity of a cannonball. I'll never forget his eyes—they were hollow, distant, and dull as he vanished under the grill.

Earl shoved it in reverse, swung the car around, and peeled out again. Fred, driving the other car, was close behind. We didn't slow down until we saw the sign: "Welcome to Forbye—Home of the Watermelon Festival." Then we all collectively exhaled.

So far the pulpit committee had made three visits, all of which were disasters in their own right. We dealt with an English fella, Alistair Colgate, who didn't like the word "preacher." We listened to a good-looking man, Gavin McGreevy, who quite frankly was too pretty and too perfect for my taste. Finally we had seen Jeremiah Carmichael, the out-of-control preacher with a magic spell that brainwashed his congregation. Time was running out. Forbye needed a preacher, and my phone was ringing off the hook. One particular call came from Rose Carter when I was trying to relax with my crosswords.

Somehow I knew who it was as soon as the phone rang. *Four-letter word for busybody: R-o-s-e,* I thought as I picked up the phone.

"Hello," I said.

"Why, Emma dear, I've found you at home."

"Hi, Rose." *I knew it.*

"Sorry to bother you, but you must tell me about the search. I've been worn to a frazzle tryin' to get information out of Hiram, but he's mum on the whole thing."

As long as I've known Rose, she's never been sorry about bothering anyone. "Well, there's not much to tell," I sighed.

"Oh, come now. It's ungodly to keep us in the dark about church matters. Do tell. Who do ya like so far?"

"I really don't know, Rose, and we still have one more preacher to see," I said.

"Well, I heard Nelly and Doris didn't even hear that British fella preach. Something about them being too sick," Rose said. "Were you sick too?"

*So this is why she called,* I thought. Nelly or Doris must have slipped up while talking to each other on the phone. You see, at the time, Forbye was serviced by party lines. Nelly, Doris, Rose, and half the town all shared the same line. Everyone in Forbye knew that when Rose wasn't talking on the phone, it was a safe bet her ear was pressed up tight, listening for grist to power the rumor mill.

"Yes, Rose, we all had a touch of a sour stomach," I said. *Please, dear Lord, I hope the girls didn't say anything about the punch.*

"I find that odd," she said. "Are you taking your liver pills? I know I can't have a good movement without my liver pills."

"If you must know, my bowels are fine," I said.

"Well, when I'm all bound up I find a good enema—"

"Rose! My pot roast is burning; I must go," I interjected, and quickly hung up the phone. To the young reader out there: if you knew where that conversation was going, you'd thank me for hanging up the phone.

The next and last week of our search led us just over the state line to Forrest Park, Georgia. The preacher on the docket was Lester B. Wadsworth. I'd grown used to not knowing what to expect since every church we had visited thus far had run the gambit from A to B—*absolutely bizarre.*

I just wanted a nice sermon from an average-looking man. It had been so long, it seemed, since I had sat in Forbye's comfortable pew and listened to our dearly departed Preacher Babcock. *I'm afraid no one can preach like that man,* I reflected during the long wistful ride to Park Baptist Church.

After the service, Preacher Wadsworth wanted the committee to have Sunday dinner at his house. *At least there's no chance of being taken hostage,* I thought. But then I never thought I'd be too drunk to attend a church service. You just never know.

Before arriving at the church, the men came up with a brilliant plan. Our car would pass by the church first to scout out anyone lurking in the parking lot. Even if the coast was clear, we would find a school or another public place to park our cars. Then, from different directions and at various times, each couple would walk to the church. But that wouldn't be enough for Earl, it seemed: he talked us into going undercover. Now understand, I'm never comfortable with lying, but this was a mission for God, so I felt confident the Lord would allow the ends to justify the means.

Earl and I (aliases Bill and Betty Webber) were passing through on our way to Atlanta. Nelly and Fred (Robert and Sarah Green) were thinking about moving their membership. Hiram (Henry) and Doris (Thelma), surname Baxter, were in town to visit her sick sister. Finally, Duncan and Martha just moved into town, and would introduce themselves as Paul and Mary Tanner.

A few blocks from the church, we found public parking by a small lake. It was around 10:30 a.m. and some sinners were already out boating. We got out of our cars, probably looking overdressed for a fishing hole, but no one seemed to notice while we planned our strategy.

"All right," Earl said. "Emma and I will head in first. I'll get a feel for things and if something smells odd, we'll abort and call the whole thing off."

"Sounds good, Earl. We'll be about five minutes behind. Fred, you and Nelly go next and then ten minutes later, Duncan and Martha head in," Hiram said.

"Remember, don't even make eye contact with each other. Got it?" Earl commanded. "Let's go, Emma."

Earl and I broke away from the group and walked down a shaded sidewalk. In the crisp spring air, dewdrops clung to dogwood branches that majestically formed a pink canopy over our heads. The street displayed blooming azaleas, fully awake from a winter slumber. Their proud exhibit was truly the Lord's splendor at work. Spring mornings fulfilled His promise of a new day, a new season, a new life. Only our Master's imagination could create such a luscious array of colors. I took a deep breath just to let God's bounty flow through my nostrils, and then I started choking. Earl had lit a cigarette.

"Earl, you need to quit those things," I said.

"You'd just find something else to nag me about."

"I don't nag; I artfully critique."

"I'll agree with you there. You're so good at nagging, it belongs in a museum," he teased as he quickly sidled away. I took my pocketbook and playfully walloped him on the backside. What can I say? I love that man.

About a block away from the church Earl said, "Now remember, we're Bill and Betty Webber and we live in Sarasota. And we're just passing through on our way to Atlanta."

"What do you do?" I asked.

"What? Oh, yeah good thinking. Let's see. Well ... I'm a farmer."

"But you are a farmer in real life."

"Everybody in Florida is a farmer, so don't worry," he said.

"What do you grow?"

"I don't know—oranges, grapefruit, sunshine, or whatever they grow down there. Enough with the questions, I'm not going to get in a deep conversation with these people, so it doesn't matter."

"Earl, they're Baptist."

"Okay, I grow oranges."

We approached the church steps. A thin, balding man watched us walk up. "Hi, strangers," he greeted us. "Are you new to our town?"

"No. Just passing through," Earl said. "I'm Bill Webber and this is my wife Betty."

"Webber did you say? Well, I'll be! My name is Webber too, David Webber," he said, and the real Mr. Webber stuck his hand out.

"Oh, we're probably not related. We're from Sarasota," Earl said.

"You're kidding me. I grew up in Sarasota. What street ya live on?"

My stomach felt like I just took a swig of Planter's Punch. *Abort, Earl, abort,* I thought.

"Orange," Earl stated matter-of-fact.

"Oh, yeah. Orange Avenue. I rode my bicycle many a time down

Orange. We probably crossed paths. Hey, you look familiar. You're not Linda's boy are you?"

"No. No, we haven't lived in Sarasota that long. I just bought the place after the war." Earl knew how to lie.

"What took ya to Sarasota?" Mr. Webber asked.

*Baptists, we're dealing with Baptists. I tried to warn you, Earl.*

"I bought an orange grove," Earl lied.

"This has got to be the smallest world. My family is in the orange business. Are you sure we're not related?"

"I really doubt it. My family is from Atlanta. That's where we're headed."

"Oh, okay. Wait a minute! Whose grove did you buy?"

*Earl Gladstone, you're going to hell and I'm right behind you,* I thought, but just smiled.

"Well, I really didn't buy a grove. I bought land and just planted the trees."

"Yeah, a lot of folks are doing that down there. I guess Webber is a common name, but how funny. Well, pleased to meet ya, and y'all enjoy the service."

*Phew,* I thought as Mr. Webber walked away. I realized I wasn't built for covert operations. Two more seconds with that man and I would have confessed to everything this side of bank robbery. Lying for the Lord sounded good, but when put to use, it felt like a sin just the same, and it was most definitely easer said than done. We went inside and settled down in a pew.

I got close to Earl's ear. "Orange Avenue, huh? How on earth did you know Sarasota had an Orange Avenue?"

"I didn't say Orange Avenue. I just said 'orange,' and Mr. Webber filled in the rest. Chances were good some road down there was named orange something. Give the enemy time and he'll be your guide."

"He's not an enemy. He's a Baptist, and I'm not comfortable with lying."

"Emma, when you've been through as many interrogations as I have, you lie to stay alive," he said.

"I guess you did a lot of that during the war."

"War? Nah, that was a piece of cake compared to *your* interrogations." Then Earl's belly jiggled. I jabbed him in the ribs, and he grunted, "Ooph!"

I pulled out my preacher scorecard and checked my pen for ink. Just then I saw Hiram and Doris walk past our aisle. Doris still had color in her face so they must have made it through any inquisition or another man with their alias, Baxter. It was odd, though, pretending not to know them.

"Quit looking at them, Emma. You'll blow our cover," Earl whispered.

"What? I'm just sitting here."

The friendly Mr. Webber made his way down the aisle and stopped right in front of Hiram and Doris. He stayed with them briefly and then headed back out the door. "Did you see that?" I asked Earl.

"Don't panic, Emma. He just welcomed them. Why don't you pull out one of your crosswords and put your eyes to good use?"

"We are sitting in church, mister, telling one big fib after another. I'm not going to provoke the Lord and compound my sins by doing crosswords in His house!" I said as loud as I could and still keep it a whisper.

I got a giant whiff of Alabaster Heaven and knew that Nelly and Fred had just walked in the door. Nelly didn't go anywhere without her special perfume, and whenever she walked by, you'd think she bought it by the gallon.

They sat down on our side, five rows up. Nelly was obviously trying to look inconspicuous, which made her look so conspicuous. She'd touch her hat, straighten her sleeve, flip through a hymnal, check the clock, and none of it looked natural. Then that man named Webber went down the aisle and stopped in front of them.

I poked Earl, but he didn't respond. The rascal was asleep. With a little more authority I poked again. He flinched awake. "God's gonna get ya if I don't get you first," I whispered.

Earl shifted on the pew but said nothing. That Webber fella had my attention anyway. I imagined him going outside checking for vehicles with out-of-county plates. *When he finds none, he'll send out a deacon to scour the town. Eventually, our cars will turn up and the whole ruse will be exposed.* Those were my thoughts as I watched Mr. Webber walk out the door.

The church was filling up nicely. I smiled at members and nodded when the occasion was called for. My outside bore no resemblance of the guilt storm turning in my gut. At five minutes before eleven, Duncan and Martha came in and found a pew near the front. At three minutes till, good ol' Mr. Webber walked down to meet with them. Church members were all around us, so very quietly I whispered to Earl, "Is it too late to call this thing off?"

"Don't worry," he whispered.

"I worry because you don't."

However, after talking to Duncan and Martha, Mr. Webber didn't leave this time. Instead, he went right up to the pulpit. I gathered up my pocketbook, ready to bolt on a moment's notice. I even slipped out of my heels; last week's great escape was still fresh on my mind.

"I have just a few announcements before we get started," Mr. Webber began. "Next Saturday is our monthly workday here at the church. We ask all able-bodied men to meet here at seven o'clock. Bring your tools and work gloves. The ladies will put on a pancake breakfast, so bring your appetites as well."

*So far so good,* I thought.

Mr. Webber continued. "Now, it isn't very often we get visitors, being our town is off the beaten path, but this morning we have eight of them and I'd like to welcome them. Bill and Betty Webber, please stand up."

*No, no, no,* I thought as Earl pulled me up.

"That's right; their name is Webber, just like mine. Not only that, they're from my hometown of Sarasota, and Bill is in the same business as my family. He has an orange grove down there. What a coincidence."

Nelly shot her head around to us. Her eyes nearly left her face.

"Remain standing, Bill and Betty," Mr. Webber said. "We also have Robert and Sarah Green with us. Robert and Sarah, stand up." Nelly and Fred stood up. "I want y'all to make the Greens feel welcome because they are thinking about moving their membership. Robert and Sarah, please remain standing."

My knees buckled a bit; there I stood supporting sin, and it was getting heavy.

"Paul and Mary Tanner just moved into town. Paul and Mary, stand up. Since the Tanners are new to town, I'd like someone from the congregation to take them home for Sunday dinner."

"I'll do it, Brother Webber," someone from the congregation offered. *This plan had seemed flawless on paper.*

"Thanks, Sister Connelly. Paul and Mary, please remain standing. The last couple with us today is Henry and Thelma Baxter. Would y'all please stand up?" Hiram and Doris stood up. "They're here on a sad occasion. Thelma's sister is sick. Some of you ladies might want to get with them after the service and see if they need food or anything."

*We are going to hell—the whole lot of us—going straight down. We will be the first pulpit committee in the history of pulpit committees to burn forever in the lake of fire!*

"So take a good look at our visitors. Make them feel welcome. Pray for Bill and Betty as they travel to Atlanta and add Thelma's sister to your prayer list."

I wanted to scream at the top of my lungs, "There is no Bill and Betty Webber! No orange grove, no sick sister! I've never been to Sarasota. We're all fakes. I'm Emma, she's Nelly, she's Doris, and there's Martha. Please have mercy on us!" However, I just stood there next to my husband—who, by the way, I'm sure had already convinced himself that he was actually Bill Webber with a little ol' orange grove in Sarasota. Men!

So there in various locations throughout the church we all stood. I dared not look up because I knew the heavenly host was gazing down on us, readying themselves for an all-out assault. I half expected the other shoe to drop and hear Mr. Webber say, "Brothers and Sisters, I give you the pulpit committee from Forbye. Now, get 'em, boys!" But he didn't. He just said, "You may be seated."

To put it mildly, I was a bundle of nerves throughout the service. The congregation sang my favorite hymn, "Blessed Assurance, Jesus Is Mine," yet I didn't enjoy a single note. I understood sins can be forgiven, but I was still sinning with at least another thirty minutes to go. Could you imagine a bank robber asking for forgiveness right in the middle of a heist?

By the time Preacher Wadsworth approached the pulpit, I'd somewhat managed to steady my hand enough to write on my scorecard. Although I was riddled with guilt, my sense to evaluate the preacher hadn't left me. Preacher Lester B. Wadsworth was a squatty little fella whose head barely protruded over the pulpit. I'd bet a pound of lard was used to slick back his tuft of twine, which some might call hair. Another oddity involved his round pasty face. It turned beet red each time he deliveredi an excitable point. At certain points during his sermon he'd get so red in the face I wondered if someone was behind the pulpit strangling the poor man. God bless him, but he was short.

The cadence of his delivery was awful. He finished each sentence with the words, "you see."

His sermon went something like this. "Jesus died on the cross, *you see*. For the sins of man, *you see*. Only through Him can you have salvation, *you see*. And I'm telling you right now, sinner, we put Jesus on the cross, *you see!*" And then his face went red.

Preacher Wadsworth scored four hundred on his scorecard, *you see*.

However, that delivery, *you see,* can be very annoying, *you see.* So, I deducted thirty points for aggravation.

After the last "Amen," Earl and I headed out the door. We didn't look back and we didn't make eye contact. If anyone tried to engage us in conversation, Earl just pointed to his watch and said, "Gotta get to Atlanta." Mercy, that man could lie.

I held my breath for two blocks. I just knew Mr. Webber was rounding up a posse. They probably already had Hiram and the others in custody, and I was certain the deacons had put up roadblocks at each end of town.

"Anybody behind us?" I asked.

"No, Emma, nobody is behind us. Will ya quit worrying?"

Suddenly I spotted a small bench underneath an oak tree. Grabbing Earl's hand, I said, "Come with me."

"Oh, Emma."

"Now listen hear, Earl Gladstone, we're going to ask for forgiveness, and we're going to ask right now! You bow your head and close your eyes, and you better not open them, Mister, until we're through."

"Okay, okay. Just get it over with," Earl sighed.

"No, no, no! One doesn't just get it over with—"

"Emma, sheesh, fine. Take your time," Earl interrupted.

I took a deep breath. "Dear Jesus, we just sinned against Thee to the highest degree in Your house, in front of Your people, the Baptists. I thought it would be okay being it was for Thee and all. But lying is never okay, and I should've known better. Please forgive me. Earl here is another story. He's simpleminded, like a child, so he doeth childlike things. Sometimes I think he'd rather climb a tree to tell a lie than stand on the ground to tell the truth. Thou created man, so I don't have to tell Thee how sinful he can be. Most of the time his heart is in the right place, yet his mind can concoct some wicked tales. Please forgive him and remove this sin from Your list. Oh, and forgive me for coveting Nelly Dalton's floral chiffon dress, even though it would look better on me. In Jesus' name, amen." I lifted my head. "Okay, Earl, your turn."

"But you just asked for me," he said.

I folded my arms and looked at him.

"Dear Lord," he said. "Forgive me for lying and please remind Emma that Eve tempted man, and she wouldn't be here today if it wasn't for Adam's rib. In Jesus' name, amen."

"You think you're real cute, don't ya?"

"I always manage to put things into perspective."

I didn't speak to my husband for the rest of the walk.

The rest of our group all made artful escapes and I believe the church members were none the wiser to our deceitful display.

Our lunch was tedious at best. Nothing happed that bears repeating. The preacher seemed lukewarm and almost inattentive at times. Maybe he had preacher guilt for entertaining the notion of leaving his flock. Perhaps he was tired, sick, or wanted to wash that pound of lard out of his hair. Whatever the case, the committee left with the impression that Lester B. Wadsworth wanted to stay put. We drove back to Forbye using our real names.

Wednesday night after prayer meeting, the committee met to discuss our search to date. Personally, I'd had my fill of eccentric preachers from oddball towns. I may not know much, but I did know this band of bellowing Baptists couldn't replace Preacher Babcock. Oh, I knew Preacher McGreevy was the odds-on favorite, but I still had a card to play, and I aimed to play it before the meeting adjourned.

Hiram approached the chalkboard and wrote, "Alistair Coalgate, Gavin McGreevy, Jeremiah Carmichael, Lester B. Wadsworth," one below the other. Immediately after writing the names, Hiram took his chalk and did this: ~~Jeremiah Carmichael~~.

"I assume everybody can agree," he stated over his shoulder.

"Absolutely," Duncan said and the rest nodded yes.

"Okay, let's talk about Alistair Coalgate. Earl, what's your gut feeling on the man?"

"Well, Hiram, I tell ya, the fella's got quite a vocabulary and he seemed sincere from what I could understand, but I'm not sure our congregation can speak English."

"I thought that, too," Fred interjected. "If I was in a dogfight with the Luftwaffe I couldn't think of a better man to have by my side. But the preacher of Forbye? I'm with Earl, we don't speak English."

Hiram huffed, "All right, guys, look. We speak English, okay? We shouldn't rule out a man just because he sounds a little different than us."

"So, you like him, Hiram?" Duncan asked.

"Absolutely not; I found him pompous and boring. Besides that, God hasn't moved me in his direction." Hiram stated.

"I still think the fella was too hard to understand," Earl said.

"Okay, Alistair Coalgate is off the list," Hiram said. "What about Lester B. Wadsworth?"

"The spirit didn't move me," Fred said.

"He seemed happy to stay put," Duncan said.

"I thought his sermon was queer. Not that I didn't appreciate the effort that was put into his performance, but he kept using the phrase 'you see.' I found it to be a nervous crutch, which might be the first symptom of an unstable mind," Earl said.

Hiram nodded. "You got a good point, Earl. I can't make a case for Preacher Wadsworth either." He surveyed us all; no one disagreed. "So he's off the list."

Their attention went to Gavin McGreevy, the perfectly good-looking man with the perfectly good-looking wife, who preached a perfectly good sermon.

"Fred, your thoughts on Preacher McGreevy," Hiram said.

"I think we ought to call him; seems like he'd fit in well," Fred said. Obviously Nelly had used some pillow talk on her husband.

"Earl, what do you think?" Hiram asked.

"Well, I don't think we should rubberstamp this guy," my husband answered. Obviously I'm fairly versed in pillow talk, too.

"Duncan, how do you feel about it?"

"I like the guy. He's certainly head and shoulders above the rest," Duncan said.

"Yeah, I like him too," Hiram agreed, "but Earl's got a point. We need to kick it around a bit. Earl, what didn't you like about the preacher?"

"Oh, he's kinda flashy. Seemed too perfect." *Tell 'em, Earl.* I hid a smile.

"Too perfect? I don't think that's a very good choice of words," Fred interjected. "We should all strive to be perfect."

"No, I see what Earl is getting at," observed Hiram. "The preacher might be hard to control. We don't want a situation like Jeremiah Carmichael."

Duncan volleyed back, "Oh, come on, now. McGreevy isn't Carmichael"

Now, dear reader, I know what you're thinking: "Emma, you haven't said a word during this debate!" I must remind you officially the pulpit committee was a board of men. All the ladies were present as nothing more than decorations or brainless support. I desperately wanted to take part in the conversation, and Nelly's tongue was trapped behind clenched teeth as well. We had to remain mum and wait for our cue. Hiram glanced our way, but I sensed he didn't want that can of worms opened... yet.

"Why not have the committee go on the road for a few weeks more? Maybe even go out of state," Earl suggested.

"I can't leave my farm for a few more weeks," Hiram said. "But I admit I'm still on the fence with McGreevy."

"You're the swing vote, Hiram. You either vote to bring in McGreevy, or we rehash this thing all night," Fred pointed out.

Hiram rubbed his chin and then shifted his eyes toward us. The room grew quiet in anticipation of, or maybe with hesitation for, what was about to unfold.

"Ladies," Hiram said, "show of hands. Who wants to call Preacher McGreevy?"

Nelly and Martha lifted their hands while Doris and I remained still.

"If I could just say something, Hiram," I volunteered.

"I want to say something first," Nelly jumped in.

"I spoke first, Nelly. I should have the floor."

"You just want to filibuster until we're all wore down. Chattering nonstop is your worst quality," Nelly said.

"My worst quality? Please, dear, your mouth has been open since the doctor spanked you on the backside," I replied.

"Hold on, ladies." Hiram held up a hand. "You'll both get your chance. Emma, go ahead."

"Thank you, Hiram. I have the preacher I think we all can agree on, and I'm quite surprised no one has mentioned him. Oliver Babcock."

"Oliver Babcock!" Nelly cried. "That boy is still in diapers!"

I shot her a look. "Like I was saying, Hiram, before I was so rudely interrupted, Oliver is schooled and very capable of serving Forbye. He knows our congregation and has his dad's sense of the gospel. No one is more perfect."

"I don't think Oliver is the direction we need to go," Hiram said. "He'd always be compared to his dad, which is unfair... No, I won't consider, Oliver."

"At least someone here can think clearly," Nelly commented.

"Just what are you implying, Nelly dear?" I asked.

"Oh, I don't know. Perhaps you get confused when you're off your liver pills."

I rolled my eyes just a little. "What's with the liver pills? Have you been talking to Rose Carter? I assure you my functions and faculties are in perfect working order, which is more than I can say for you. And I can prove it!"

"Hiram, listen to her rattling on like a child," Nelly said in a dismissive voice.

"Hold on, Hiram," I called, grabbing my pocketbook. "I know more about Preacher McGreevy's sermon than any of you, especially Nelly Dalton."

"Oh, Emma, what could you possibly know that I don't? We all were there!" Nelly snorted.

"What was Preacher McGreevy's sermon about?" I said. "Can anyone tell me?"

"Well, ah," Hiram stammered. "He... I'm sure he mentioned sin and the Bible... and..."

"Good heavens, Hiram. That's quite a stretch. Even the Pentecostals mention sin and the Bible in their sermons, too. How 'bout we call one of their preachers? Maybe we can get some snake handling on the side." I reached for my scorecard. "Here it is—my preacher scorecard."

"Oh, that old thing. You can't be serious tallying up a preacher like he was a beer-swilling ball player. Utterly ridiculous," Nelly criticized.

"Okay, Nelly Dalton. Tell me, did the preacher read out of the book of Revelations?"

"You're completely batty, Emma," she replied.

"Don't know, do ya? How many amens did the preacher get? Did he pound the pulpit three times or four times? And what about the all important Heaven-to-Hell ratio?" I asked.

"Heaven-to-Hell ratio? What must go on in your mind? Why must you be such a contrarian?" Nelly turned to the others. "Put an end to this balderdash, Hiram, and get on with calling Preacher McGreevy. The man did have a vision about coming to Forbye."

"Jerry Carson had visions, too, and they locked him up in the crazy bin," I muttered.

"Scorecard, huh? Emma, can I take a look at that?" Hiram asked.

"Of course, Hiram; I think you'll find it helpful." I handed my scorecard past Nelly's turned-up nose and then shifted politely on my chair. I could tell Hiram was impressed. I casually rocked back, satisfied with my homework.

"Excellent work, Emma! This certainly captures the preacher's sermon in a nutshell," Hiram said.

"I know," I said as I admired my fingernails.

"So, how did he stack up against the rest of 'em?" Hiram asked.

"Well, ah, that's why we need to call on some more preachers," I said.

"He scored the best, didn't he?" Nelly guessed.

"That's not the point of the scorecard. I wanted to prove you didn't know what the preacher said. And you clearly didn't!" I snapped.

"You have here, Preacher McGreevy scored 540 total points and 100% on his Heaven-to-Hell ratio. Now I don't know exactly what that is, but you circled it and wrote, 'a perfect sermon,'" Hiram said.

Friends, it was true. I did write that. It was a magnificent sermon, but the committee missed my point. None of them knew what the preacher said. My theory held true: Gavin McGreevy was too pretty for anyone to be able to comprehend his message. The women would become lost in his startling blue eyes, while the men would look at his all-too-beautiful wife and daydream of younger times. I'd bet the devil could sit in the front pew and I'd be the only one to notice.

"Well, well, well. A perfect sermon by Preacher McGreevy," Nelly gloated. "I do believe those were your exact words."

"Emma, your scorecard idea was brilliant. In fact, you should be the head of this committee," Hiram said.

"Why, Hiram, I—"

"But you're not, of course," he cut me off. "However, I've taken your scorecard under advisement, and I put forth a motion to bring Gavin McGreevy in view of a call."

"I second that motion," Fred said.

"Earl, you want to confirm and make this thing unanimous?" Hiram asked.

"Better not, for the sake of domestic tranquility. I have to go home with Emma," Earl said.

"Understood, and that settles it by three to one in favor of Gavin McGreevy. Duncan, would you close us in prayer?" Hiram concluded.

"Wait just one minute," I said.

"Oh, please, Emma," Nelly complained.

"Nope, I'm saying my piece. I find it hard to believe none of you have any trepidation about hiring a man whose sermon you couldn't remember! Don't roll your eyes at me, Nelly Dalton; you're gonna hear the truth whether you like it or not. We're talking about out-of-control preacher worship fueled by sex appeal. There—I said it! Could you imagine voting for a President based just on his looks? Don't answer that, Nelly; it's rhetorical." I turned back to the men. "Y'all have been sideswiped by the devil—hoodwinked by the sultan of darkness. Preacher McGreevy may be a fine man and all that; I'm sure when all is said and done, he'll rest comfortably at the feet of Jesus. But the First Baptist Church of Forbye isn't a testing ground for handsome preachers delivering the Gospel." I was really getting going. "And I'll tell you another thing! You men had better not take that man fishing. Oh, don't think I've forgotten about that! I guarantee you, one look at that preacher in his under-britches, and you'll have a line of women from Fort Myers to Forbye coming to camp out on our pond!"

I stopped briefly to catch my breath. Earl took it as an opportunity to say, "I'm gonna get her out of here so y'all can close in prayer."

Unmoved, I continued, "You said it yourself, Hiram, I should head this committee. Well, as titular head of this committee I renounce the last motion. I put forth a motion to expand our search. Mississippi is full of God-fearing, homely preachers. I say we start there."

Earl picked me up and then flopped me over his shoulder. He carried me towards the door while I continued to let the committee have an earful. "You're making a mistake if you think Preacher McGreevy won't cause spiritual upheaval. You'd better get Brother Johnson down at the funeral home to stop making fans and start making blindfolds, because that's the only way the congregation will hear this preacher!" I yelled from the bent position of a fireman's carry.

"We'll see y'all Sunday," Earl called, and then closed the door behind us.

I smacked his back with my pocketbook. "Put me down, Earl Gladstone!"

"Nope, you'll run back in there. I'm carrying you all the way home."

You're probably looking at these pages with a condescending sneer, fully judging my petty interjection towards a man who did nothing but acquire remarkable genes. So, while you sip your tea and delicately nibble on a watercress sandwich, or whatever high-society snack a character like you enjoys, feel free to judge away. Oh, how the view must be, perched in an ivory tower, breathing rarefied air, casting aspersions disguised as the arbitration of morality! That may work at your ladies' bridge club, but I reject any pejorative connotation that might suggest a petty motive on my behalf. I'm dedicated to serving the Lord. He gave me a mind to speak, so I speak my mind: that's my role. And quite frankly, I'm good at it.

That said. The committee had spoken, and as a good Christian woman I would begrudgingly accept their decision. It's no secret that I love the opportunity to say, "I told you so." I really do. Given my sense and acute ability to foresee problems before they exist, I was as certain as sunrise that sooner or later I would utter those four words, "I told you so." Nothing and no one was perfect except Jesus, and I didn't see sandals on Preacher McGreevy's feet.

Sunday morning was the event everyone in Forbye had waited for since Preacher Babcock went home to meet the Lord. In my mind, I knew Preacher McGreevy would be confirmed the minute his handsome face made it through the doorway. Yes, he did have to preach, and, yes, there would be a vote. He could give a series of grunts and rattle off "Blah, blah, blah," and the congregation would think it was the best sermon this side of Billy Sunday.

The morning was clear; not a cloud hung in the sky. The temperature was pleasant: brisk, but comfy inside my shawl. A spring shower had passed the night before, leaving the air fresh and alive. Dare I say the atmosphere was perfect for the perfect preacher? Earl dropped me off in the front of the church and then motored around back to park the car. Nelly was waiting for me in front of the church steps.

*New dress, different shade of lipstick, and a gallon of Alabaster Heaven soaked into her skin? She is ready to greet the preacher,* I thought. "Nelly," I smiled.

"Emma, it's just a delightful morning! Don't ya think?"

"Close your mouth, dear. Drool is unbecoming on a Sunday morning," I admonished.

"Why, Emma, you can't possibly still be upset. God looks down on animosity," she puffed.

"God looks down on coveting, too. So if I were you, I'd wipe that smirk off my face before the preacher's wife sees it," I puffed back.

"Well, at least I don't need—what was it again? Ah, yes, a scorecard to judge my preacher," she snapped.

"Pearls before swine, my dear. Enjoy the service," I brushed past her.

"Oh, I will."

"Oh, how I know," I whispered under my breath from a good fifteen feet away—still not far enough to escape the cloud of Alabaster Heaven that smothered the foyer. I bet she had such a supply of that stuff, it could fuel Earl's tractor for a month.

The church was half-filled as I made my way in. It had been four weeks since I'd worshipped at our little church; it felt so good to be home. Suddenly I remembered that the last time I was there, I left my umbrella. I hoped some good brother or sister stored it in the back closet where we kept the lost and found. I knew I'd forget about it later, so while it was still fresh on my mind, I headed through the doorway behind the pulpit that led to a small hallway where extra hymnals and various odds and ends were stored. The same doorway also served as a side entrance to the preacher's study. *I hope someone didn't throw out my umbrella,* I thought while pulling on the closet door.

I felt a warm hand touch my shoulder. The hand was firm yet soft, authoritative yet timid, commanding yet humble. Yes, I garnered all that from a touch. I turned around and my knees suddenly felt like half-churned butter, for I was inches away from the most perfect face God had ever created. Preacher McGreevy stood before me. He smiled and, my heavens, those eyes flashed a blue that would make the sky jealous. In a split second, vertigo took me. The last time I felt like that, I had five Planter's Punches in me. I lost my balance, but the agile preacher caught my fall.

"Hold on. I gotcha," he said.

"Oh, Preacher, I don't know what came over me," I said as he propped me up against the wall.

"It's a little cramped quarters in here and the air is stuffy," he replied.

"Yes, that must be it. I just came for my umbrella."

The preacher lifted one of his massive paws to the top shelf. "Here it is," he said.

*Old Spice,* I thought as he handed me my umbrella.

"Actually, Sister Gladstone, you're the one I want to see."

*Oh, no. Had word got out? What did Nelly tell Rose Carter? The party line, the party line. Please, dear Lord, not the party line!* I thought.

"I heard a rumor and I have to know if it's true," he continued.

*That blasted party line.* "Oh? What rumor might that be?" I asked.

"That you make the best boysenberry pie in the state," replied McGreevy.

"My boysenberry pie? Oh, I wouldn't go that far... well... maybe the county. Of course, I'm not the type of woman who plays into rumors," I demurred, fanning my face.

The preacher looked at me with those blue eyes. A woman of lesser faith would've dived into those limpid pools and taken a few laps. He said, "You must promise to bake me a pie so I can put those rumors to rest."

"And what if I don't?" I said playfully. *My word, am I flirting?*

"Then we'll stay in this closet until the Lord comes home," he said. *Oh, my, is* he *flirting?*

Of course, he was happily married, and I had, you know, Earl. I was, however, taken back by his unique ability to converse on a personal level. Perhaps I was a little hasty in my judgment. After all, he was a man of God; I was a godly woman; I really saw no reason to continue a fool's errand. I still felt, if I had my druthers, that Preacher McGreevy needed a snaggletooth or a lazy eye to penetrate the eardrums of his followers. Hopefully, time and a few liver spots would dent Adonis' armor.

"I'll do you one better," I offered. "I'll have your wife over and I'll share my secret recipe with her."

"It sounds like you're as astute at politics as well as baking," he noted.

"I've collected a few petitions in my life."

"I pity the mayor."

"The ex-mayor," I shot back, and then we shared a laugh.

"Well, I'd better head on out. We can't let the service start without a preacher," he winked.

"Oh, goodness no! Look at the time! Earl will wonder where I went."

We walked toward the door. "I hope the congregation is ready to hear about the Last Supper," he said.

*Honey, they ain't gonna hear a word,* I thought. "I'm sure they are."

The preacher pulled open the door, exposing him and me to the rest of the congregation. Betty Parker was softly playing "What a Friend We Have in Jesus" on the piano; she hit a sour note as she first laid eyes on the preacher. She recovered gracefully, but I wish you could've seen the look on Nelly Dalton's face when the preacher and I popped out of the doorway. Nelly knew good and well how cramped and intimate that hallway was—and Nelly's favorite hobby was minding other people's business. What wild thoughts must have scrambled through her brain, on Sunday no less, over an innocent encounter by happenstance! I glided down the aisle, unashamed, and the preacher took a seat next to the pulpit. As I passed Nelly, I sensed her narrowed eyes trying to burn a hole in my fireproof dress. I found my seat next to Earl.

"What were you doing back there with the preacher?" Earl asked.

"Oh, just telling him about our wonderful orange grove, Mr. Webber."

Shortly thereafter we sang the Doxology, and women throughout the congregation put forth quite an effort praising God from whom all blessings flow. We sang a few more hymns, Hiram made some announcements, and the potato portion of the service concluded; the meat waited briefly before approaching the pulpit. I glanced around; you'd think somebody had just rung a bell, because all at once the ladies grabbed their fans. The worshipping had begun before the preacher opened his mouth.

I could go on and tell you Preacher McGreevy gave a wonderful sermon. Would you care if I said he pounded the pulpit at just the right moment? Does it matter that he had a perfect Heaven-to-Hell ratio? How about the fact that he shook his Bible while quoting Revelations? A truly impressive stunt I'd never seen before. Nope, none of that matters to you, just as it didn't to the congregation at the First Baptist Church of Forbye. You knew, I knew, and everyone reading this knew Gavin McGreevy would be the new preacher since he was first introduced in this story.

However, formalities were in order. Hiram asked the preacher and his family to step outside while the church voted. The man barely got out the door before Hiram said, "All those in favor say, 'Amen.'" A thunderous "Amen" echoed around the sanctuary. I'm sure the preacher and his family heard it through the walls. I'd even bet the Pentecostals heard it four blocks over. And, yes, I said it, too.

"Any against?" Hiram had to ask. I think one cricket disagreed.

"Someone bring in our new preacher, and we'll get down to bartering," Hiram said.

Preacher McGreevy, his wife, June, and their two boys, Jake and James, walked down the aisle and stood in front of the congregation. "Preacher," Hiram said. "I think you'll be happy with our arrangements. Forbye takes care of our own. To start things off, in addition to the pastorium, the church will set aside twenty-five dollars a week for your salary. Now the floor is open. Let's start with the farmers."

"A dozen eggs a week and two fryers a month," Ross Hamilton offered.

"I'll give a gallon of milk and a pound of butter a week," Frank Smith added.

"I'll make weekly drops of whatever is in season—corn, tomatoes, turnips, mustards," Earl said.

This went on for about an hour as each church member pledged something to the McGreevys: haircuts, doctor visits, new clothes for the boys, and so forth. The preacher was truly overwhelmed from the outpouring of generosity towards his family. He graciously accepted our offer, and the First Baptist Church of Forbye finally had a preacher—too handsome a preacher, but a preacher just the same.

I would be remiss if I didn't include an ironic twist to the whole reason we needed a pulpit committee. I'm sure you haven't forgotten about dear Preacher Babcock and the sermon that took him home. It was the television set, the devil's tool, which angered the minister into a manic display of heart-stopping proportions. The man died on the spot fighting Satan's newest battle.

Now, friends, I will fast forward to the next Sunday, our new preacher, and his first official sermon as Preacher Babcock's replacement. After the hymns, the offerings, and the tension building one might expect from a newly appointed preacher, the congregation fell silent as Preacher McGreevy approached the pulpit he would now call home.

"I'd like to share something with you I saw on television the other night," were his first words.

The congregation gasped.

Oh, how I love to say, "I told you so."

# God Will Clear a Path

"Not one nigger will step foot in this church!" Prescott Kotter shouted from the fourth pew.

Did I shock you, dear reader? That wasn't my intent, although I confess I spent many hours thinking about how I should open this story. I just wanted to put you inside the First Baptist Church of Forbye on a hot July night, 1960. I will return to that night shortly, but first I'll share with you the events leading up to the day those words were uttered.

Calling it summer would be an injustice to lazy days and breeze-filled nights. That year, the sweltering months from June through August were the worst Forbye had ever experienced. Humidity, thick with malice, unbearable and unbreakable, walled the morning air like freshly mortared bricks across the doorstep. It was the kind of summer when blooms hung languishing on the vine, and spry creatures of the wild roasted to delirium and wandered down Main Street, unaware of their surroundings. The heat, that gosh-awful heat, never flinched, never rested, and never discriminated. Everyone and everything suffered from its brutal blow. The mood was ripe for sluggish bodies to propagate indignant thoughts. And when those thoughts were left to fester, it was only a matter of time before anger engulfed the town.

The phone rang while Earl and I were watching television. Yes, you read correctly. We bought a television set after Preacher McGreevy assured us it wasn't a sin as long as we didn't watch game shows or soap operas. Earl liked to watch ball games, and my favorite show was *Bonanza*. Anyway, that particular night we were watching Richard Nixon as he was nominated for President during the Republican National

Convention. I always thought Nixon to be a shifty sort, beady eyes and all, but I had no choice. Dick Nixon would get my vote because that Kennedy fella was just too good-looking to be President. Of course, Nelly Dalton had a Kennedy bumper sticker on her car, in case you hadn't figured that one out.

Oh, yes, the phone rang, and Rose Carter was on the other end. "Have you heard the news?" she asked before I could even say hello.

News to Rose could be anything from her bursitis acting up to Luther Roberts beating his wife again. I figured I'd confuse her with the obvious. "Dick Nixon just got nominated for President," I said.

"Huh? No, this is big news!" she announced. "There is a Negro over at Preacher McGreevy's house!"

"Okay," I said.

"Well, what do you think he's doing over there?" she asked.

"Uh, talking to the preacher, I suppose."

"But what about? What could it possibly be?" she hounded.

"How would I know, Rose? You called me."

"Aren't you curious?"

"No, not really," I admitted.

"Well, I just thought you'd like to know, so good-bye," she said, and hung up.

Poor Rose! I didn't play the gossip game with her. I took two steps away from the phone but then had an idea. I walked back over and gently lifted up the receiver. "There is a Negro over at Preacher McGreevy's house," I heard Rose telling someone on the party line, and then I dropped the phone clumsily on the cradle just to rattle her ears.

"What was that about?" Earl asked without looking up from the television.

"Oh, Rose got wind of a black fella over at the preacher's house."

"Unbelievable. You can't trust 'em," Earl said, still looking at the tube.

"Earl, don't be that way!"

"Well, you can't trust 'em. They just nominated Nixon!"

"The coloreds just nominated Nixon?"

"No, Emma, the Republicans nominated Nixon," Earl explained, "but I'm sure the preacher doesn't have a problem with 'em."

"The Republicans?"

"Emma, try to keep up. I'm talking about the black fella at the preacher's house."

"How 'bout I wait until your conversation circles around, and I'll jump in," I suggested.

"All right, the black man. Now jump in," he said.

"Rose is calling all over town about the man being inside the preacher's house," I told him.

Earl rocked back on the couch and rubbed his chin. "She's probably stirring up Old Man Kotter," he said.

"I bet he was first on her list."

"I'm afraid Rose just dumped gas on some smoldering rags. This summer just got hotter," Earl stated.

Although he owned most of Forbye, Prescott Kotter was an angry man. His list of enterprises included Kotter General Store, Kotter Gas Station, Kotter Seed and Feed, Kotter Tractor Sales, and of course his prized possession, Kotter Lumberyard. What Mr. Kotter didn't own, he controlled. The folks of Forbye knew if their taxes went delinquent, Old Man Kotter would be at the courthouse steps waiting for the doors to open. If he was in a good mood, he'd work out arrangements and maybe rent the property back to you. However, catch him on a bad day, which was usual, and he'd just send the sheriff to your door.

I don't know why bitterness consumed the man or if he even considered himself ornery. In his view he was a family man, a pillar of the community, and a God-fearing Christian. He'd tell you that with a straight face and a steady jaw. If one could buy his way into heaven, Mr. Kotter would enjoy a first class ride to the Pearly Gates. After all, no one tithed more than he. Just ask him.

Mr. Kotter's appearance reminded me of that colonel who ran those fried chicken joints. He had a chubby face with a belly to match and always wore a white suit. He sported a mustache and a goatee, which surrounded his thin lips and crooked teeth.

I'm sure in Prescott Kotter's mind he thought of himself as a plantation owner. He, for lack of a better word, employed several black families to work in his various businesses around town. He used something called "Kotter coins," cheaply minted metal pieces, to pay his workers. Now, where do you think one could spend Kotter coins? That's right—only in Kotter's general store. I know that sounds awful, but there was more to Mr. Kotter's wage agreement. A black person couldn't just walk into his store. No sir! They had to wait until a storefront sign that read "Whites Only" was flipped around to read "Negros Accepted," and then they could enter. The sign was usually turned over between the hours of four and five o'clock, but Old Man Kotter loved playing games with that sign. Some days he'd walk to the window, grab the sign, and then set it back down and walk away without flipping it over. Yes, indeed! Oh, but let's not forget, Prescott Kotter was a *fine* Christian man.

The next day Earl had to pick up some feed, and I decided to accompany him down to Kotter's store. Earl really didn't like to trade with the man, but Mr. Kotter let the local farmers have credit until harvest or slaughter time. I always joked that first the steers were butchered, and then Earl was slaughtered by Mr. Kotter's simple interest plan.

A bell rattled against the glass pane as Earl and I walked through the door. Mr. Kotter was holding court by the old checkerboard table where men usually gathered to sip coffee and complain about the weather. However, that wasn't the topic on Prescott Kotter's mind. The only air moving in the stuffy store came from a small fan propped up on the counter and the wind blowing out of Old Man Kotter's mouth.

"Looks like that preacher needs to be reminded we still got Jim Crow laws in this county," I heard him say.

I needed blood meal for my roses, so I went down one aisle while Earl headed for the counter to order up some feed. Although he was out of view, I could still hear Old Man Kotter pontificating on Jim Crow etiquette. "You know, the other day one of 'em tried to walk past me without removing his hat," he said.

"What did you do?" someone asked.

"Well, the boy was across the street, so I shouted, 'Hey boy!' The colored boy's eyes got as big as watermelons because he saw who I was. He flopped that hat off fast as anything and hung his head. I proceeded down the street with one eye on the boy just to make sure he knew his place." Kotter chuckled, then turned to Earl. "How 'bout it, Earl? You know anything about a colored boy stepping inside the preacher's house?"

"Nope," Earl said. "I need a hundred pounds of oat-barley mix and a couple of salt blocks. This heat is rough on my mama cows."

"Well, you know McGreevy better than me. Has he ever shown a reason to cohort with 'em?"

I glanced around the aisle and over a burlap sack of corn seed to watch Earl's reaction. I knew Kotter was trying to size up Earl's loyalties, and Earl knew he needed credit on the feed. "Cohort with 'em?" Earl asked.

"Yeah, cohort. You know, treat 'em as equals," Kotter explained.

"No idea," Earl said, "but I need to get this feed back to the farm and cool down my calves."

"Well, I'll tell ya what; we gonna find out! You let one of them darkies through the front door, and the next thing you know Forbye will be overrun with uppity nigras claiming equal rights when they already have their own rights. Like they've never heard of separate but equal!" Prescott Kotter said those words as easy as falling off a log.

If I'm totally honest with you and myself, in those days I didn't want to be bothered with civil rights. I wasn't a racist, mind you. I was just a simple woman with my own concerns. Some might call me ignorant, while others would claim I was part of the problem. I got along fine with black folks simply because I'd never really been around black folks. Earl always hired a few during harvest or to help out with cattle, but they never came up to the house. I was troubled, though, by the ugliness that seemed to consume otherwise rational and decent men. However, when men like Mr. Kotter went off on bigoted rants, I could sense fear tucked deep inside the bellowing brew of adjectives.

Earl threw the feed into the back of our pickup truck and then plopped down on the seat. He pulled out his kerchief and wiped the sweat off his brow. "This thing's gonna have legs," he said as he exhaled.

"Oh, Kotter is just blowing steam. All we need is a good summer shower to cool things off," I said.

Earl popped the clutch in our old truck, and we rumbled down the cracked clay road. Earl seemed troubled. His eyes were focused behind the wheel, but I sensed he was clueless to his surroundings. We drove past Myers Lake, which usually brought the comment, "Wish I had my fishing pole," but Earl just bounced along with indifference to a lake that was known for its five-pound bass. Our truck shook and rattled down sandy washboard roads without one complaint about the county's road maintenance program. *Something is definitely eating at Earl,* I thought as my head bobbled around the dust-blown cab.

"Up here on the right, you see that old barn back there?" Earl finally said. I looked out to a pasture where a few cows were huddled under a shade tree. In the distance I saw a weather-beaten barn with an old gray wagon sitting out front.

"The one with the wagon?" I asked.

"Yeah. That's where they have Klan meetings."

"Klan meetings? No, Earl! Not in Forbye!"

Earl just nodded. "And you know who owns that property?"

"Don't tell me, Earl. Not him."

"Yep—none other than Prescott Kotter." Earl lit a bouncing cigarette as the old truck hopped down the beaten dirt path.

"How do you know this?" I asked.

"Reach in the glove box and pull out that envelope," he said.

*What on earth could Earl have in his glove box to prove such a thing?* I popped open the door and plucked out a plain white envelope. "This?"

"Yeah, read 'em. Start with the one on top."

I unfolded the first note. "Dear Brother Gladstone," I read out loud. "Many men who are organizing eventualities have been watching you. You are being judged by your every move. A summons is in the waiting. Are you ready and willing to respond? Mention this to nobody." I closed the note. "What's this about, Earl?"

"It was left on my windshield about a month ago. Read the second note."

My hands felt clammy. "Brother Gladstone, we contacted you because we have faith in you. We are on your side and you will need us on your side. The dense shroud of secrecy is nigh. Are you a man or mouse? Open your eyes to the blazing cross and abate not, but move toward the light. Mention this to nobody."

I felt my heart in my throat as I opened the next note. "That one came a few days later. It was taped on my tractor," Earl said.

"Dear Brother Gladstone," it read. "Our judges like you. Are you sturdy enough to heed the call? The ministers of the kingdom will shortly issue their call. Be wise, strong, and accepting. You are not alone. The Brotherhood protects its own. The Brotherhood turns a blind eye on the weak. Don't be a weak man! The circle waits for your signal. Place a lit lantern in your barn loft on the first night with no moon. Mention this to nobody." I pretty much knew what all the notes were about, but it didn't seem real until Earl confirmed my fears.

"The Klan wants to recruit me," he frowned.

"Oh, no, Earl! And you think Kotter is behind this?"

"I know he is," Earl said. "Pull out that invoice from Kotter's store."

I reached in and found a bill for last month's charges. "Okay, now what?"

"Look at the letter M on the invoice and then look at the letter M on the notes. You'll see the M key is chipped at the top corner."

"Oh my goodness! You're right, Earl! They came from the same typewriter."

"So much for the cloak of secrecy, huh?" Earl scoffed.

"Still..." I mused. "The notes didn't say anything about them meeting at that old barn."

"No, but I've had my suspicions about that old barn for the longest time. Something about the place just didn't add up. Once in a while when I'd drive by it late at night, usually on my way to early market over at South Creek, there would be a bonfire out back and several horses tied up by the wagon. It seemed strange to me because the place looks deserted in the daytime."

"Have you talked to Hiram or Duncan about this?" I asked.

"No," he replied, staring straight ahead.

"Earl, you don't think they're in the Klan, do you?"

"I don't know," Earl admitted, "but I do know one thing. Tonight is the first night with no moon."

Earl lumbered the truck into our driveway; its brakes squeaked to an eventual stop. The morning was already a scorcher even without this newfound news. Heat consumed the breezeless cab, but we just sat there, baking in our own thoughts. I wondered what had happened to Forbye—or perhaps nothing new had happened; maybe I had just denied it all these years. I mean, we'd never had a cross burning in our town. Our streets were always quiet, and everybody seemed to get along. The dreadful thought of angry men running around in white robes looking for black men to lynch painted an ugly portrait of my picturesque town. The world was changing; I knew that for sure. And I guess Forbye really didn't have a choice in the matter.

"Well, all we can do is wait and see how this thing plays out," Earl sighed at last.

"What about the lantern? If you reject them Earl, there could be trouble."

"You think Old Man Kotter scares me? Let me tell ya something, Emma. Cowards hide behind masks. Under those white sheets you'll find a yella man."

Although Earl did not place a lit lantern in the barn loft that night, he did keep watch with his shotgun. But, thanks to the Lord, the night passed without a disturbance. We spent the next several nights on little sleep and gallons of coffee.

Rumors continued to swirl around town during the days leading up to Sunday's service. I heard murmurs in the grocery line and whispers down at the beauty parlor. And Rose—good gravy, Rose Carter was working a double shift on the party lines. Come Sunday, if Preacher

McGreevy didn't explain why the black fella had been at his house, then the town would surely combust from curiosity.

Each day seemed hotter than the day before, and Sunday morning was no exception, which made my usual go-to-meeting attire quite unbearable. Oh, I don't mind dressing up for the Lord, but nylons and a girdle in that heat! I should've earned points that day. Earl threw on a sport shirt and loose trousers, and then had the nerve to complain about wearing hard shoes! Men!

Naturally, we had a good turnout for Sunday service. I think we ran about seventy in Sunday School and probably had around eighty-five in attendance for preaching service. Preacher McGreevy was delivering a wonderful sermon on loving thy neighbor, but he made no mention of the black man who was spotted at his house. I kept glancing at Mr. Kotter. He bobbed his head from side to side; sweat poured down his jowls and pooled around his neck. We all were perspiring, but Kotter's sweating looked agitated, restless, and angry.

In the final minutes of service, Brother McGreevy read from the Book of Mark, chapter 12, verses 28-34:

> And one of the scribes came, and having heard them reasoning together, and perceiving that he had answered them well, asked him, Which is the first commandment of all?
>
> And Jesus answered him, the first of all the commandments is, Hear, O Israel; The Lord our God is one Lord.
>
> And thou shalt love the Lord thy God with all thy heart, and with all thy soul, and with all thy mind, and with all thy strength: this is the first commandment.
>
> And the second is like, namely this, Thou shalt love thy neighbor as thyself. There is none other commandment greater than these.

Brother McGreevy stopped and focused out into the congregation. His perfect hair dripped with sweat. The summer's tantrum held little respect for our house of worship. The hot air that moved through the open windows seemed to stop and hang on the preacher's gaze. Perspiration, abundant and bothersome, rolled freely down his tanned face and gathered around the cleft in his chin.

"Let me repeat that again," he said. "'Thou shalt love thy neighbor as thyself. There is none other commandment greater than these.'"

He paused and looked at a handkerchief lying neatly on the pulpit. The preacher slowly reached out, grabbed the fabric, and mopped his brow. He placed it inside the pocket of his sweat-soaked jacket.

"I know there have been rumblings about a colored man visiting my house," Brother McGreevy began.

The wooden funeral-home fans stopped in mid-breeze. Several members shifted in their seats, while Prescott Kotter leaned foreword in anticipation of receiving the answer he'd craved all week. "The man was Pastor Lucious Hightower, and he is the preacher at Bethel Baptist right here in Forbye. In other words, Bethel Baptist is our neighbor," Preacher McGreevy intoned.

A collective inhale went throughout the congregation and held for whatever was next.

"Now, some of you might not like this, but the world is changing," the preacher continued. "Just as the New Testament gave us a new covenant, the civil rights movement will bring forth a new day. As Christians, we must lead the way by not only being color blind towards our black skinned brothers, but also by standing up when we see injustices masked by the phrase 'separate but equal.'"

*Snap*! Old Man Kotter's head jolted back like he'd received an uppercut to the jaw. The back of his neck turned fire-engine red. I was sitting two pews behind and could only imagine what contortions flashed over his face. However, Preacher McGreevy wasn't finished with his round of flurries as he went on to say, "Preacher Hightower and I have discussed on several occasions the best way to bring this community together. After many hours in prayer, we've been given an answer from God. Next week I will preach the message over at Bethel Baptist, and Preacher Hightower will be right here, behind this pulpit, preaching to this congregation."

Hushed rumblings went throughout the congregation, and then Prescott Kotter bolted straight up, "Now hold on, Preacher!" he blurted out. "We cannot allow that!"

"Please sit down, Brother Kotter," the preacher requested. "This is Sunday worship, not a debate." He looked coolly out over the pews. "Now, I figured this news might be upsetting to some. So we will have a calm and cool discussion about this during Wednesday night's prayer meeting."

Old Man Kotter turned on his hard, polished heels. The sound of his beating hoofs echoed down each pew until he flung the door open and stormed out. Stunned silence gripped the room.

"Brothers and Sisters, I ask that you go home and pray about this. Dig deep into your souls and ask yourselves what it would be like to walk in the shoes of a colored person. Discrimination is the ugliest form of hatred. Yet we think nothing of eating at a whites-only lunch counter, shopping at stores where blacks can't trade, or even worshipping in a house that doesn't welcome all of God's people. How silly the notion is that black schools are just as well funded as our schools! In your hearts, you know this isn't right. Jesus taught us to love one another, and hatred is an emotion with which Jesus cannot co-exist." The preacher stopped briefly to dab at his forehead, as well as to let the congregation absorb those last words.

"The world has come to Forbye's doorstep," he continued. "It's time we show the world how Christians treat their neighbors. And as your pastor, I will not segregate this church. Now, you can run me out of town, but it won't change a thing. Jesus did not die just for you, but for all races. The sooner we accept this, the better off we'll be." Preacher McGreevy dropped his head and stood in silent prayer.

Whether the congregation liked it or not, the preacher was right. I looked around. Members' mouths were agape, fixed eyes glazed over. I suppose I had the same look. *Budging on old habits and lifelong practices might be too much to swallow in one gulp*, I thought.

Brother McGreevy lifted his head. "I realize this is short notice, but sometimes the Lord needs us to move quickly in order to conquer the devil before he has a chance to move. Preacher Hightower and I decided on this approach. We will preach at each other's churches to kickoff a weeklong tent revival in Battlefield Park. Together, standing side by side, we will share the gospel with all people, of any color. If no one shows up, then we'll preach to empty chairs and open-minded mosquitoes." Again, he coolly surveyed the congregation. "We will meet here Wednesday night for a rational discussion about Brother Hightower delivering his message here, but the revival will happen, with or without this church's blessing. We will not have Sunday night service tonight. Instead, I ask that you spend time in prayer. Listen to the still, small voice. Open your souls to his word. You are dismissed."

Preacher McGreevy walked down to the first pew, gathered up his family, and left through the side door, leaving us to reflect on the weight of his message. The atmosphere was heavy with thought. Members filed out; mouths remained mum. I couldn't judge the attitude. Had Brother McGreevy won the hearts and minds of the congregation? Or did he just set into motion his own departure? Time would tell.

Earl said nothing on the way home. Gauging that man's emotion had always been a particularly hard nut to crack, but this—this *thing*, this elephant in the room, bottled him up tighter than Nelly Dalton's girdle. Everybody had to have an opinion, right? I know I did. Maybe I didn't at first, but since the preacher spoke, the Lord laid it on my heart to clear my soul of any hatred toward anyone based on their color. That's what I kept trying to tell Earl on the way home. He never agreed, disagreed, or even responded to my newly found conviction. It was almost like his mind was in some distant Korean foxhole.

We spent Sunday afternoon and evening just trying to keep cool. The heat wave was taking its toll on our farm. We lost a momma cow and her calf due to dehydration. Best we could tell, the heat affected the cow's senses, and she went batty. They must have wandered the back forty searching for water and ended up lost. The poor calf died at his momma's side. What was left of our crops was holding on, barely. That summer's scorcher reached deep into Earl's wallet, and most of Earl's wallet was on credit to Mr. Kotter.

Late that evening, after Earl had hosed down the cattle and made his rounds, he showered, picked at a bowl of peach ice cream, and wandered off to bed. I decided to stay up in hopes of catching a breeze on the front porch while doing my crosswords. I guess at some point I drifted off, because suddenly the ringing phone jarred me awake. Still a little confused as to my whereabouts, I heard Earl fumbling around inside the house.

"Earl?" I shouted. He didn't answer, so I got up and walked to the door. Just as I reached for the knob, Earl met me coming through the screen door.

"The preacher has a cross burning in his front yard!" he yelled, bolting through the door.

"What? A cross?" I responded. Earl was headed to his pickup truck. "Wait for me!" I was just in my night coat, but there was no time for shoes, so I had to run barefoot through the damp grass and to the truck.

Earl gave the old truck a foot full of floorboard, and we tore out, kicking up dust in our wake. Before he hit third gear, he said, "That was Hiram on the phone, so at least we know he's not part of the Klan."

"You can be sure?"

"Yeah, he said the preacher just woke him up with the phone call. Plus he was too shook up to be part of this."

We turned the corner on Brier Street and that's when I saw it: a cross burning right in the middle of the preacher's yard. I raised my hand to my face. I couldn't believe it, but my eyes captured the worst vision of hate. That symbol, the cross, where the Savior was crucified for all mankind, stood enraged, blazing the devil's fire through means of intimidation, terror, and downright ugliness. I sat in the truck—I couldn't move.

Hiram and a few other men arrived at the scene just as Earl popped out of the truck.

"Go up to the house and make sure the McGreevys are okay!" Earl shouted to Hiram. "I'll grab a hose! As dry as it is, this thing might catch the house on fire!"

Earl and the fellas hustled about pulling at hoses and spraying out flames. In short order, the cross was a smoldering ash.

Still in his nightclothes, Preacher McGreevy walked outside. He stepped around the mass of gray lumber without so much as an acknowledgement and came over to the truck where Earl and the men had gathered. "I heard something hit our door, and I ran to the window," he said. "When I pulled open the curtains, I saw the cross burning and five men on horses. They wore white hoods and robes, and each of them had a shotgun. That's when I called you, Hiram. I wanted to go outside, but my wife and kids begged me to stay inside. Deep down, though, I felt I should've gone out. I should've made them shoot me on the spot, right there."

"Preacher, you did the right thing," Hiram said.

"I don't know. Maybe," the preacher sighed. "But they just sat on those horses... staring at me, wanting me to come out... wanting to teach me a lesson, I'm sure. They didn't move until they saw your headlights, Earl, coming around the corner. Then, they smacked their horses and disappeared into the darkness."

Somehow, Calvin Tibbs got wind of the cross burning and drove up with an investigative sneer. His round belly popped out first as he swung the car door open. He was wearing baggy trousers and a shirt that until twenty minutes before was lying wrinkled in a hamper. The shirt was buttoned up unevenly to his neck. He relit his used cigar, fumbled through a spiral notepad, and then barked, "We got a cross burning?"

"No, Calvin, we always meet at the preacher's house at two o'clock in the morning," Earl said in a sarcastic tone. Earl was in no mood for the press.

"I see. Well, Rose Carter called me and said—"

"Yes, Calvin," Earl interrupted, "a cross was burned on the preacher's yard."

"Oh, okay then, so there was a cross burning. Good!" Mr. Tibbs said.

"Good?" I shot back at Mr. Tibbs.

"No, I mean good that there was a—uh, that my informant was correct," he stammered.

*Oh dear Lord, Rose is known down at the* Telegraph *as the informant. I guess it fits,* I thought.

"So, does anyone have an idea who might have done this?" Mr. Tibbs had pen in hand, ready to scribble down names to this caper.

"It was a cross burning, Calvin! Who do you think did it?"

"Just trying to get the facts here, Earl. So ya think it's Klan related, do ya?"

Earl sighed. "Oh boy, you majored in journalism, didn't you?"

"Yeah, and I minored in criminology," Calvin replied. "Now, 'bout these Klan members. Did anyone get a description of them, like what they were wearing, scars or tattoos?"

"Tibbs! They were wearing white hoods and robes, for crying out loud!" snapped Earl.

"Gee, Earl, you don't have to get snippy," Mr. Tibbs huffed.

Earl lit a cigarette, a gesture, I'm sure, designed to help him avoid punching Tibbs right in the jaw. Preacher McGreevy moved in. "Come on, Calvin. Walk with me and I'll tell you what I saw."

The preacher and the reporter moved away from our truck about the same time that Jed Burton, the Sheriff of Forbye, pulled up in his squad car. He opened the door and slid out in one motion. I'd never seen the sheriff out of uniform, but there he stood in his bathrobe and black cowboy boots, a holstered pistol around his waist. He slammed the car door shut and then reached through the window to pluck his hat off the seat. It settled loosely over his crew cut, providing an official look despite the bathrobe. He squared his shoulders and leveled his eyes dead at the preacher and Calvin Tibbs standing a good twenty yards away.

"Tibbs, what are you doing here?" Sheriff Burton growled.

Mr. Tibbs waddled over, belly before feet, until he reached the bumper of Earl's truck. Breathless, he wheezed, "I got a tip there was a cross burning."

"Rose called you too, huh?" the sheriff said. "Does the woman ever sleep?"

"I think she might take cat naps—"

"Tibbs!" the sheriff interrupted. "It was a statement, not a question! Now, stay out of my investigation, or I'll shut the press out of here."

"By press, do you mean me?" Mr. Tibbs asked.

"Yeah, Scoop! He meant you," Earl chimed in.

"Now look," said the sheriff. "I don't know what all happened, so give me the what, when, and where."

"Cross burning, about an hour ago, right here," Earl informed him.

"Okay, now we're cooking," the sheriff said.

Sheriff Burton pushed past Mr. Tibbs and stepped over to the charred remains. We all watched from the truck as he bent down, stuck his finger in some ashes, and then brought it to his nose. "Yep," he said to himself. Standing up, he kicked at a piece of burnt wood. "Uh-huh," he muttered. Then, while staring at the burnt lawn, he backed up about ten paces, shook his head, and crinkled his nose. For several minutes, the sheriff stood motionless, fixed on the burnt woodpile, his investigative senses churning, his mind focused on any little clue that an untrained civilian wouldn't recognize. He tilted his head to the right and then to the left, almost like he was receiving a mental image of the villains responsible for this terror. Keeping his eyes locked on the scene, he shouted, "Hey, Tibbs!"

"Yeah, Sheriff?"

"Go to my car and fetch me that big tackle box I got on the seat," the sheriff ordered.

"Got ya, Sheriff," Mr. Tibbs said, and then he turned to us. "Probably wants me to help with some evidence gathering." Calvin Tibbs went as quickly as his legs would allow over to the sheriff's car. The top half of his body disappeared through the window. The view wasn't flattering for a man of his carriage, belly propped up by the car door, trousers losing gravity with each stretch of his chubby arms. Finally (and thankfully before the sheriff would have had to handle another crime—indecent exposure!), Tibbs's sausage-like fingers found the box. "Told ya I minored in criminology," he chirped as he went by us.

The sheriff pointed to the ground, and Mr. Tibbs set the box down.

"Thanks, Tibbs. Now beat it," Sheriff Burton said.

"Oh, well. I guess I can just wait over there, then."

"Yes, Tibbs you can just wait over there... then."

Poor Tibbs. He shuffled back with his minor in criminology dragging the ground. The sheriff bent down, flipped open the box, pulled out a thermos, and poured a cup of coffee.

"Well, Calvin, not only did you minor in criminology, you lettered in water boy," Earl chuckled.

The sheriff downed his java, grabbed a flashlight, and then walked a good distance beyond the scene. He studied the ground for clues. It looked quite bizarre, the sheriff poking at the ground while wearing a bathrobe, his boney knees at liberty just below the hem. After a few minutes of prodding in the dark, he made his way back to us.

"Yep, it was a cross-burning all right," the sheriff stated.

"I told you that a half hour ago," Earl said.

"Now hold on, Earl. A lawman can't take a civilian's word. If we did, ol' Tibbs here would be under the jail," Sheriff Burton announced. "Right, Tibbs?"

"Oh, come on, Sheriff," Mr. Tibbs said. "There's no evidence I was peeping in Betty Turner's window."

"Betty Turner? I was talking about Molly Sanders," the sheriff replied.

The blood left Mr. Tibbs's rosy cheeks, followed by uncomfortable silence.

"Just messing with ya, Tibbs," the sheriff finally burst out, and then slapped the journalist on the back. The puffy cheeks of Calvin Tibbs returned to their rosy nature. "Well, I best be going," said Burton.

"Wait, what are you going to do?" asked Earl, amazed.

"Well, breakfast is still a few hours away, so I'll catch a few z's before the day starts," Sheriff Burton said.

"No, about this." Earl pointed to the burnt cross.

"I already told ya. It was a cross-burning, probably the Klan," the sheriff said. "Y'all have a good day, now." The sheriff flipped his hat onto the seat, swung his bathrobe around, and plopped down behind the wheel. He left as quickly as he came.

Nothing much happened over the next couple of days, but you could sense the tension building towards Wednesday night's prayer meeting. I guess you could say it was the calm before the storm. Collectively, the town wondered if the cross-burning was the first drop of rain from a hurricane brewing off the coast.

It was a hot July night. Humid air, sticky and stifling, filled the car as Earl and I drove to prayer meeting on Wednesday night. Angry and hateful passion suffused the First Baptist Church of Forbye as we stepped through the door—not a very Christian atmosphere. The church was full, much fuller than a normal Wednesday night service, so we had to settle in towards the back. It really didn't matter, because Mr. Kotter had the floor and could be heard from the moon.

"It would be quite amusing, Preacher, if not for the simple fact that a Negro minister isn't properly ordained to preach to a superior race. And I, for one, will not entertain such an outlandish idea. The sanctity of this church must be preserved. Our Southern Baptist brethren forbade such activity, knowing it would surely lead to our undoing. You go mixin' races, and you'll have opened a box that you can't close," Mr. Kotter informed the preacher.

"I understand your concern, Brother Kotter, but God has placed it in my heart to accept all people. The human soul has no color," Preacher McGreevy stated.

"Preacher, you're right on that one," shot back Kotter. "White is not a color, and Negroes have no souls!"

*He said what? Negroes have no souls?* I was half-sure I'd misheard.

"No more than a mule or a workhorse has one," Mr. Kotter continued. "You should know this, Preacher. Noah cursed Canaan and his descendants into slavery because of his father, Ham. We all know Ham was black; it's right there in the Bible."

"That's antebellum thinking when you parse out the Bible to the way you want it to read," Preacher McGreevy said.

"Antebellum thinking, huh? This church does belong to the Southern Baptist Convention. Need I remind you why the Southern Baptist Convention was founded?" Mr. Kotter spouted.

"Brother Kotter, man is not perfect. And, yes, I know the Church's history."

The packed church was witness to a debate between just two men. Oh, Kotter had his corner, but no one spoke openly. I'd guess most of the farmers were deep in debt to Prescott Kotter and feared the old man would cut them off or demand balance due if they sided with the preacher. Also, I'm sure some liked our church the way it was—white.

"Let me just remind everyone why we're Southern Baptist," Prescott Kotter said turning to the congregation. The damp air plastered his thin hair wildly about his forehead. His cheeks, round and sweaty, grew red as he began to speak. "The Southern Baptist Convention was founded because of slavery. Look it up! See, the Baptists up north didn't want missionaries to be slave owners. That was just unacceptable to a Southern gentleman. After all, throughout our history godly men had owned slaves—Washington, Jefferson, and so forth. Why should a

Northerner concern himself with our property? Because that's what a slave was—property."

"Brother Kotter, we're enlightened men now," Preacher McGreevy said. "Man used to think the Earth was flat and leeches cured all ills, but man evolves when ignorance is rectified. Our Baptist brothers were wrong, and it's time we admit it."

Mr. Kotter pointed his bony finger towards the preacher. He was eaten up with rage, a mad man dizzy from his own venom. "What you're doin', Preacher, just ain't right," he spouted. "I will write a letter to Dr. Ramsey Pollar, the president of the Southern Baptist Convention. And Dr. Pollar will receive this letter stating your intentions to have a colored preach behind this pulpit. Brother Pollar is already none too happy about the chances of a Catholic becoming President of the United States. I imagine when he hears this news, you'll be taken to the woodshed."

When Kotter finished, Preacher McGreevy looked at him and said in an even tone, "I encourage you to write that letter, but it will not change my mind. Ramsey Pollar is not my judge. One day, though, each of us will be judged for our actions here tonight. I pray your judge will be merciful."

That comment from the preacher made the angry man even angrier. Mr. Kotter clinched his fist and went off on a bizarre tangent. "You're out of your colored-lovin' mind. The measures our Baptist brethren went through to preserve the Southern heritage will not be mocked in this church. We all know blacks can't control their sex drive. This is not a theory; it is a fact, borne out by history. The men slaves were used as studs on the plantation; now that urge is in their genes. You go turnin' loose a black man on a white congregation full of women… well, Preacher, nothing would please the Negro more than to have forbidden fruit."

"Careful, Brother Kotter, you're getting out of line," Preacher McGreevy warned.

"*You've* been out of line, Preacher, ever since that black fella went to your house!" Kotter shouted, fist shaking.

"Brother Kotter, please calm down."

"Not one nigger will step foot in this church!" Prescott Kotter raged from the fourth pew.

"Enough!" roared a voice, and everyone turned and looked in my direction. I couldn't believe it—the voice was Earl's. He stood up and walked down the aisle. All eyes followed my husband as he stepped up to the pulpit. There was awkwardness about him as he fumbled his hands across the pulpit's oak framework. In all the years we had worshipped at that church, I don't think Earl had ever stood behind the holy podium, and it showed. His body language spoke insecurity. He looked as if he'd rather be any place than where he was. He tugged nervously at his sleeve before speaking.

"His name was Sergeant Jeffery O'Boyle," Earl began, "but we called him Sarge. We were Gladstone and O'Boyle, just a couple of Scottish brothers that got thrown together during the war. I served in his squad along with eight other men. There was Joey, a Jewish kid from Brooklyn, and a guy named Donny whose grandparents emigrated from Italy. Then there was Leo, a Catholic boy, who wanted to become a priest after his hitch was up. We even had a Mexican, Manny, who joined the army the day after he became an American citizen. Can you believe that? Oh yeah, and Carlos! How could I forget him? Carlos was an odd sort. His heritage was Cuban, but he couldn't speak a lick of Spanish, and he loved bluegrass music." Earl laughed. "I remember Manny trying to teach Carlos Spanish. It was the funniest thing. I probably picked up more of the language from just overhearing them than Carlos did. We also had a fella named Paul in our group. He was born in America, but he had relatives that died in one of Hitler's concentration camps, and Paul wasn't even Jewish. Rounding out our squad was Stefan, a Polish lad and a third-generation American. During lighter moments, if war really has any, we busted Stefan's chops with every Polish joke we knew. He actually liked them and told a few on himself." Earl stopped and his smile slowly withered away.

"You're probably wondering why I'm telling y'all this," Earl said. "I told ya about the Sarge, and this is a story about him and what he did for those men I just mentioned," Earl paused to clear his throat. "Sarge used to carry one of those pocket-sized New Testaments with him everywhere he went. He'd read it in foxholes, chow halls, latrines, and sometimes in between tossing hand grenades. He hated the thought of taking another man's life, especially when the enemy had a lost soul. I saw him cut down a line of Koreans single-handedly and then weep over their corpses while praying for forgiveness. That's the kind of man Sergeant Jeffery O'Boyle was.

"The Sarge was my kind of man, and we hit it off the day we met. Maybe it was because we both shared Scottish surnames, or that we were country boys at heart, with the same dream of owning a farm one day. The big difference, the only difference I guess, was the fact that Sarge was a Christian, and I was not. He'd always ask me, 'Are you going to heaven, Stony?' That's what he called me, Stony. And I always told him, 'I doubt it; God doesn't like drunk soldiers.' His response was always the same. 'God loves everybody,' he'd say. He wasn't pushy, but he always invited me to chapel and that sort of thing.

"Well, I had just made corporal, but was still a kid and far from battle-hardened when our squad went out on patrol one night. Nine of us were supposed to coordinate a brief sweep through the jungle, with another squad flanking our right. As things go in the army, about a mile into our hike the radio went dead, and for you guys out there who served, you know it was a snafu. Anyway, we continued, with our heads on a swivel and rifles ready. Suddenly, Sarge threw up his hand. We froze." Earl stopped to mop his brow. The congregation hung on his words; even Old Man Kotter leaned in a little closer to hear Earl continue.

"Everything got quiet," Earl said. "I heard my heart beating. Sarge whispered, 'Somethin's not right.' No sooner had he spoken those words, than the night sky lit up with gunfire. We had walked into an ambush. We scattered the best we could, but fire came from all sides. 'Retreat to the right and find our flank!' Sarge yelled. It was the only move we had. But without radio contact, our flank took us as hostiles, and they opened up on us.

"Joey took one right between the eyes and was dead before he hit the ground. The earth rattled and explosion after explosion bounced us around like rag dolls. Above the artillery blast, I heard somebody scream. It was Manny. I couldn't believe my eyes. 'Manny is hit!' I hollered and then I just locked up—I couldn't move. The noise, the smell, the disorder, the sight of Manny's innards hanging out of his uniform, all paralyzed me. I could sense men running around, I could hear Sarge barking out orders, but I just stood there with chaos raining down. Through this haze of confusion, a Korean somehow appeared right before me, ten yards, maybe closer. Our eyes met. My weapon stayed on my side, while he drew his. I remember thinking, *You're dead Gladstone; just get it over with!* But before the thought left my mind, the enemy was riddled with bullets. So many rounds were pumped into his belly that it nearly cut him in half. His blood hit my face, I was that close. Things were happening so fast around me, but I still couldn't move. I heard, 'Stony, get down,' and then this massive body grabbed me and together we launched into a makeshift foxhole. My helmet caught a bullet on the way down.

"'Stony! Stony, snap out of it!' I heard a voice say. The battlefield roared with anger above us. The ground would not stop shaking, but I managed to gather my senses. 'Sarge,' I said.

"'You back with me, Stony?' Sergeant O'Boyle asked. I was back with him, but we were in no better shape. We didn't know where our men were; the enemy was advancing; friendly fire kept pounding our position with mortar shells. We hunkered down, hoping the firestorm would ease up a bit, but a lull never really happened. 'We got to find a way out of this, Stony, and save our men,' the Sarge said. He popped his head over some brush to observe the landscape. The sky lit up like a flashbulb. *Pop! Pop! Pop! Boom! Boom!* I felt a constant rumble in my chest. The Sarge ducked back down. 'There's at least three of our men pinned down about fifty yards due west. They're sitting ducks and must be getting close to running out of ammo.'

"'Now listen to me, Stony, and listen good,' Sarge said. 'I don't know how far I'll get, but I'm gonna try to draw the enemy's fire by sneaking behind them. Now, give me all your hand grenades.' I clipped two off my belt and placed them in his hands. The Sarge reached into his pocket and pulled out his New Testament. 'Take this, Stony. If something happens, here's a map to see me again!' He shoved the small Bible inside my jacket. 'Don't make me go to hell looking for ya, boy,' he said. And then the Sarge grabbed two grenades off his belt. He fiddled briefly with the four grenades before placing two each in the palms of his huge hands. 'Now, pull the pins out, Stony,' he ordered.

"'Don't do this, Sarge,' I pleaded.

"He hollered, 'Stony, pull the pins!' More gunfire rattled over our heads. The sound of battle ripped through my ears and shook me to the core. Trembling, I pulled the safety pins out while the Sarge kept his hands clamped down on the live grenades. He looked at me, 'This will knock the fire out of them,' he said. Then Sarge closed his eyes and started praying to himself. I'm not much of a lip reader, but I could tell the Sarge was preparing to meet God. Then just before he opened his eyes, a big smile flew across his face and I heard him say, 'Thank you, Lord, I'll be there shortly.' Just as sure as I'm standing here, I knew right then and there that God's voice told Sergeant Jeffery O'Boyle, 'Come home, son. My Kingdom is yours.' No, I didn't hear it, but I know the Sarge did because to this day, I've never seen a smile like that," Earl stopped.

The memory became painful. I'd known the man for years and this was the first war story I'd ever heard him tell. Watching his expression told me why. His face revealed the torture his soul was going through.

Hidden battle scars he'd kept buried deep inside opened up like fresh wounds on a salty face.

"'Now, Stony,' Sarge said. 'You're gonna hear a loud blast when these grenades go off. I don't know how many of 'em I'll get, but they'll know I'm behind them. When I engage, you hightail it over to our men; keep your butt low and your head lower. Do not, I repeat, do not fire your weapon; it will only give up your position. When you're within earshot of the men, start shouting the code word.' For those who don't know, we always used a code word to identify a friendly. That particular night our code word was Ted Williams. So, the Sarge looked at me one last time and said, 'God will clear a path. Stony, the Lord will take care of me—you take care of my men.' Then the Sarge jumped to his feet and took off with both hands full of grenades. For some reason I closed my eyes and started countin' one... two... three... four. Before I reached 'five,' a huge explosion rattled the ground, followed up by an array of machine gun fire. I bolted from my cover, the coming dawn giving enough light to help me navigate through the battlefield without tripping up. Rapid gunfire continued behind me. I half expected a bullet to catch me at any time, if not from the Koreans, then from my buddies that I was running towards. A lump was building up in my throat, but somehow I managed to yell, 'Ted Williams—Ted Williams!' The battlefield went silent." Earl paused.

I felt the congregation holding their breath. No one moved, not even to fan or swat at mosquitoes.

"Just like that, the battle was over. I heard someone yell back, 'Ted Williams,' and the sound echoed around the calm combat zone. Through the mist of dawn, I could see soldiers walking slowly out of the woods. My eyes began to focus. They became clearer as the Sarge's men gathered around me. There was Leo, pale and still shaking. Stefan joined us with that same petrified look. I glanced to my right and saw Carlos wandering out of the thick brush, holding his hands over his ears. Not long after that, Donny and Paul walked up with absolutely no expressions on their faces, just blank stares." Earl stopped. Weariness consumed his face. The man seemed to age with each sentence that fell out of his mouth. He looked weak, frail, and almost unrecognizable, yet all eyes remained on him.

Earl cleared his throat and continued, "So, there we stood, all six of us. Day was beginning to break and from first light we could see that the battleground was littered with dead Koreans. Donny asked, 'What happened? We were goners not more than ten minutes ago. Then boom! Just like that, they're all dead?'

"'The Sarge happened,' I said.

"'Sarge! Where is he?' someone asked, and I dropped my head.

"'No!' Paul shouted, and then he started running around, calling out, 'Sarge... Sarge... *Sarge*!' I think somehow Paul believed if he screamed it long enough and loud enough, the ole Sarge would come walking out of that jungle. Well, Sarge didn't. We found him lying in some tall grass about forty yards away. I don't know how long we stood there looking at his lifeless body, but some of us cried, some of us threw up, and all of us cursed. We cursed the war, cursed the Koreans, and cursed God. And then the strangest thing happened." Earl looked up to the ceiling as if to seek guidance from above.

Earl spoke more deliberately when he finally continued. "With all the commotion going on, I had forgotten about our right flank. You know, the squad that was mistakenly firing at us during battle. Why did they stop? I could explain the Koreans; the Sarge blew most of them up with his grenades and then finished them off with his rifle. I imagine the Sarge was killed with a bullet fired from a dying man's gun. But Sarge could not have stopped friendly fire, which was a good distance from our location. At least it didn't make sense until Sergeant Baylor came walking up with his squad.

"'Sorry 'bout the fire, Stony. Where's the Sarge?' he asked.

"I just looked at him and tilted my head down to the tall grass. Sergeant Baylor's pasty white face turned a lighter shade of pale when he saw Sarge's lifeless body.

"'Stony, I just saw him. What happened?'

"'What do you mean, you just saw him?' I asked.

"Sergeant Baylor went on and told us that he didn't know we were anywhere around because we didn't answer our radio. In fact, he thought we went south. So when fire broke out, he assumed it was the enemy and unloaded on us. They didn't stop until the Sarge appeared, from what seemed out of nowhere, and started waving his hands. Sarge told them to hold their fire because his men were in the jungle, and then he pointed in our direction. Sergeant Baylor turned to his men and yelled, 'Cease fire,' and then the strangest thing happened. When Sergeant Baylor turned back around, Sarge was gone." Earl paused to gain a little composure; his damp eyes had a steady cast of red. His bottom lip quivered while his mind sorted out the next sentence.

"I remembered Sarge's last words, 'God will clear a path.' Those words keep running through my mind...God will clear a path...God will clear a path. At the time I didn't know it, but it became so clear after hearing Sergeant Baylor's story. Now I may not know a lot of things, but I do know this—there is no way Sarge's earthly body could have traveled over to Sergeant Baylor's squad. God will clear a path..." Earl's voice trailed off. "There is no mistake about it; Sergeant Jeffery O'Boyle took on the form of an angel and stopped Sergeant Baylor's squad."

The weight of Earl's story could be felt throughout the congregation.

"Battlefield cleanup is always a messy detail, but that one hurt more than any other. We lost three men that day: Joey, Manny, and Sarge. I saw two of 'em die right before my eyes. But what were we? What were they? Joey was Jewish and Manny was Mexican and probably neither would be welcomed in this church. What about Leo, the Catholic kid, I told ya about? Or Carlos, who was American through and through, but his skin was a little brown? Would this church feel uneasy if they sat down in one of our pews? While you think about that, think about this—our country doesn't call up white men, brown men, Catholic men, or Jewish men. No! Our country calls up men. And if you've ever been in a foxhole with a buddy, the last thing on your mind is his religion or his skin color." Earl stopped briefly. "You know, I should have died that day. Only God knows why I didn't. Maybe I was spared for this moment right here—right now; I don't know. But all this week those words kept running through my mind: God will clear a path." Earl stopped and fumbled around in his shirt pocket. He pulled out a small book.

"This is the New Testament Sarge stuffed into my pocket that day." He held the Bible up high. "Sarge saved my life twice that day, once in this life and once for the life after this. See, I took this book and I read it because I wanted to see the Sarge again. I became a Christian through Christ who saved me, through Sarge who saved me. See how that works?" Earl took a deep breath. "Now, does anyone here believe I will see Sarge again?"

The whole congregation, even the ladies, said, "Amen."

"I am glad we all can agree on something," Earl said. "And you know, there is one thing about Sarge that I forgot to tell ya about." Earl looked up to the heavens. "He was a black man." He paused, then said to the sky, "Sarge... God will clear a path."

Nobody saw that coming. Some shifted uncomfortably in their seats. Some nodded their heads with approval. And one turned beet red—Prescott Kotter. The old man's head bobbed, his shoulders shook, and then he leaped up. "Earl, that's got nothing to do with this! If there is a black heaven, then I'm sure your friend is there," he said without realizing how ridiculous he sounded.

"I thought you said black people didn't have souls?" Earl responded.

"Well, you don't need a soul to go to black heaven," Kotter huffed and fell deeper into the absurd.

"Look, Kotter," Earl said. "I'm not gonna debate you on this thing. And I'm not gonna make any threats, but I am gonna tell ya how it's gonna be. Now, Preacher," Earl looked to Brother McGreevy and said, "don't worry about us. We're not gonna have any trouble here because, come Sunday morning, I'll be standing out in the parking lot waiting for Preacher Hightower to arrive. When he does, I will escort him to the door and to the pulpit if I have to. I'm prepared to do this alone, like the Sarge did. But a soldier never turns down volunteers. Will anybody stand with me?"

Dead silence screamed from the congregation and lasted for a few uncomfortable moments.

"I'll stand with ya, Earl," Hiram Humfinger said and then made his way up front. I thought I might have imagined this, but I felt a cool summer breeze slip through the chapel's windows.

"I'll join ya, Earl," Duncan Bennett said, and then he went up front and stood by Earl and Hiram. No, it wasn't my imagination. Goose bumps ran up my arms; the room was cooling off. Slowly, men rose from their pews and joined the fellas up front. It looked like the invitation at a Billy Sunday revival; it was a sight to behold, indeed. Go figure: a war story from a quiet and humble man defused a powder keg itching to explode.

The last man, the only man, left sitting was Prescott Kotter. His mouth was agape. His body twitching, he was obviously in some kind of discomfort. The man saw his world suddenly disappear. He walked into a segregated church and thought that through power, influence, and intimidation, it would stay that way. Trouble was, he didn't count on an old farm boy with dirt under his nails and a sudden gift of gab to make common sense out of a senseless situation.

*A black heaven! My word!* I thought as I looked at the pathetic creature in the fourth pew. It was quite a contrast to the men up front. They were smiling, slapping each other on the backs, and, it seemed, collectively exhaling. The endless summer was ending. Sure it was hot, but the heat rested solely on Mother Nature's whim.

"So, this is how it's gonna be?" Mr. Kotter said jumping up. "Well, this church has seen my last dime. If fact, all you farmers up there, I want my money by mornin'!" He wagged his old bony finger at the men. "No more credit!" he shouted as he huffed out the door.

I can tell you what happened next only because Earl told me this on the way home. When Prescott Kotter left the church, Earl followed him out. As Earl said, "I wanted to catch him alone to clear something up." Mr. Kotter was about to drive off when Earl slammed both hands down on the hood of Kotter's car.

"Hold on, Kotter," Earl said.

"You're dead to me, Gladstone," Prescott shot back.

Earl went over and flung the car door open. He reached into his back pocket and pulled out Kotter's last invoice. "I'll eat beans and rice for a year if it means owing you nothing," Earl said and then pulled out two hundred and eighteen dollars from his billfold. Then he fiddled in his front pocket and came out with four pennies. "Here!" Earl slapped the money down on the dashboard. Earl said he then got right up to Kotter's face. "If you're gonna send out K.K.K. recruiting letters, you best buy a new typewriter." Earl stuffed the invoice into Kotter's shirt pocket. "But more importantly, you best know who you're sending them to. See, Kotter, the whole time you've been watching me, I've been watching you. I know it was you that burned the cross on the Preacher's lawn."

Earl told me that when he said that, Kotter's face turned whiter than the sheet he hides under. "You're a coward, Kotter, and a miserable man. But you know what? This is a free country, and you can be as ignorant as you want to. Men like Sarge believed that, cherished that, and died for that. And don't you ever forget it!"

Earl said Kotter just looked at him, and then drove away.

When Sunday rolled around, the whole church waited in the parking lot for Preacher Hightower to arrive. It was a lovely sight: smiles, handshakes, and pats on the back. We surrounded the preacher with love, and he returned our actions.

The preacher was a portly man with a receding hairline. He wore wire-rimmed glasses that looked dignified on the bridge of his nose. And let me tell you something: the man could preach. It reminded me of the time I got drunk and stumbled into a black church. Oh dear, I just typed that, didn't I? Well, it's true; he had us shouting for Jesus and making all kinds of joyful noise. If we had spoken in tongues, we could've passed off as Pentecostals—it was that lively. Nelly Dalton, of course, got a little too carried away, and her slip fell down around her ankles. But all in all, it was a very spiritual service.

The tent revival was just as powerful, if not more so. The week long services were a celebration of brotherhood. Preachers McGreevy and Hightower stood shoulder-to-shoulder, presenting an awe-inspiring message. Black folks sat next to white folks; we shared hymnals, Bibles, and God's love. The only thing segregated under that tent was the devil—we left him pouting in the corner.

Forbye seemed to change overnight. Oh, we still had a few with the old mindset. As long as humans are breathing on this planet, some group is going to hate another; the devil will see to that. But Forbye did change. To use a phrase the kids today say, Forbye was "cutting edge" when it came to race relations. Our church started a member exchange program with the folks over at Bethel Baptist. On the first Sunday of each month a few of our members went to their house of worship, and in return, a few of them came to ours. It was wonderful. Earl and I became friends with several families over at Bethel Baptist. I learned that people are the same no matter where they come from. They laugh, they cry, they celebrate, and they struggle. You know the saying, "Beauty is only skin deep?" Well, skin color is even thinner.

That summer left like a quiet whisper fading into the wind. Many seasons have come and passed since those days, but I think of them often, and wonder what all the fuss was about. It seemed so silly. Towns and cities across this nation protested, rioted, and filled their bellies with hate. From television sets, our living rooms blared out news of unrest and strife. Anger, like a disease, infected suburban neighborhoods and inner-city streets. What a turbulent time it was. However, little ol' Forbye seemed immune to it all.

God cleared a path.

# Emma and Earl: A Love Story

I wasn't always a Gladstone. My given name was Emmaline Bernadette Baumgaertner. It doesn't exactly roll off the tongue, does it? Well, this story goes way back to when I was known as Miss Baumgaertner. The year was 1948, when I was just seventeen years old and a senior at Forbye High. I'll give the curious a few moments to calculate my age.

What I'm about to tell will shock some, and others will just say "Hmm," under their breaths as the next sentence unfolds. Nelly Wilkinson was my best friend back then. Perhaps you know her as Nelly Dalton. Yes, reader, Nelly Dalton was my friend.

Even though we were opposites—Nelly smacked gum and listened to swing music, while I was more inclined to Lifesavers and the dulcet tones of Vaughn Monroe—we did everything together. I can't count the times we sat at the counter inside Dickinson's Pharmacy drinking root beer floats and chatting about Nelly's favorite topic: boys. Anytime there was a cute soda jerk behind the counter, Nelly suddenly didn't know what to order off the menu. One time, with a particular good-looking boy, she actually asked him to describe the ingredients in a hot fudge sundae—twice! She even went as far as ordering a banana split without the banana, just to see the look on the lad's face.

Trying to keep up with Nelly's romances was a daunting task. *Whimsical* would be one word to describe her, but *fickle* would be a better one. During the course of our senior year, Nelly went through two soda jerks, a gas hop down at the filling station, one set of twins (that means both of them), and the stock boy over at the Piggly Wiggly. And that was before Christmas recess.

On the other hand, for the most part, I stayed true to my class studies and spent my free time preparing for the county's annual crossword puzzle tournament. There was a boy who courted my affections, a boy you may know of: Calvin Tibbs. You know him as the ace reporter for the *Forbye Telegraph*. Back then, Calvin had most of his hair and all of his teeth. Or was it most of his teeth and all of his hair? Gosh, it's been so long I can't remember, because eventually he ended up with neither. Anyway, back then he was thinner and had dreams of being a reporter for the *New York Times*. (On a side note, I still weigh the same and never dreamed he would... but I digress.) I tolerated his occasional advances as a trade off for a Coke and a bag of popcorn at the picture show. Calvin, however, was just an amusement to pass my idle time. Whatever you may have heard him say otherwise would fall under the category of journalistic embellishment.

During Christmas break that year, Nelly became infatuated with her newest fella whom she found during a shopping spree over in South Creek. Two days before Christmas we met for a soda, and she filled in all the details.

"Oh Emma, I've met the most wonderful man," she said while eyeing the new soda jerk.

"Man? What happened to Sam, the boy over at the Piggly Wiggly?"

"Yesterday's news, dear, and you said it yourself. He's a boy. Need I remind you that we are reaching the marrying age? A gal needs to start planning her future," Nelly said.

"I thought our future included nursing school in Atlanta. Besides, we're only seventeen, and my concerns right now are my school studies and the crossword tournament."

"Oh, child, to be so naive. Being a nurse would be fun if there wasn't so much blood and sickness involved." Nelly waved her hand. "Besides, you have Calvin."

"I most certainly do not! What did he tell you?" I shot back.

"Nothing," she giggled.

"I'll ignore that," I said. "Now do tell about this, ahem, man you've found."

Nelly took a big gulp of her chocolate malt before she launched into a lovesick narrative. "It was a perfectly glorious day. I'd spent the whole afternoon window-shopping, you know, eying the latest fashions. I decided to go into Stapleton's because they had a lovely sale on foundations, and I needed a new brassiere. So anyway, I was going through the Maidenform rack when out of the corner of my eye I saw him—"

"In the women's underwear department?" I interrupted.

"No, darling, he was over by the nut stand. You know that little booth where you can buy fresh nuts?" Nelly explained.

"Great analogy, but go on," I said.

"Quit being silly! Do you want to hear it or not?" Nelly shot back.

"Yes, yes, nut stand! Go ahead, dear."

"So anyway, again! I saw him out of the corner of my eye, and I thought, *Now there's a nice-looking fella.* Well, he turned and our eyes met. Oh, goodness gracious, my heart jumped up to my throat! I could see those blue eyes clear across two rows of girdles and a stack of Firestone tires. He looked so cute holding that little bag of nuts in his hand. And then he started walking my way. Of course I had no choice but to leave the foundation department. I mean, he couldn't see me with a brassiere in my hand. What if he found out I'm a C-cup?"

"B-cup," I corrected.

"Not in Maidenform, honey," Nelly said. "You know they run small."

"Huh, I never noticed."

"You know what? I'm going to pretend you're not here and finish telling this story to the malt."

"Oh, don't pout. I want to hear it," I said while patting her hand.

"Okay!" She perked up. "So, I started walking toward him. My heart was racing; I had no idea what I would say to him, but I didn't care. I'd figure it out. Well, he moved closer, so I batted my eyes a little."

"Of course you did," I muttered

"What?" Nelly threw her hands up.

"Nothing; go ahead."

"Thank you. So, we got closer. In fact, we met face-to-face right in front of the jewelry counter, maybe an omen, you know. Wedding rings were off to the right."

"Wedding rings? You haven't even spoken to this fella yet! You're bonkers, Nell."

"Maybe, but my momma married my daddy only after a week of courtin'. Short engagements run in my family," Nelly said.

"So does divorce."

"Emma! That was uncalled for! You know daddy had a problem," Nelly complained.

"You're right. I'm sorry, dear. Please tell me about this fella."

"Okay, so we were facing each other. He's awkward in a cute kind of way—maybe shy, maybe mysterious, but dreadfully handsome. His blue eyes could put out a fire or start one in a gal's heart. I was smitten before he spoke..."

Nelly continued talking, but my mind started to wander. *I wish Nelly wouldn't do this. Within two weeks, she'll tire of this fella and move on to the next. What makes her act like this? Last week all she could talk about was Sam. Today it's nut-boy, tomorrow the soda jerk. Nod your head and act like you're listening.* I nodded my head. *I do love her though. She's a good egg, and nobody makes me laugh more than she does. So I shouldn't rain on her parade, even though this will be the fourth boy she's paraded around this month. Nod your head again.* I nodded my head. *Even though it's fun, I don't want to be the one who always says 'I told you so' to her. No, not this time, Emma. I'll just play along. It's her life. What's she talking about now? Pay attention, Emma.*

"So he finally spoke," I heard Nelly say, "And his first words to me were, 'Want some of my nuts? They're warm!'"

I couldn't help it—I started giggling.

"What's so funny?" Nelly questioned.

I tried to say, "Nothing, dear," but I couldn't stop giggling.

"All he did was ask if I wanted his warm nu—" Nelly clapped her hand to her mouth. "Emma!"

Then we both giggled.

Finally Nelly caught her breath. "They were cashews, and they were lovely. So, we chatted a while in the store. He's nineteen years old and his name is Barth."

"Barth?" I interrupted "What on earth kind of name is that?"

"Isn't it dreamy? Like a name out of a dime-store novel." Nelly batted her eyes.

"Yeah: cheap." *That's not playing along.*

"Now Emma, don't be fussy. Especially since Barth could be the one."

"One what?"

"My husband, silly. I told you we met in front of the wedding rings."

"Nell, you've gone kooky! You just met this—this Barth!" *Okay, I can't play along. She can't seriously be thinking of marriage.*

"And you're gonna meet him, too. He's driving up from South Creek next week. What say you and Calvin double date with us?"

"Calvin? I don't know. I feel like I'd be leading the poor boy on if I asked him for a date. He might get the impression I'm carrying a torch for him."

"Oh nonsense. Just tell him you need to chaperone us. Call it an investigation. Calvin likes that sort of thing," Nelly coaxed.

"Well, I do need to see this Barth fella, and Calvin is always good for a free soda," I agreed.

Since school was on recess, we set the date up for the following Tuesday, which was a few days before the New Year. We would meet at the drugstore for a soda and then catch a show. After the movie, we would head over to Nelly's house and listen to some Glenn Miller records. Of course, all of these plans hinged on Nelly's ability to keep her attention on Barth for a week. The gal never seemed satisfied; I've seen her change dates during intermission. What was that word again? Ah yes—fickle.

I had the loveliest Christmas. Momma and Daddy gave me a completely wonderful school dress, a pair of bobby socks, and some perfume that I'll tell you about later. But the best gift of all was a book of crossword puzzles. The book had over two hundred puzzles I could use as preparation for the crossword tournament. It was printed in New York, too—the crossword capital of the world!

Now about that perfume. I understand it's the thought that counts, but that stuff smelled like axle grease with a little bit of orange blossoms thrown in for good measure. I didn't want to hurt Momma's feelings, so I dabbed a little behind each ear and held my nose. Well, within two hours my ears were red and starting to blister. Turns out I had some kind of allergic reaction to the fragrance in question. Momma wanted to return the perfume, but I had a better idea... one that I would regret for the next sixty years. I rewrapped the perfume and gave it to my best friend, Nelly. Yes, I gave Nelly her first batch of Alabaster Heaven, a scent that literally lasted a lifetime.

The night of our double date was cold and wet. Rain came down in buckets most of the day, and a cold front blasted Forbye like it was Santa's backyard. I even saw a few snowflakes from my window as I waited for Calvin to pick me up. He was running late because his old jalopy wouldn't start—again. By the time we arrived at the drugstore, Nelly was already sitting at a booth with her date. Through the window I could see her smacking her chewing gum and twisting her hair in a playful manner around her finger. That always seemed to be Nelly's flirt move, and this new beau was no exception. When we stepped inside, Nelly's boyfriend had his back to us, but I assumed he was doing something amusing because Nelly's cackle traveled across the diner.

"There they are," Nelly said when she saw us.

As we approached the waiting couple, Calvin leaned over my shoulder and said, "Dutch treat, right?"

"Dutch treat? Only if you've got on wooden shoes," I said as I turned to the table. "Well, hello, Nelly." The young man sitting next to Nelly looked up at me. He had two paper drinking straws up each nostril and about five silver spoons jammed in his mouth. Think of a walrus with braces—that was the look that greeted me.

"Emma, this is Barth. Barth, this is Emma, my best friend," Nelly introduced us.

"Pleased to meet you," I smiled. *When are you due back at the nut-house?* I thought. Barth untangled the silverware from his mouth, removed the straws from his nose, and then stuck his hand out.

"Not until you wash those hands, buster," I said.

"Emma!" Nelly scolded.

"What? It's flu season, and those straws were just a dipstick to bacteria," I said. I slid into the bench across from them. "Oh, this is Calvin Tibbs, my...date." Naturally, Calvin didn't care about germs, the flu, or the puddle of drool Barth left from his walrus stunt. Calvin stuck his hand out.

"Barth, huh?" Calvin said while shaking his hand. "That's an interesting name; not sure if I've ever heard it." *Calvin, what an investigative journalist.*

"Oh, it's short for my middle name, Bartholomew, but everybody just calls me Barth."

"You wouldn't happen to have a full name, would you?" I asked. I was clearly irritated with the boy. He slouched in his seat, had fundamentally flawed grooming habits, and a casual demeanor that I found disrespectful on the occasion of first acquaintances.

"Earl Bartholomew Gladstone," he said, and then winked at me.

"Is there something in your eye, Mr. Gladstone? Because we're not on familiar enough terms for that to have been a wink. I also see your barber is still on holiday, but you could have at least run a comb through that mop of yours," I snapped.

"Oh, Emma, Barth is just being funny," Nelly laughed.

"You seem to have quite a spirit packed into—what? About ninety-five pounds, I'd guess," said Barth. "And don't call me Mr. Gladstone; call me Barth." He winked again.

"I imagine you have a very lucrative career guessing weight with a carnival sideshow, but if you wink at me one more time you'll be guessing with one eye, Mr. Gladstone!"

Nelly was giggling at the repartee between her boyfriend and me, although I found nothing amusing, witty, or charming about the beast sitting across from me. "You're right, Nelly," Barth said. "She's a feisty one."

I know what you're thinking, so I might as well stop this story briefly and talk about the elephant on these pages. Yes, I married the beast that was sitting across from me. Did I steal Nelly's boyfriend? Technically, no. Is this where the rift between Nelly and I started? To be precise, yes. Am I a strumpet? I'm not going to answer such an outrageous question.

Over cherry Cokes we got into a big debate over which movie we would see. Nelly, naturally, wanted to drive over to South Creek and experience the latest craze, a drive-in-movie. In those days, drive-ins were popping up all over the country, and Nelly just loved the thought of watching a giant screen in the cozy confines of an automobile's bench seats. To further Nelly's excitement, the South Creek Drive-In was playing *Every Girl Should Be Married,* starring Cary Grant and Betsy Drake. The title alone had Nelly there. Cary Grant was just more enticement. Of course, Calvin liked the idea of a long drive over to South Creek, a two-hour movie, and then a long ride back to Forbye with me just inches away, in the backseat, in the dark. Strangely, Barth (oh, I'll just call him Earl) agreed with me. "There's no sense in driving over to South Creek just to watch a show in the rain," he said.

"Who said anything about watching a movie?" Nelly said as she cuddled up to Earl.

"Yeah," Calvin said and then tried the same move on me. My elbow landed between his third and fourth rib. Then my glare finished him off.

"What's playing at the Forbye Bijou?" Earl asked.

*"The Treasure of the Sierra Madre,"* Calvin said.

"Humphrey Bogart," Earl and I said at the same time and then the rascal winked at me again. I ignored it.

"Oh, *Treasure of the Sierra Madre.* That old thing has been in and out of the theater all year. Let's see something new," Nelly whined, adding, "and preferably more intimate."

"Well, I haven't seen it, and the Forbye Bijou is quite intimate enough, thank you," I said.

"Emma, you've never seen *Treasure of the Sierra Madre*? Then that settles it," Earl said. "We're going to the Bijou. I hope y'all brought your badges."

"Badges?" I asked.

Earl went into what is best described as a Mexican accent and said, "Badges? We ain't got no badges. We don't need no badges. I don't have to show you any stinkin' badges." Then Earl tipped back his head and laughed so hard I could count each of his teeth. None of us knew what on earth was so funny, but nevertheless, Earl seemed to enjoy saying the word *badges*. A strange lad indeed.

"Okay, fine," Nelly gave in. "*Treasure of the Sierra Madre* it is, but next week the drive-in," she insisted.

Suddenly it hit me; I knew why Earl was so appealing to Nelly. She couldn't control him. As long as I'd known Nelly Wilkinson, she'd always run the show. In other words, she got her way. Earl Gladstone was a wild horse, a loose cannon, an unpredictable storm, or any other analogy you might think of. Earl's casual approach to Nelly's demands intrigued her, baffled her, and most importantly, challenged her to tame the tiger.

Earl threw seventy-five cents on the table and told the waitress to keep the change. Calvin, after seeing that move, quickly added up the bill in his head and figured Earl left enough tip for all of us, so he went to the counter to pay just our bill. Nelly excused herself to the ladies room, which left me in the company of Earl Gladstone. I was none too happy. We slowly walked toward the door.

"You're gonna love *Treasure of the Sierra Madre*. I've seen it four times," he said.

"Well, I suppose you can't go wrong with Bogart," I said. *Come on, Nell, get out of the bathroom,* I thought.

"You like movies, do ya, Emma?" Earl said.

*Calvin, what are you doing—counting every penny in your pocket? Get over here!* I pleaded in my head. "Oh, I've seen a few, but it's not godly to see more than one a month. And I never watch a Betty Grable movie," I said.

"So you're one of those," Earl said and then rolled his eyes.

"One of those what?" I narrowed my eyes.

"Goody two-shoes, home by nine o'clock, say your prayers at night," he shot back as he reached for a cigarette.

"Well, I'm a Christian gal if that's what you mean. My shoes, good or otherwise, are simply none of your concern," I grabbed the unlit cigarette from his hand. "And I detest smoking!" I threw the cigarette on a busboy's tray as he went by.

The move set Earl back for a moment as he studied me. "I like you, Emma," he finally said. "Have you ever been kissed?"

"That's none of your business, and I find your conduct simply abhorrent! Now wipe that smirk off your face, mister!"

"Boy, you sure are wound tight. I'm just having some fun."

"Well, take your fun along with your disrespectful attitude outside, buster. I'm going to check on Nell." I turned quickly and ran right into Calvin, who had his head down still counting the change in his hand. The coins flew up and then jingled on the floor. "Calvin, you clod! It doesn't cost anything to pay attention!" I left in tears. *Men! Boys!*

I rushed into the restroom and found Nelly primping in the mirror. "Oh, Nell, this is dreadful, just dreadful," I sobbed.

"What is it, dear? What happened?"

"Oh, it's Calvin. He's such a drip. He ran into me and money flew all over the drugstore. I think a nickel landed in someone's egg cream. Oh, I'm so embarrassed. And then, Earl—"

"You mean Barth?" Nelly said.

"Barth, Earl, or whatever that goon you brought for a date is called."

"Goon? Emma, what could have possibly happened in the last five minutes?"

"He mocked my Christianity and said some very rude things in my company."

"Now, dear, it can't be that bad. You always overreact in these situations." Nelly took her handkerchief and dabbed under my eyes.

"Calvin is such an idiot. I don't like him, you know."

"Yes. There, there, dear. Let it out," Nelly continued to console me.

"And Barth, tell me you don't like him, Nell. Tell me he's just another beau you'll soon tire of." I blew my nose on her handkerchief.

"Oh, darling, I can't. I have a feeling there is something special about this one."

"No, Nell, no. He's wrong for you. I can just tell," I sobbed.

"Oh, Emma, you haven't had a chance to get acquainted with him. Now get that silly notion out of your head. Barth is wonderful. Trust me, you'll see," Nelly stroked my hair.

"Nell, I don't want to grow up. I don't want to think about boys or men or you wanting to marry. Can't we stay in high school forever?"

"Time waits for no one, dear. In a few days it will be 1949, and before you know it, we'll be two old ladies wondering where our life went," Nelly said.

"Yes, sudden. Too sudden," I said.

"So, you'll give Barth a chance?"

"Oh, I suppose so." I managed a smile.

That's my gal," said Nelly.

"But will you promise me one thing?" I pushed.

"Anything, dear."

"That we will stay friends forever," I said.

"Of course we will. Nothing can ever come between us," Nelly promised.

We walked out of the restroom and the drugstore to find Calvin and Earl talking cars. Boring drivel, but better than whom I have or haven't kissed. I must confess, Earl rattled me a bit. Up till then, all the boys I'd been around were clumsy, pimply, and insecure. Although Earl was goofy, crude, and brash, there was a certain air about him. It unsettled me. It stirred me. Did it really attract me?

We decided to take Earl's car because, naturally, Calvin's wouldn't start. Once all the doors were closed in Earl's '41 Chevy, he said, "Oh, no. She's leaking oil again."

"What's leaking?" Nelly said.

"My car. You smell that? Maybe it's not oil. It smells more like axle grease. I'd better hop out and take a look."

I knew it wasn't axel grease. The offensive smell was none other than Alabaster Heaven making its pungent announcement. As Earl crawled beneath his car looking for the greasy odor, Nelly thanked me once again for her Christmas present. She reached back and stuck her forearm under Calvin's nose. "Isn't it a lovely aroma, Calvin?" she asked.

"I can't smell a thing, Nelly. I had an ammonia accident when I was a child and it took my sense of smell with it," Calvin said as he sniffed her arm. "Nope, nothing."

*Every accident has a silver lining,* I thought.

"Well, there's nothing leaking," Earl said as he popped back into the car. "I guess I have some grease on my shoe or something because I still smell it."

During the short ride to the movie house, Nelly got acquainted with Earl's shoulder. I bet you couldn't have slid a matchbook between them. That was always my rule. Anytime a boy got close to me, I pulled out a matchbook and placed it between us. If they persisted, I lit it. I burnt plenty of dungarees in my day. They didn't call me "Matchbook Emma" for nothing—a name I wore as a badge of honor.

I decided, for Nelly's sake, that I would give Earl another chance. Maybe I was too hard or judgmental, even though that was a trait I'd seldom shown. If this boy, Earl, was the love of Nelly's life, then I'd better get used to him being around. I still couldn't imagine what she saw in the fella, but blooms do flower on the thorniest rosebush.

Nelly and I stood off to the side while Calvin and Earl purchased our tickets.

"I'm gonna pull Calvin aside when we go in so you and Barth can get to know each other," Nelly said.

"Nell, don't. Please," I begged.

"Relax, it will be fine," Nelly said. "Just follow my lead." Earl and Calvin walked up. "Barth, darling, would you and Emma go find us a seat while I take Calvin to the refreshment stand?"

"Sure, you need some money?" Earl asked.

"No, since you drove, the treats are on Calvin," I said.

"Hey, wait! What?" Calvin protested.

"Nice thinking, Emma," Nelly said. "It's only fair."

"He drove a half mile. How much gas could it have been?" Calvin said as Nelly turned him toward the concession stand.

"Don't forget the Jujubes," Earl said. "Well, it's just you and me, again. Shall we?" Earl and I walked into a darkened theater. The room was cold and damp, just like the day.

"I guess the heater isn't working," I said.

"That's what Calvin is for," he replied.

"Puh-lease!" I said. "How 'bout this row?"

"Suits me."

When we sat down, I left one seat between us. *The Treasure of the Sierra Madre* was not exactly a first run movie, so the theater was only half full, but Bogart always drew in a few. *Okay, let's see what makes him tick.* I thought. "You're tied to that Barth name, then, are you?"

"Yeah, I like it. Kinda different, don't ya think?"

"Well, I'm calling you Earl from now on," I said. *That will rattle him.*

"Okay," he said.

"I said, 'I'm calling you Earl.'"

"Yeah. Earl. I got it. Fine," he said. "I know you don't watch a lot of movies, but who's your favorite actor?"

*I'm supposed to be asking him the questions.* "Oh, if I had to pick, I'd guess Spencer Tracy," I said.

"Spencer Tracy, really? Ya know some people think I look like Spencer Tracy." He did. I thought that when I first saw him, and maybe subconsciously, that was why I said it. Of course, to my knowledge, Spencer never had two straws jammed up his nose or a mouthful of silverware crammed down his throat. However, I wasn't going to play into his wild fantasy.

"Spencer Tracy? Maybe if you combed your hair and I closed one eye and squinted out of the other, then I might see some resemblance of Mr. Tracy," I said and then closed one eye and squinted out of the other. "Why, Spencer, fancy meeting you here," I said.

Earl let out a laugh. I could count all of his teeth again. "Oh, Emma, you're feisty and funny, a deadly combination."

*Hmm.* "So Mr. Gladstone, what are your intentions with Nelly? She's awfully fond of you."

"You think so, huh? Well, my intentions are to watch this movie with her."

"Funny, mister, but you know what I mean. I don't want to see her hurt."

"Oh, I'm not gonna hurt her. I won't be around long enough. I report for duty in three weeks."

"Duty for what?" I asked.

"The army."

"Nell never told me this."

"She doesn't know. It's not like she's my steady girl," he said.

*Not his steady girl? Oh dear, Nell,* I thought. Just when I opened my mouth, though, I heard, "There you two are." It was Nelly and Calvin standing by our row.

"Here's your Jujubes, Barth. They were a nickel," Calvin muttered.

"Thanks, Calvin. I'll catch ya next time," Earl said.

"So, did you two have a nice conversation?" Nelly asked as she slid into the seat between Earl and me.

I felt it wasn't my place to tell Nelly something she should already know about. Poor Nelly. I suddenly realized that friendship had gray areas. If I were thirteen years old, then of course I would have belted Earl one, grabbed Nelly's hand, and left the movies right then and there. Maybe I should have done that at the ripe old age of seventeen. I do know that this story and my life would be quite different had I stood up right then and said, "Nell, there's something you need to know." Oh, Nelly would eventually hear those words come out of my mouth. However, they would be the prelude to the end of our friendship.

Through most of the movie, I had a nervous stomach that was brought on by Earl's frivolous attitude over his relationship with Nelly. To make matters worse, Earl talked through the entire show. He knew every Bogart line and very distractingly would say them before Bogart did. Nelly loved it, though, and her giggles encouraged Earl even more. During one particular part in the movie, some Mexican bandits surrounded Humphrey Bogart and his men. One bandit said they were the "federalies," the mounted police. Bogart asked to see their badges.

Right on cue, Earl, sitting there in the theater, said, "Badges? We ain't got no badges. We don't need no badges. I don't have to show you any stinkin' badges." Earl laughed and then turned to me. "See, I told y'all to bring your badges," he said.

*He is kind of cute,* I thought, smiling to myself.

After the show, we all headed over to Nelly's house. The heater in Earl's car wouldn't work, which made Nelly happy. She cuddled up next to Earl without much thought to road safety or the flu season.

We pulled into Nelly's driveway, all of us eager to sip hot chocolate and listen to records by the fire. Well, Calvin was a little too eager. I opened the car door, and he nearly pushed me out of the way.

"Hold on, Calvin," I said. In my haste to climb out, my legs tangled together and I fell face first into a giant mud puddle. *Splash!* Calvin laughed, and I believe Nelly snickered too. I was a dripping mess, but my two friends found humor in my embarrassment. My date just stood there while Earl ran over to help me up.

"You okay, Emma?" Earl said as his massive hands gripped me under my arms. I eased up. My body was freezing, with the exception of where Earl's warm hands still gripped me.

"She's fine. She won't melt," Nelly said. "I've got some dry clothes you can change into, dear."

Earl looked at Calvin. His expression plainly said, "Aren't you going to do something?" Calvin returned his look with just a clueless stare. Earl took his jacket off and placed it around my shoulders.

"That'll keep you warm until we get inside," Earl said. *Chivalry isn't dead!*

I was so humiliated. Had Earl not stepped up, I might have been worse for the wear.

Nelly's momma had retired for the night, so we had the house to ourselves. Nelly went to put on some cocoa; Calvin went to the record player; and I went down the hall to change in Nelly's room. "Anything you want to wear, Emma! You know where my things are!" Nelly hollered down the hall. I shut the bedroom door. I was freezing, so I peeled out of my wet garments before finding dry clothes in Nelly's closet. I stood there without a stitch of clothes on until I heard the doorknob turn. I assumed it was Nelly. My assumption was wrong. "Ahhhhh!" I screamed.

"Yikes!" Earl screamed. "I guess the bathroom was to my right, not Nelly's right," he said.

"Shut the door!" I said with one had covering my lower half and my other arm flung across my chest.

"Uh—right. Sorry." Earl slammed the door.

*This night just couldn't be any worse!* My bottom lip started to quiver. I quickly grabbed a robe and tied it snugly around my body. I saw another robe. I grabbed it, too, and wore it over that robe. I felt embarrassed. Not falling-in-a-mud-puddle embarrassed, but never-wanting-to-show-my-face embarrassed. Nakedness was for wedding nights, perhaps even the day after. It wasn't a sideshow for some lug who didn't know his right from his left! The whole event left me feeling dirty. I immediately plundered Nelly's closet. I put on a pair of her dungarees, some wool socks, and an overcoat. Then I tied a thick scarf around my neck. I didn't want one inch of my bare flesh exposed. I grabbed a knit cap on the way out of the door.

As I walked down the hall I saw him, the bane of my humiliation, sitting comfortably and sipping cocoa like nothing happened.

"Where you going dressed like that, Emma, the North Pole?" Calvin asked.

"I'm cold, Calvin," I said as I folded my arms. "Would you get me some cocoa, please?"

"Uh, sure." Calvin left the room.

"Emma, I heard you scream, dear. Did you see a cockroach?" Nelly said.

"Yes. Yes, I did." I looked straight at Earl.

"I figured so. They seem to be lurking around lately," she said.

"They sure are," I continued to glare at Earl. "You wouldn't mind if I killed one, would ya?"

"By all means, dear, I can't stand to look at the things. Just make sure you clean up his guts. Momma hates to see—"

We heard a crash from the kitchen.

"Uh-oh," Calvin muttered. "Nelly?"

Nelly jumped up, "Calvin!" She left the room.

I went over to Mr. Gladstone and bent down inches from his face. "You listen to me, mister. If you tell one soul what you saw, I'll squash you like the roach you are."

"I'm sorry—"

"Shut up! What on earth were you thinking?" I asked.

"Well, I—"

"Shut up! You planned that didn't you?"

"No, I—"

"Shut up! You like looking at naked gals, do you?"

"I was just—"

"Shut up! What did you see?"

"Nothing," Earl said, finally getting a word in edgewise.

"Nothing? So now I'm nothing, huh?"

"No, you're something, Emma. Really something," he said.

"Ah, so you did see something!"

"No, I mean, I saw...uh, I can't win this, can I? Do you want to see me naked?" he asked.

The palm of my hand shot across his face, and I slapped him before I realized it. "You'd like that, wouldn't ya?" Before another word was spoken, Nelly came around the corner.

"Oh, Calvin broke Momma's..." Nelly started, and then stopped. "Emma, why are you sitting on Barth's lap?"

My debate was so heated, my anger was so intense, that I didn't realize the precarious location I had fallen into. Somehow my posterior had found a lateral position on Earl's thighs. Anyone who didn't know the nature of my business with Mr. Gladstone would assume, as Nelly so rightly pointed out, that I was sitting on Earl's lap. That would clearly violate my matchbook rule, right? So, I did what any gal would do who was caught sitting on the lap of her best friend's boyfriend. I lied.

"Oh, my eye. I, uh, had some mud or something in it from the fall. Earl here was trying to see if he could find it," I managed to say. I'm glad my neck was wrapped in that thick scarf. I could feel the lie turning my flesh red.

"Yeah, here it is," Earl held a finger up and then wiped some imaginary dirt on his trousers.

"Well, I'm glad you two are finally getting along. Just don't keep any secrets from me," she giggled.

*Secrets like Earl doesn't consider you his steady, he's going into the army, and he saw me naked—those kinds of secrets?* "What secrets could we have?" I asked. We all laughed, and then Nelly cleared her throat. I was still sitting on Earl's lap.

"Oh, my goodness," I cried, jumping off.

"What'd I miss?" Calvin asked, returning to the room. *He's gonna make a fine journalist.*

We finished out the night listening to the Andrews Sisters and playing charades. The evening ended with Calvin walking me to my door. What a night! My head didn't hit the pillow before eleven o'clock. *So much for Miss Goody-two-shoes, home by nine o'clock,* I thought as I drifted off to sleep. Yes, I said my prayers.

The next morning I woke up to the sound of Daddy's voice.

"Eunice, get me my shotgun. There's a stranger parked out in the yard!" Daddy called. Eunice was my momma's name.

I jumped up and peeked out my window. To my surprise, I saw Earl sleeping behind the wheel of his car. "Daddy, wait!" I shouted and then quickly threw on some presentable clothes. I opened up my bedroom door. "Daddy, I know who it is. I'll go see what he wants."

"What's he doing here?"

"I don't know, Daddy. That's why I said I'll go see what he wants."

"Well, tell 'im to get out of here."

"Oh, don't worry, he'll beat it." I was still upset over his bumbling escapade the previous night.

What I did next, I can't explain. Without even thinking about it, I found myself standing in front of my bathroom mirror applying a small amount of makeup to my face. I fussed with my hair until it looked just so, brushed my teeth, and then finished off the look with a touch of red lipstick. I know—red. No, I didn't get all gussied up for Earl, but like I said, red lipstick. Oh, and I splashed on some perfume before I walked outside. The morning air was cold, probably about thirty-five degrees. The sun, already up, was the only object in the perfect blue sky. I could see Earl fast asleep, tucked under what appeared to be a sleeping bag. I grabbed a nearby rock—*right through the windshield*—but then I thought better of it and dropped the rock.

*Tap, tap, tap*—I knocked on his window. Nothing. The boy was in another world—so much so that drool was rolling out from the corner of his mouth. I viewed his quiet surroundings. His car was calm and serene, a comfortable cocoon for his blissful slumber. He looked so peaceful, so relaxed, so tranquil. I paused briefly.

*Bam! Bam! Bam!* I wacked on the glass with the ball of my fist, "What are you doing here, Earl Gladstone?" I shouted. He jumped forward and his face hit the horn. Dogs started barking throughout the neighborhood. He got out of the car, holding his head.

"What's the matter, ya didn't get a good enough peek last night?" I took my hands and pushed on his shoulders. Earl fell back against his car. "So now you're back to look in my windows?"

"Emma, no, it's not like that," he said.

About that time, Daddy, with his shotgun, stepped outside. "Honey, is everything all right?" he hollered from the front porch. I'm not sure if anyone ever measured Daddy, but he was a big man. He had to duck his head to fit through most doorways, and turn sideways to walk down some halls. Boys always got real nervous around Daddy, even when he didn't have his shotgun. One time Calvin Tibbs wet his britches when Daddy made a sudden move to swat at a fly.

I looked up to the house where he stood. The door was no longer visible behind his frame. I turned to Earl and quietly said, "Do you want to tell him you saw me naked, or should I?"

White wrestled all the color from Earl's expression. If white had a lighter shade, then that would be the pigment to describe his face. "You—you… you want me to…what?"

"Yeah, tell him. Tell my daddy you saw his little girl in her birthday suit," I said out of the corner of my mouth. I then waved at Daddy and yelled, "Daddy, I got some news for you."

"No! No, Emma, don't do this. Let me explain," Earl whispered as fast as he could.

I figured the bumpkin had suffered enough, so I yelled, "Daddy, Earl said it might snow tonight." Daddy nodded and then went inside. I giggled and pushed Earl again.

"You're crazy, Emma," Earl said after he released a lungful of air.

"You deserved it." I looked away. "How did you find me and what do you want?"

"Well, I drove to every house in Forbye until I saw Baumgaertner on the mailbox. Small town, odd name. I figured I'd find it sooner or later."

"Too bad I don't live in Atlanta and my name isn't Smith," I muttered.

"What?"

"Never mind," I said. "Does Nell know you're here?"

"No, but what does that matter?" I balled up my fist and gave Earl a roundhouse to the shoulder. "Why do you like to hit me?" he asked.

"Oh, I don't know. Why do you like to spend the night in my driveway when you're Nell's fella?"

"I'm not exactly Nell's boyfriend."

"I had a cousin one time that said she wasn't exactly pregnant. Should I tell ya how that turned out?"

"Okay, okay. Just don't hit me," he said. "But Nelly assumes things."

He was correct. Nelly assumed a lot of things. C-cup was the first that came to mind. "I'm listening," I said.

"It's about last night. I couldn't drive back to South Creek without clearing the air. I feel we got off on the wrong foot."

"So that's what they call gawking in South Creek, huh? The wrong foot?" I challenged him.

"Emma, just hear me out. I don't talk much because I tend to say exactly what I think. Most folks can't handle the truth, so I get along by being quiet. But last night, for some reason, I said some rude things to you. That's not me, and I'm sorry for that. As for walking in on you, it was an honest mistake. I asked Nelly where the bathroom was and she said first door on the right. Well, I was standing in the hallway facing her and opened the door on my right, which was actually the first door on the left. No one was more surprised than me to see you standing there."

"Wanna bet?"

"Can you forgive me?"

"If Jesus can, I suppose I should."

"The truth is, Emma, you make me anxious. I could tell right away that you were special. Here I go again, saying what I think. But from the moment I first saw you my heart quickened and hasn't slowed down since."

"I bet it really raced when you saw me in all my glory!"

"You're not gonna let that go are you?"

"Just hold on, Earl Gladstone! I don't know who you think you are or how many gals you've thrown that line to, but it ain't flying with me, buster! My goodness; Calvin Tibbs stutters, but yet he's more suave than that. You got your cheap thrills. Now scram!" I was tough.

"Well, ah, but—"

"How easy do you think I am? You think you're some hot shot from South Creek who can do anything behind his girlfriend's back. Nelly is my friend, and it's not right for us to be having this conversation. Now, beat it. Go on. Beat it!"

Earl hung his head and slipped in behind the wheel of his fancy Chevy. He closed the door and gave a bewildered stare. I motioned for him to roll down the window. Thinking I was giving him a second chance, he quickly cranked down the window. I stuck my head inside. "Do you even own a comb?" I said and then I popped him on top the head.

I turned around and walked up to the house—smiling the whole way. I think I was falling for Earl Gladstone.

Do you want to know when I was smitten by the smooth talking Earl of South Creek? Go ahead, guess. That's right, when I fell down and he came to my rescue. Something snapped in my head and I finally understood what Nelly meant about growing up. A school girl slipped into that mud puddle, but a man grabbed a woman's arm and lifted her out. Of course Earl ruined it five minutes later by seeing the bare facts, but I was a tough gal—I could get over that. Plus, he paid. He had paid dearly!

Oh, yes, that part where I ended up on Earl's lap? It was purely coincidental. Honest, it was. I was mad and totally unaware of my actions. However, maybe subconsciously I saw an opportunity to rest or get comfortable during my tirade. And that, dear reader, is the closest you'll have me to admitting that I purposely sought intimacy on the lap of Earl Gladstone.

I'm well versed in human nature, and I pretty much had it figured out after Earl drove away, totally devastated over my harsh rejection. He would skulk back to Nelly. He would feel so ashamed for calling on another gal, me, that he'd find comfort in Nelly's sickly-sweet and often annoying personality—so much so, that Earl would begin to fall for Nelly. Then the trap would be set. Nelly, as Nelly always did, would tire of Earl in about two weeks and throw him aside. That would leave one week before Earl went into the army for me to pick up the pieces if I so desired. I would tell Earl that I'm awfully busy, but I'd try to write him once a month, unless Calvin Tibbs objected. Of course, Calvin wouldn't object—he was clueless. But a little jealousy goes a long ways. During the course of Earl's enlistment, we would court via the United States Postal Service. This was how we would get to know one another, and I must confess, I could write a killer letter. So, if Earl thought I was special after one night, then just wait until he opened a letter that began with "My Dearest Earl."

You see, I had patience. Love, true love, waits. There was no sense in rushing anything. Earl's hitch in the army was the best thing for our relationship to brew. I wanted to complete my studies and then go on to nursing school. And of course, my crossword tournaments and farm chores would occupy my time nicely.

I bet you're thinking, "Emma, you'd only met Earl twice; you were no different than Nelly." Well, first, you know how this story turned out. It's not a secret that I married Earl. (And by the way, I'll remind you that you're still reading about it.) And, second, it was Earl that slept all night in my driveway. A woman's intuition is truly a gift, and men will never understand that.

After sorting all this out in my head, I felt pretty good. I decided to work on my crosswords—you know, bone up for the big tournament. Yep, everything was falling into place. *A five letter word for love Italian style? Ah yes.* "Amore," I wrote on the puzzle. Before I read the next clue, I heard a knock at the door. Daddy was out on the farm, and Momma was doing laundry out back, so I let out a huff and put my book down. *Probably Mrs. Abbot looking to borrow some sugar,* I thought as I opened the door.

"I did it, Emma. I did it," Earl said standing at the door.

"Did what? And why are you back?" I looked in the driveway. "And where is your car?"

"Oh, I didn't want your daddy to see me parked out front again, so I parked it down at the filling station," he said. "Come on, grab your coat and walk me back."

"I'm not going anywhere with you, mister. Now what did you do?"

"Nelly. I broke it off with her so we can be together. Now come on, let's go get the car and go for a drive," he said.

"Wait! You broke it off with Nelly? No, that's not how it was supposed to work!"

"Huh?" Earl said.

"Get inside before someone see you," I said.

"Can I have some water, too? I ran all the way from the filling station."

We went to the kitchen. Earl sat at the kitchen table while I let tap water from the spigot run into a small glass. I needed to think. With all my savvy in understanding human nature, I had miscalculated one thing. Evidently, my spell was too strong. *You had to put on red lipstick!* I thought as I plotted out my next move.

"Earl Gladstone, I don't even know you. What part of 'scram' did you not understand?" *My gosh, he's so cute standing there. I do want to go for a drive!* "What on this planet would lead you to believe that I would be your gal?"

"Come on, Emma, don't kid yourself. You feel this too," he said.

*Drats! How smart is this guy?* "Balderdash. I have no idea what you're talking about!" *Don't you smile and show me your dimples.* Earl smiled and those dimples popped up. *Oh Emma, don't get wobbly. Look away!*

"Emma, look me in the eyes and tell me you want me to leave," he said. *He's calling my bluff. Keep the upper hand. Think. Think.*

There was a knock on the door, which broke a very tense moment. "Stay here. We're not finished!" The break would afford me a chance to get my thoughts together. Just as I reached for the doorknob I heard, "Emma, hurry! I need to talk to you. Barth just broke up with me!" It was Nelly's tearful wail.

My eyes nearly left their sockets. *No!* I turned to Earl. "Did you tell her anything about us?" I whispered.

"No! I'm not stupid," he said.

"Well, you're not very bright. Look what you've done!"

Nelly knocked again. "Oh Emma, please answer," she cried out.

"Uh, just a minute, dear," I said through the door. "Earl, hide," I whispered."

Earl threw his hands up. "Where?"

"My bedroom. Quick,—it's the first door on the right," I said. Then I grabbed his arm. "The first door on the *right*, got it?"

"Yeah, yeah, I got it ... Oh, I get it. Funny ..."

"Just go!"

I quickly adjusted my appearance and gathered my thoughts. I let out a deep breath. *Stay calm, stay calm. Act surprised.* I opened the door. "Nelly, what's the matter?"

"Oh, Emma," Nelly fell into my arms. "Barth dumped me," she wept.

"Honey," I patted her back. "It will be all right. You didn't know him that long."

Nelly kept blubbering on my shoulder. I could only make out about every other word. "He ... the ... one ... me," she said.

"I know. I know. That's right," I agreed to whatever gibberish she just said.

"And then ... said ... going ... without," she sobbed.

"Nell, dear, you need to calm down so I can understand you. Come sit down." I guided her over to the sofa. The poor thing, I'd never seen her this shook up before. Well, there was that time in third grade when she lost the watermelon seed spitting contest, but that was long ago. I took her hand, and even though I was fully aware of what had occurred between her and Earl, I said, "Nell, tell me what happened."

Nelly stiffened up her lips and let out a few nose clearing sobs. "Barth came over to the house and said he never went home last night because he needed to think. I mean, where could he have possibly spent the night?"

*Two hundred yards right behind you, dear.*

"So, I thought he was thinking about a marriage proposal," she stopped. Her bottom lip started to quiver and then she clouded up. Tears fell like water over Niagara Falls. "I just don't understand," she howled.

I really didn't follow Nelly's thinking. It was preposterous to think that Earl would seek an engagement after only a few weeks. They barely knew each other, for crying out loud. She'd probably had a bout of diarrhea that lasted longer than their courtship! I did know one thing, though; the longer she sat there bawling uncontrollably, the more my stomach twisted. Earl had really thrown a wrench into how our courting was all going to work out. All he had to do was wait until Nelly dropped him. And as sure as the devil wears a red suit, she would have. Patience—no one had any! Now our friendship was in jeopardy; Earl was hiding in my bedroom; and I was becoming a liar.

"Well, maybe it's for the best since he's going in the army," I told her.

Her tears stopped. "Army? I never said anything about the army. What do you know about the army?" she asked.

*Oh, no! She didn't say anything about the army, you idiot!* "Yes, you did. I remember you saying he was leaving for the army," I lied, feeling horrible.

"No, Barth never said anything about joining the army," she looked puzzled.

*Barth, Earl, whoever you are! You're the idiot. The perfect excuse, and you say nothing about it!* "I was sure you mentioned it when you first came in the door." I maintained the lie.

"No; if that were the case, then maybe I could understand. I think it's something else. I think Barth found him another gal!" Nelly went from tears to anger. She couldn't fathom the idea of any girl being more attractive than she. She would absolutely flip her wig if she knew that gal was sitting across from her lending a consoling ear. "Who could it be, Emma? Did you see him talking to anyone last night at the movies?"

What was I to tell her? Yes, he talked to me? Or perhaps, yes, he helped me out of the mud puddle and we fell in love? Maybe the simple fact that she caught me sitting on his lap would be a good clue to start with. How about the seedy underbelly of all this, the one that you, the reader, find so amusing: he saw me ... naked.

"Well, I talked to him." I threw it out there.

"My stars, no dear," Nelly laughed. "Good heavens, I'm talking about someone that Barth would find attractive."

"I'm so glad to see you laughing." *Earl's in my bedroom.* "Looks like you're coming around."

"I didn't like him anyway!" Nelly snapped.

"That's my girl," I said.

"Barth—that's a stupid name."

"Yes, dear, yes." Finally I said something that wasn't a lie; Barth *was* a stupid name.

Nelly just flew through the stages of grief. She gave a good five minutes to shock; her denial phase was brief; and finally she faced acceptance. Emotions always ran quickly through her system, with the exception of one: revenge.

While Nelly prattled on about her superior qualities and how Earl wasn't good enough for her, my mind began to drift. Her mindless chatter always had a rhythmic cadence that lulled me into other thoughts. It was a trait I liked best about Nelly.

*I don't know what I'm going to do. Nell's my friend. In her time of need she came to me for comfort. How could I possibly date Earl under these conditions? No, I'd rather keep a friend for life than risk a flyer on a hick from South Creek. But those dimples. My goodness! He is sweet, too. Yeah, a little thick in the brains department, but what man isn't? Who does Nell think she is? I can't believe she made that comment. What am I, chopped liver? Obviously Earl finds me very attracti—Oh, what did she just say? Just agree and nod your head.* "Yeah, that sounds good," I said.

"Good, let's go," Nelly said.

"Go where?"

"To your bedroom, silly. How else can I try on your clothes?"

*Oh, of course. Anytime Nell feels blue she likes to try on clothes ... what? Try on clothes!* "Nell, wait!" I was too late. She bolted through my bedroom door. I quickly followed and waited for a scream that didn't come. The room was empty of one Earl Gladstone. *Phew!* Nelly ripped open my closet doors.

"Let's see, I feel like putting on a Sunday dress. Where's that number you wear with that frilly Easter hat?" Nelly asked.

*Where did Earl go? The window is still locked.* "Um, it's in the back where I keep my formals," I said. Just then I saw Earl's dusty boots in the back where I kept my formals! I had to think, and I had to think quickly. One wrong maneuver or a hasty disrobe by Nelly and Earl would view his second naked gal in as many days. What were the odds?

"Nell, wait!"

"What's the matter, dear? You look like you just saw a ghost."

"Uh, I just remembered, that dress needs to be mended."

"Well, I can do that," she said reaching for the dress. "It'll give me something to occupy my time."

"A cockroach!" I screamed. I had to think of something. I hit her shoulder. She jumped back with the dress in her hand. Earl was in full view, but Nelly was facing me.

"Where? Where is it?" Nelly hated roaches, remember?

I grabbed her by both shoulders. Now I controlled her movements. "Be still. Don't move." I held her tight. She was looking down for the roach. Earl began to creep slowly from the closet. He was just a few inches behind Nelly's back. With careful guidance, I turned Nelly the opposite way as Earl moved toward the door.

"I don't see him," Nelly said.

*If I'm lucky you won't.* "Hold on. I don't want it to run up your leg." I gripped Nelly tighter.

"Emma, what's wrong with you? You're hurting me. Let me go!"

"Not yet, dear. I want to make sure he's gone." I wasn't about to let her go. Earl was just inches away from the doorknob. Suddenly, I heard the backdoor of our house open.

"Emma, you in the house?" It was Daddy coming in for lunch. Earl retreated and dove under my bed. I turned Nelly loose.

"Emma, what's got into you? I think you bruised my shoulders," Nelly complained.

My mind was racing. Nelly knowing Earl was in my bedroom was one thing. If Daddy found out—that would surely be quite another! "We're in here, Daddy," I called to him.

He poked his head in the door. "Oh, hey, Nell. What are you gals doin'?" Daddy asked.

"Just girl stuff, Daddy. You want me to make you a sandwich?"

"Nah, you gals have fun. I'll make it myself," he said. Then he started to turn around, but stopped and looked at my bed. "You nasty buzzard, what are you doing here? I'm gonna kill you!" Daddy yelled as he headed for my bed.

"No, Daddy! I can explain!" I really couldn't, but I said it anyway.

It all happened so fast. Daddy rushed to my bed, lifted up his shoe, and then drove it down on the hardwood floor. *Thwack!* "That'll teach ya," Daddy said. "Don't tell your momma I found a roach in here. You know how she hates those things."

*Phew*! My heart started beating again. I was saved by a cockroach. That beautiful nocturnal creature, which scurries about striking fear in man and child alike, was no less than my knight in shining armor, truly a gift from God. In my mind, God knew this was just a series of unfortunate circumstances. God knew I wasn't a strumpet. God knew I wasn't stealing my best friend's boyfriend. God knew I was a good girl. And I was president of the Bible club, student fundraiser for Lottie Moon, and lead contributor to the monthly newsletter, "Jesus, the Devil's Nightmare." I wasn't the backstabbing liar that my bedroom was depicting. Yes, I truly believe God inspired me to yell, "Roach!" and then manifested that creature to preserve my dignity. The cockroach—God's magnificent creation! From that day forward, I always thanked a roach—right before I smashed its guts out.

The crisis was over. I just needed to get Daddy out to the kitchen, find an excuse for Nelly to leave, and then sneak Earl out the window. All I wanted to do was to rest my head. This whole affair had left me quite dizzy.

Daddy gave the dead roach one finale twist with his work boots before exposing the fate of what happens to an intruder in his house. "Yuck," Nelly said observing the remains. "Look at the size of that thing. Emma! Do you think your daddy could do that to Barth?" she laughed.

"Who's Barth?" Daddy asked.

"Oh, he was my boyfriend," Nelly said.

"Emma, wasn't that the boy who was in our driveway this morning?"

*You really hate me, God, don't ya?* "Uh, no." *Think, think, Emma.* "You mean, Calvin?" I managed to say.

"No, you called him Ernie or Darrell," Daddy said.

*I called him Earl, and he's under my bed.* "No, Daddy, you heard wrong. You know you're hard of hearing." *I'm getting too good at lying.*

"Well, whoever. I didn't have my specs on, but he didn't look like that Tibbs boy."

"Oh, Daddy, you're so funny!" I laughed. "I bet you're hungry, too." I changed the subject.

"Yeah, I better go scrounge up somethin' to eat."

"Wait just a minute!" Nelly interjected. "There was a boy here this morning?"

"Y-e-e-e-s," I said more like a question than an answer. I could see

Nelly's mind quickly putting everything together. Earl and I talked alone at the picture show; he pulled me out of the mud puddle; she caught me sitting on his lap; and finally, the evidence beyond reasonable doubt—Earl never went home last night!

"Mr. Baumgaertner," Nelly turned to Daddy. "Would you please excuse us? I need to talk to Emma about a personal matter."

I tried to take a big gulp, but it stayed in my throat like a loaf of stale bread.

"Boys, huh?" Daddy said and then chuckled as he left the room.

"You're not fooling me anymore, Emma," she said. Then she fixed her eyes on me and gave a hard look up and down. What could I say? Nothing. I started preparing for my asking-for-forgiveness speech as Nelly slowly circled me. "So, there was a boy here this morning, huh?" she pried.

"Yes, I already told you that," I mumbled.

"And you call me your best friend," she said. "You are truly unbelievable!"

Nelly always had a flair for the dramatic, and she was milking this for all that it was worth. I wanted to ask for a blindfold and cigarette just to get my execution over with. "This really explains everything. Your denials will not be accepted, so don't even try!" Nelly leveled her eyes on me. "I should have figured it out when I saw you this morning. Come over her and look in the mirror," she said while pulling on my arm.

*So this is how she's gonna do this. Make me look at myself in the mirror.*

We stood in front of my dresser. "What do you see?" Nelly asked.

"You giving me an evil look," I said.

Nelly busted out in laughter. "I'm sorry. I can't keep a straight face any longer."

"Huh?"

"Look at you, dear. The makeup, the red lipstick, and that subtle perfume you're wearing. You like Calvin Tibbs. He was here this morning and you got all dolled up for him."

*Phew. No, double phew!* Okay, Nelly wasn't as smart as the credit given.

"So when did you know, huh? Was it last night?"she asked.

"No, Nell, it's not like that."

"Oh, yes it is, but that's okay. I'll never believe you."

*I bet you will.* "Please, you make too many assumptions."

"Well, now I need to find a fella so we can double date. I think that new soda jerk is a good place to start," Nelly said.

*She's* finally *over Earl? What was that, thirty minutes?* "There ya go! That's the spirit!" I encouraged her.

"Oh, Emma, you make me feel so good! I don't know what I'd do without ya. Hey, let's go down to the drugstore and flirt with the boys."

"Nah, I'm not up to it. Besides, I'd be a fifth wheel with that new soda jerk. Go ahead without me, dear."

"Oh, that's right; you're with Calvin now, and I do flirt better on my own. No offense, dear, but you can be a prude."

*Did I mention Earl was under my bed?* "None taken, love. That's my role." I faked a headache just to hurry Nelly along. (What? So I lied. Do you think a little lie about a headache would worsen my fate in the eyes of the Lord at that particular moment? You have been keeping up with this story, right?)

With Nelly safely gone and Daddy back on the farm, I closed my bedroom door. "Earl Gladstone," I said. He slithered out from under my bed. His face was red, and his clothes wringing wet. The boy had a severe case of the flop sweats.

"I hope you're happy," I said with my hands on my hips. He stood up and I belted him one right in the midsection.

"Emma, you're gonna have to stop hittin' me."

"Well, you keep askin' for it." Then something happened to me. Maybe it was the emotional events of the day, or perhaps the woman in me breaking through my school-girl skin. But whatever the case was, I said, "You're right. I'm sorry. Women don't punch. It won't happen again." I looked into Earl's gorgeous blue eyes and a thousand thoughts went through my head; most of them, I can't repeat here. I will tell you this—Earl was the only man for me. Right there, right in my bedroom, Cupid landed an uppercut of his own. Not a shallow punch, the kind girls get—no sir. This was real, so real I felt my face glow; I felt my knees buckle; and without a doubt I heard a beautiful voice singing in my ears. Earl heard it, too. It was Momma coming down the hall—she had such a lovely voice.

"Quick, back under the bed," I told Earl. He disappeared before I finished saying the words. Momma opened up my door.

"What are you doing cooped up in here? You need to enjoy that brisk breeze blowin' outside," Momma said as she hung a few clothes in my closet. I sat on the bed. I think I heard Earl grunt.

"Oh, just thought I'd work on my crosswords," I answered.

Momma turned around and looked at me. "Why, Emma, you're glowing. You have a new boyfriend, don't ya?"

"Mother, please. I don't know what you're talking about."

Mamma smiled and sat down beside me on the bed. Earl didn't grunt this time; perhaps he was passed out. "Honey," Mamma said. "You're growing up so fast. When I was your age, me and your daddy were already married. We didn't have a long courtship either."

"Oh, boy. You sound like Nelly."

"Well, it's true. I reckon we were made for each other, and I knew it the first time I met him. You'll see, dear. One day your thoughts are on school days and crosswords, and then all of the sudden the moon falls in your lap and all you can think about is him."

"So that's it? You can't control the feeling?"

"Not if he's the one," she said. Then she brushed my hair away from my face. "You're such a pretty woman. You're gonna make same man very happy."

*Um, there's a man under my bed.* "Oh, Mother, you act as if I'm ready to walk down the aisle."

"By that glow on your face, you might be," she said. Momma kissed me on the forehead and then went to leave my room."

"Momma?" I stopped her. "There's really a glow, huh?"

"Yes, dear. The same one I had many years ago," she said. "Now, if that fella you got under the bed is the one, then you better get him out before he suffocates," Momma winked and closed the door.

"What? Earl, did you hear that? She saw you!"

He scrambled topside. "Yeah, pretty neat, huh?"

"Pretty neat?" I went to slug him, but I remembered my new manners. "Oh, I'm so embarrassed."

"Look, you're gonna have to face it. You're feeling the same thing I am. Your momma was right. It's on your face."

Everything was happening so fast. I never knew love could be so sudden, but it was true. The option of playing hard to get obviously got lost in the shuffle. Momma was right. Earl was right. My face was right!

"Earl, this is crazy! I mean we haven't even kissed, for goodness sakes!"

Earl reached out and grabbed the back of my head and then brought his lips to mine. Oh, the feeling! Words can't express the sensation, but I'll give it a try. Imagine a wet brick wall coming at you at ninety miles per hour. *Thud*! I thought my nose broke. Cast iron was more pliable.

My cheeks compressed on impact. Earl didn't steal a kiss. He assaulted one! However, it was the sweetest kiss I'd ever had. (And I'd had a few, thank you.) Nevertheless, the move took me by surprise. I broke his lock and slapped him across the face.

"What did ya do that for? And you said you'd never hit me again," Earl said rubbing his cheek.

"Girls hit, but women slap, and don't you forget it," I said. "And I wasn't ready."

"Oh, well ..."

"I'm ready now," I said. Then I grabbed the back of his head and our lips met going ninety miles per hour, again. It was fun. We did it over and over and over again. My lips changed color and lost two layers of skin from the workout. My mouth may have been numb, but my heart was alive more than ever. Earl could have said anything, and I would have agreed with him.

"I need to talk to your daddy," Earl said.

Except that! "What? Oh no, Earl. I'd like to keep you alive for at least a day or two."

"No, Emma. I have to ask him if I can take you out on a date."

I've told you how tall and wide daddy was. Well, let me tell you about his strength. The previous spring we'd had a bull that was an ornery cuss. Nothing made that old bull happy, not a pen full of heifers or a trough full of feed. He'd snort up a storm if you so much as looked at him. Daddy got him cheap because every farmer in town hated that bull, and their momma cows hated him even more. Anyway, one day I was coming out of our henhouse with some eggs when I heard a thunderous rumble coming from the pasture. I looked up and saw Daddy walking across the field. Right about the same time, that old bull had set his sights on Daddy and went charging after him. I hollered, "Daddy, look out!"

But he just kept walking, almost clueless about the bull's existence. I panicked and drew my hands up to my face; surely this was not going to turn out well. On a dime, Daddy wheeled around right when the bull got there. *Smack*! Daddy hit him square on the nose. The force of his blow knocked the bull backwards and then onto the ground. Daddy stood over him like a prize fighter, daring the bull to get up. The bull finally did, but only after Daddy walked away. After that, we never had a lick of trouble out of that bull and he never looked Daddy in the eye again—respect.

So you understand my trepidation at the thought of Earl meeting Daddy. Although Earl weighed maybe one hundred and seventy pounds and only had two legs to run with, he insisted on talking to my daddy, and that's when I realized I had fallen for the dumbest man in America.

Before I would allow Earl to meet Daddy, I figured we should do a trial run with Momma. A simple test, really. Momma was a sweetheart who could find kindness in John Dillinger; and besides, she'd already met half of Earl while he was under my bed.

I straightened up my hair, for I didn't want Momma to think we were smooching or something. It was bad enough Earl was under my bed. What would her thoughts be if she knew he was all over my lips? We walked out of my bedroom and found Momma in her chair mending an old pair of Daddy's overalls.

"Momma, I'd like to introduce Earl Gladstone. He's from South Creek," I said.

Momma tilted her head down and looked up over her sewing glasses. "I thought he was from under your bed!" Momma always had a quick wit. "So nice to finally see the front of ya, Mr. Gladstone."

"Uh, nice to meet you, Mrs. Baumgaertner," Earl managed to say.

"Momma, it can easily be explained," I said.

"Well, I really wasn't going to pry, dear. I trust you. Your virtue is never in doubt with me. But now I'm fascinated. I want to hear how easy it is to explain a boy under your bed. Go ahead," Momma said.

"I ... well ... see, it started when Earl slept in our driveway last night," I said.

"Oh, you and Earl had a sleepover, did ya?"

"No, Momma, Earl slept in his car and I slept in my bed."

Momma pulled back the curtain and looked outside. "Huh, there's no car out front."

"That's because Earl didn't want Daddy to see him. Wait! That didn't sound right." *Maybe we should have bypassed Momma and gone straight to daddy.* "Look, Earl was hiding from Nelly!"

"Well, I'll be—you're right. That was an easy explanation. All you had to do was mention Nelly's name."

"So, do you want to hear the rest?"

"I think I got it figured out. Let's see..." Momma always had an odd gift. Some folks called her psychic, and a few Pentecostals believed that she was a witch, but she never believed in that nonsense. She called it logical perception, whatever that meant. Nevertheless, anytime a cat went missing or a neighbor fell ill, Momma always knew the outcome before the bodies were discovered. It went further than that. One time, Daddy had his car up on jacks and was about to crawl under the thing when Momma came running out of the house. "Wait! It's gonna fall!" she hollered. And sure enough, just as Daddy stood up, the car tumbled down. She'd do silly stuff too, like telling expectant mothers the sex of their babies, and I don't think she ever got one wrong. She could even predict twins long before the doctor could. So it was really no surprise that she saw the glow on my face or Earl under my bed. Momma just had her ways. "Since you said Nelly was involved in all of this, I think I know what happened," Mamma said. "Nelly and Earl were on a date, and you tagged along with that other boy. What's his name?"

"Calvin."

"Yes, Calvin. So somewhere during the night Earl got sweet on you. Something happened, and it probably had something to do with those wet clothes you brought home last night." She stopped and raised her eyebrows over her glasses.

*If you know Earl saw me naked, I'm gonna scream!*

"Now, knowing Nelly," Momma continued, "she was clueless to Earl's feelings for you. She probably even thought Earl would want to marry her."

*Momma, you're unbelievable.*

"So after Earl took Nelly home he drove back to our house because he wanted to tell you his true feelings. When he got here, all the lights were out so he fell asleep in his car. This morning you found him out there—or, first, your daddy and his shotgun found the boy. Well, I know you pretty well, Emma. So, you told him something like, 'You're Nelly's fella, and I'm not going to talk to you.' I bet you hit him too, just to cover up any feelings Earl might have discovered. Anyhow, Earl decided he'd take care of Nelly and went over to her house and broke it off. Then, on Earl's way back, he stopped and bought some flowers and then parked his car. He thought about driving up to our house, but thought better of it because he didn't want Daddy to see him in the driveway again until he had a chance to talk to you. So he walked back to our house, which turned out to be a good thing, because shortly after he showed up, Nelly came a-knocking at our door, crying her eyes out over Mr. Gladstone here. You told Earl to hide in your bedroom until you got rid of her. A tough act to do, I might add. Nelly can be a bit dramatic, bless her heart. She gets it from her momma's side, poor thing. Oh, I suppose in her situation, Nelly wanted to do something girlish, like try on clothes to make her feel better. And that's when Earl bolted under your bed."

I told you momma was amazing. It was almost like she was there.

However, I had to set her straight. "You're wrong momma, Earl didn't get me flowers."

Momma looked up at Earl. "Do you want to tell her?"

Bewilderment overtook Earl's face. "Emma, I got some flowers waiting for you in my car," he said.

"Momma how did you—?"

She held up a hand. "Logical perception, sweetheart. Do you want me to tell you how your lips got chapped?"

"Momma, no!"

"Well, there's ointment in the cupboard if you kids need it," Momma smiled.

"I think we'll be fine," I said.

We left Momma to do her sewing and went out to look for Daddy. I was used to Momma and her logical perceptions. That's why I never drifted toward inappropriate behavior. I always knew that Momma, like Jesus, was all-knowing; the difference was that Jesus couldn't look you in the eye. Earl, however, left that conversation a bit mortified, somewhat petrified, and a whole lot sanctified. After meeting Momma, I doubted Earl would ever think of a sin again, much less commit one.

I told you that Momma saw good in everyone. Well, Daddy took a different approach. He was suspicious of everybody. Thank goodness he wasn't blessed with logical perceptions or the whole town would be rounded up on one charge or another. Not that he was hateful or mean—he just wanted to protect his property. He really was a teddy bear, once you got to know him. However, his quick-to-judge attitude made that feat a positively difficult task. He always said that there are two kinds of snakes: dead ones and live ones. Daddy's shovel took care of the live ones.

Earl grabbed my hand as we walked down to our barn looking for Daddy. It was a cold, breezy afternoon, and his hand provided all the warmth I needed. Nothing ever felt so right. How strange, though, that the previous day Earl Gladstone was the last thing on my mind. Nothing more than an idiot with a couple of straws up his nose, really. Love is many things, but unexpected might be the greatest.

We could hear Daddy's voice before we went into the barn. "Dagnabbit! I'm gonna shoot you!" Daddy yelled. No, he wasn't cursing Earl. It was his tractor.

Earl and I stepped inside. Daddy was hunched over his tractor and up to his elbows in grease. He'd spent all week trying to get that thing running, and by the looks and sound of him, fixing it wasn't going well. I gave Earl one more chance to get out of it. "This isn't a good time. Maybe we should come back later," I whispered.

"Are you kidding me? This is the best time! His tractor's broke," he grinned.

*Yep, I fell for the dumbest man in America.*

Earl went right up to Daddy and stood behind him. "Hello, Mr. Baumgaertner." The sound startled Daddy and he bumped his head on the inside of the tractor hood. *Quick to judge. Good-bye Earl.*

"Dang it! What's wrong with you, boy?!" Daddy grumbled while rubbing his head.

I jumped in. "Daddy, this is Earl Gladstone."

Daddy slowly uncoiled himself from inside the tractor. Earl's eyes grew bigger and bigger as daddy's frame kept extending further and further upward. When Daddy reached his full and natural height, all Earl saw was Daddy's chest. Earl had to back up just to look him in the eye.

Daddy looked down and then looked Earl over. "Gladstone, huh? You that fella that was in my yard this mornin'?"

"Yes, sir," Earl stuck his hand out. "I'm sorry if I frightened you. I just wanted to talk to Emma," Earl said with some confidence.

Daddy wiped some grease off his hand and then grabbed a hold of Earl's hand. "Son, did I look frightened to you?"

"No. No, sir. I meant ..."

"Emma," Daddy interrupted. "You told me that Tibbs boy was in our yard. Now, Gladstone here says it was him."

"That's because I didn't want Nelly to know," I said. "It's a long story. Momma will fill ya in."

"You cat around a lot, do ya? I don't recall any Gladstones in Forbye," Daddy finally removed the grip from Earl's hand.

"No, sir, I'm from South Creek, born and raised."

"So what's your business in Forbye?"

"Well, ah ... with your blessing I'd like to take Emma out on a date tonight."

"What happened, did South Creek run out of girls?"

"Well, no sir, but Emma doesn't live in South Creek." Earl's words hung in the air. Our barn felt like an icebox, but the weather outside had little to do with it. Daddy studied Earl with a steely glare. This maneuver sent most boys staring at their shoes. God bless Earl, though. He hung in there and fixed his eyes right back at Daddy. The standoff was a bit odd because Earl had to tilt his head back a good forty-five degrees to make eye contact. Both men stood their ground, waiting for the other to blink. Earl, the youthful contender with a heart full of romance, was either too much in love or too stupid to look away. Daddy, the seasoned veteran, wasn't about to let a runt from South Creek win a staring contest. The standstill made me want to jump out of my skin. The old barn cracked and creaked from a wind gust that whipped against its weathered sides. No one moved or was about too. I had to break the showdown that stalled at a stare. Young or old, men are stubborn creatures!

"You know," I said, "Earl has to go into the army in three weeks. Will y'all be through eyeballing each other by then?"

"Is that true, son?" Daddy asked with his same fixed glare.

"Yes, sir." Earl kept his glare.

Daddy broke his stare and looked at me, giving Earl a small victory. "I respect a man who serves his country. Emma, has your momma met Earl?"

"Yes, and she took a liking to him."

"Well, your momma knows how to read 'em. I reckon a date would be okay," Daddy said and winked at me. "Now I gotta get this tractor running. My fields need tending."

"That's an old Farmall F-20," Earl said.

"You might call it that, but I call it a piece of junk." Daddy wacked his hammer on the tractor. "I've been working on this thing all week, but she just won't crank."

Earl looked the tractor over. "Mr. Baumgaertner, it's New Year's Eve. If I get your tractor running, can I keep Emma out past midnight?"

Daddy laughed. "Son, if you get it running you can marry her."

"Emma, hand me that wrench, and I need a small nail," Earl said.

I found a nail on the workbench and handed Earl both items. *Nothing says romance like working on a tractor.*

"Now, Mr. Baumgaertner, give the engine a small turn till I tell you to stop." Earl waited. "Right there." Earl started fiddling around with some gizmo on the engine. He pulled and pried and talked to himself in a weird language. He spoke about rotating the impulse coupling and lifting it off the pawl. "Ah-ha! Just as I thought!" Earl shouted like he'd discovered America. Daddy looked at me and shrugged his shoulders. "The magneto was out of adjustment. It needs to fire at thirty-five degrees ahead of top dead center," he explained. "It should click into place ... right ... there!" Earl quickly bolted a few parts back together. "Mr. Baumgaertner, give it a crank now. She should fire up."

I think Daddy was still unconvinced when he walked to the front of the tractor. He grabbed the bar and gave it a quick turn. The old tractor came to life, purring like it was sitting in the showroom. Earl grinned, and Daddy was thunderstruck. Either Earl found a few extra inches in his boots, or Daddy suddenly shrank, because somehow when Daddy came over to thank Earl, they seemed the same height.

"Thanks, son. I'd'a been fiddling with that thing till the cows came home," Daddy spoke over the tractor's growl.

"Ah, it was nothing," Earl said.

"Yeah it was. You saved me money. How'd you know what was wrong with her?"

"I'm a tractor mechanic. I can adjust magnetos with my eyes closed," Earl said.

You could have knocked Daddy over with a feather. He just realized he'd played cards without knowing the game. Earl, however, knew the game very well and kept an ace up his sleeve until the right moment. *Yep, I fell for the smartest man in America.*

"So, I can keep Emma out past midnight and marry her?" Earl said with buoyancy. Daddy was many things, and a man of his word was perhaps his best quality. However, Daddy had also offered Earl my hand in marriage if that tractor started, which was an awful predicament for an honest man. Daddy stammered and stuttered around. The Earl of South Creek had the upper hand. To be quite honest, I found it all amusing, so I figured I'd have a little fun before I bailed poor Daddy out.

"Daddy, looks like you got yourself in a pickle. Should I go tell Momma about your horse tradin'?"

"Oh, now, Emma. I was just ..."

"No, no," I interrupted. "A deal is a deal. Honestly though, swapping your one and only daughter to get a rust bucket runnin'? What would Preacher Babcock think? That's okay, don't worry about me. I'll just stay with Earl until he loses me in a card game. Then the next fella will probably trade me for some magic beans." Daddy and Earl just looked at each other. "Now listen, you two," I continued. "I'm not some chattel that can be bartered about. I'll marry who I want to—when I want to. Not by the agreements made between you two! Now, come on, Earl. We got a date to get to." I turned and Earl quickly came to my side. As we walked out I hollered back at Daddy, "Don't wait up."

With each second that passed, I fell deeper for Earl. I quit trying to understand it. How could I? The ridiculous nature of it all! I mean, who falls in love after one day? That kind of stuff happened in trashy romance novels, the kind Nelly was so fond of reading, but it didn't happen in Forbye, and certainly didn't happen to me. Yet, it did.

Earl and I drove to South Creek for various reasons. Earl was in need of a shower. The poor boy had spent a good twenty-four hours in the same rumpled clothes, and although love was blind, it wasn't odorless. Another reason, just as important, was Nelly. I wasn't ready to confront the inevitable. Heaven forbid if we happened to run into her, or worse yet, Rose Carter (you may remember Rose from my previous stories. If not, two words—town gossip). I owed Nelly the respect of letting her hear the news from me, but on my terms. Also, our trip to South Creek would allow me the opportunity to meet Earl's mother. *A saintly woman*, I was told. *A raving lunatic*, I concluded, but you can be the judge. Furthermore, South Creek had a drive-in picture show. Need I say more?

During our drive to South Creek, I found out several things pertaining to Earl Gladstone. For instance, he was delivered at home by a country doctor, and his daddy died during childbirth. I know, I thought that was a mistake too, but it did happen. The way I understood it, Earl's daddy had a taste for moonshine, which was a polite way to call him a drunk. Anyway, he got liquored up on the night Earl's momma went into labor. Only he didn't know she was in labor because he'd spent all day and most of the night swigging from mason jars. He finally came home and heard screams coming from the bedroom. Just before Earl popped out into this world, his daddy burst through the bedroom door and saw a man betwixt his wife's knees. He was too intoxicated to realize the other man was merely the doctor who was there to deliver his baby. He thought he'd come home to find his wife in the company of another man. He let out a scream and charged the doctor. The doctor, startled and armed with a pair of scissors, quickly spun around. Earl's daddy stumbled forward and landed in a most unfortunate position, right on the doctor's scissors—heart level. The doctor managed to kill one Gladstone and deliver another in less than three minutes. I'm sure that has to be a record of some kind. So, if you ever find yourself in the middle of a boring conversation just turn to your guest and say, 'Did you hear about the man who died during childbirth?' Chances are you'll get an audience.

We pulled up to a modest house on a small lot. Obviously I didn't fall for a Rockefeller. "You're just going to love Mother," Earl said as he opened my side of the car door.

"I don't know. I'm a little nervous."

"Nonsense," Earl replied. "She'll love ya. She's never met a stranger and has never made an enemy. Salt of the earth, my mother."

"Well, you had to face my daddy. I guess nothing can compare to that!"

"Yeah, mother is only five feet tall with the personality of a lamb. Your daddy, on the other hand …" *Crack*! My elbow jabbed Earl's rib.

"Hey, I thought you weren't gonna hit me anymore," Earl said.

"That wasn't a hit; it was a jab, which is like a slap."

"I need to bone up on your definitions."

"Just don't say anything boneheaded, and you'll be fine," I warned. We stopped at his front door.

"You look beautiful. Mother will adore you," he smiled and then opened the door. "Mother, I'm home."

"Earl, honey, is that you?" a voice called, and then an elderly woman appeared from the hallway. Earl's mother looked more like a grandmother. Her hair was thin, short, and very gray, almost blue. Her skin had a tawny cast to it and hung off her bones like the underside of a turkey's neck. Squinting through a pair of oversized eyeglasses, she shuffled towards us.

"Oh, Earl, it is you. I was worried sick because you didn't come home last night," she said.

"Mother, I called you, remember?" Earl said and then turned to me. "She forgets sometimes."

"I don't recall. My mind ain't what it used to be," she mumbled.

"I'm here now," Earl said, "and I brought someone for ya to meet."

"You did? Where?" she looked everywhere except where I was standing, which was right next to Earl.

"Mother, I'd like for you to meet Emma Baumgaertner. She's from Forbye," Earl said.

Finally the woman found me. "Oh," she placed her face up to mine and then slowly gave me the once over. "Pleasure to meet you, sweetie. Any friend of Earl's is welcome here."

"The pleasure is mine, Mrs. Gladstone. You have a lovely home."

"Oh, you're too kind," she tried to wave her hand, but she stopped and grimaced. "My arthritis is acting up. Come, dear, sit. Tell me all about yourself." She pointed to an old couch and chair in a tiny room just off the kitchen. It was quaint, really, with a few old photographs of Earl as a child that were neatly placed on a doily-covered table. The smell of old books and mothballs wafted slightly through the air. A few china pieces were displayed on a wall just above an upright piano.

Earl's mother seemed sweet, folksy-like, with smooth molasses charm, when she didn't stutter. She was a bit absent-minded at times, often fumbling with names or dates, things like that. Not the quickest wit either, but I was used to my momma, so on that level it was hard for her to compete. She loved to talk about Earl, though. If I didn't know any better, I'd think Earl was the product of a virgin birth, the way she worshipped the boy. It was cute in one way and odd in another. Earl seemed to dote on her just as much as she doted on him. Since I was an only child, maybe I didn't understand the mother and son relationship. However, loving a momma is a good quality to have, and Earl loved his mother.

The three of us talked for a good hour. When Mrs. Gladstone wasn't talking about Earl, she was complaining about her health. I don't think there was an infirmity she didn't have. From carbuncles to migraines, she had them all, but her arthritis drew the most attention. Poor thing, she'd move her arm and wince with pain before letting out a groan. I hurt just watching her. I don't know how the woman got out of bed each morning. Finally, Earl decided to take a bath. Lord knows he needed one. He left the room, and Mrs. Gladstone watched her son disappear down the hall. I heard a door squeak and then close. I was alone with Mother Gladstone.

"Lovely day, isn't it, dear?" she said.

"It's a tad cold for my liking," I replied without much thought. Earl's mother slipped off her shoe and threw it at me. I could not believe my eyes. Not only did it shock me, but she had the arm of Dizzy Dean. The shoe whizzed past my ducking head and hit one of the china plates that hung on the wall. *Crash!* The plate broke into several pieces and scattered about on top of the piano.

Stunned, I froze in my seat. Did I just witness a mental breakdown? Had the old lady snapped right there on the spot? I thought about running to find Earl, but with my luck, he'd be naked in the bathtub—too risky, especially with our history.

"Look what you did! You broke my favorite plate!" she yelled. The sweet little old lady was gone. Her replacement wasn't frail, absent-minded, or half-blind. She sprang up from her chair. "I bet you're a prostitute!" No, she was none of those other things; all she was, was crazy.

I'd been raised to respect my elders; however, my respect had limits. "I beg your pardon. You threw a shoe at me, and I won't dignify your assumptions."

"It doesn't matter. When I tell Earl you broke my plate, he'll throw you out!" She brushed past me with effortless motion. No shuffle, no stopping to catch her breath, and no sign of the arthritis that riddled her when Earl was in the room. She retrieved her shoe, quickly grabbed a broom, and cleaned up the broken plate. Her pace was remarkable. "I bought that plate at the 1939 World's Fair," she said with faculties in perfect working order. "It cost three dollars and fifteen cents, and now it's gone."

Then oddly, she bounced around the room in a taunting fashion, hopping on one foot and then the other. She bent down and touched her toes while naming every President from Washington to Truman. I'm not sure I could've done that! At some point during her bizarre jig she stuck her tongue out, placed a thumb in each ear, and waved her fingers at me. I don't know what looked more ridiculous, her or the look on my face as I sat dumbfounded.

I didn't know what I was witnessing or why. Did I fall through some portal and land in Crazyville? Was I threatening her because I was with Earl and she wanted to scare me off? Maybe so, but that wouldn't explain her pitiful hoax that had taken years to hone. And then why reveal it to me? I guess I should've been angrier than I was. After all, the old woman, a stranger really, threw a shoe at me, accused me, and insulted me with a name I wouldn't call my worst enemy. However, I found myself more curious than mad. I think I was even amused, in a carnival freak-show way. I wanted to ask her a few things and tell her many things, but I decided to keep my mouth shut and wait for her to make a baseless allegation towards me in Earl's company. If that happened, then I'd have plenty to say, and I wasn't afraid to hitchhike back to Forbye in order to say it. My righteous indignation can get up at times, and my ire, as you know, is well documented. So, let the old lady dance. I'd bide my time. If Earl and I had any future, which now, suddenly, seemed shaky at best, I'd have ample opportunity to sort this woman out.

I heard a door squeak from down the hallway, and Earl's mother sprinted, yes sprinted, to her chair. "Now shut up and don't say a word," she said.

Earl walked into the room. *Okay, Mother! The stage is yours!* I thought.

"Oh, Earl, something terrible happened," she said in a sickening, weak voice.

"Mother, did Emma jab you?" he laughed as he patted his ribs.

*You have no idea how close I came.*

"No, my plate ... it ... it broke," she uttered.

*And the Oscar goes to ...*

"We were just sitting here talking ... and ... it just fell off the wall," she said.

*Just fell off the wall?*

"Did you get hurt?" Earl went to his mother's side.

*Oh, please! Maybe she threw her arm out of socket.*

"No, I'm fine," she said. "Emma was a dear and cleaned it up."

*What?*

Earl looked up to where the plate used to hang. "That was your World's Fair plate."

"I had a World's Fair plate? How? I've never been to the World's Fair," poor Mrs. Gladstone said.

"Yes you have; we went together," Earl told her.

*And you paid three dollars and fifteen cents for it—oh brother!*

"I suppose so. If you say so," she said and then stared off. The perfect blank expression. *Brava!*

"Thanks for cleaning up," Earl said to me. "I don't know what Mother would have done if she were by herself."

"I'm sure she would've managed," I said looking into the vacant eyes of Mother Gladstone. What an act! To look at her, you'd think she was brain dead: hollow pupils, a little drool on her chin. She held that gaze while Earl patted her arm. I had to close my eyes just to keep them from rolling. I wasn't about to play into the old lady's warped game—whatever it was. We all sat there for a good twenty minutes, looking, staring, and gazing. As far as I was concerned, my conversation with Mother Gladstone was over.

"Well, Mother," Earl finally said. "It's gettin' late, so we best be going. I'm taking Emma out to ring in the New Year."

Mrs. Gladstone redirected her eyes from the fixed state. "Oh, is it New Year's Eve already?"

"Yes, Mother, we've been talking about it all afternoon," Earl said.

"My goodness, where did the year go? I can't believe tomorrow will be 1947," Mother Gladstone said.

"No, Mother, it will be 1949 tomorrow," Earl corrected.

"Oh, I see. They moved it up a year," she said.

*Brilliant! That line was absolutely brilliant!*

"You could say that," Earl chuckled. "So, Mother, are you gonna be okay if we leave?"

"Of course I will. You kids go have fun and don't you worry about me," she said.

It was about time, because I couldn't wait to get out of that place. The shine hadn't come off Earl completely, but my feelings for him had dulled a little since we arrived. How could he not see this woman for what she was? Surely, at some point, he had to catch her dancing or doing some other activity that involved mobility. Her scheme had to have cracks somewhere. How credulous was he? How blind was he? How dumb was he? But the more important question: How much in love was I?

Earl and I went to leave; sanity was only a doorknob turn away. I stood at the threshold anticipating fresh air when Mother Gladstone halted my deliverance. "Wait ... before you leave," she said and began her shuffle to us. It was like waiting for Christmas during a July heat wave. It would have taken less time if Earl and I just walked back to her, but Earl, God love him, stopped my movement.

"No, let her come to us. She needs the exercise," he said. I don't need to tell you what I thought about that statement, so I'll just leave it for you fill in your own italic thought. Finally, she reached us.

"Emma, could I give you a hug?" Mrs. Gladstone asked. Then she moved toward me. My first instincts were to recoil—I half-expected vampire fangs to pop out of her mouth. She was probably due for a feeding after all that dancing.

"Yeah, Emma, give Mother a hug. She likes you," Earl said. My mind raced. Maybe Earl was in on this, too. At this point, anything was possible. I remembered reading about a couple of girls that were missing in South Creek. Perhaps this mother-and-son duo had a crawlspace jammed full of dead girls. I braced myself and said a quick silent prayer: *Help me Jesus.*

Mother Gladstone slowly put her arms around me. I returned a stilted embrace. She produced a faint squeeze around my shoulders and brought her lips right up to my left ear. Then she did something just as lethal as a vampire's bite. She whispered under her breath, "He'll never believe you." She pulled back. "So glad you dropped by. You're welcome here anytime." She smiled, but it wasn't a friendly smile. It was more like the evil smile a villain reveals after he has tied the hero to the railroad tracks. I did my best to return a shrewd smile of my own. We stood there briefly, eye to eye, knowing what the other one knew. Of course, Earl saw none of that. The gullible lunkhead saw his mother and best gal share a friendly moment.

"And you were nervous about meeting Mother," he said. "Look at you two smiling at each other."

*She's right. He'll never believe me.*

We left, and I knew one thing; Dorothy from Kansas didn't have anything on me. Two days ago Earl was Barth, Nelly loved him, and I was a carefree farm girl. Quick wasn't the word for how I got from there...to here. Momma told me many things about growing up, but she never mentioned anything about crazy women, their sons, or the abruptness of it all.

Earl and I settled in for a drive. We were headed to some greasy spoon that Earl claimed had the best hamburgers in Florida. Of course, that was the same man who said his mother was a saint. If Earl couldn't spot his own disingenuous mother, then how could he gauge the quality of ground beef?

If you remember an earlier conversation I had with Nelly, then you know I have an uncanny ability to nod my head and act like I'm paying attention when it's the furthest thing from my mind. Earl was rambling on about one thing or another, which afforded me an opportunity to mull over our relationship, his mother, and what it all meant. *Emma, what are you doing? Basically, this romance is only hours old. And in the grand scheme of things, Earl could die right there behind the wheel, and as long as he coasted to a safe stop, I doubt I would mourn him for more than a day. If he doesn't coast to a safe stop, I hope Momma buries me in my pink Sunday dress. It really brings out my color ... I should nod and say something.*

I nodded my head and said, "Yes." *So, who is Earl Gladstone and why am I attracted to the rascal?* Just then my lungs filled up with smoke. I looked over at Earl. He was going to town on a cigarette, just puffing away without a care in the world. "What do you think you're doing, mister?" I demanded.

"Drivin', enjoyin' a smoke."

"You know what I said about you smoking!"

"Yeah, you just said I could," he told me.

"I said no such thing. Give it here!"

"Yes, you did. I said, 'Can I smoke?' and you nodded and said, 'Yes.'"

Okay, my uncanny ability did have a few flaws in it. Regardless, Earl knew better than to ask me that question. Something was beginning to snap inside my head. My mind disengaged, and I felt lightheaded. "Give it here," I said, reaching for the cigarette.

"No," Earl pulled back. "I haven't had one all day."

"I haven't had one in seventeen years, and I've managed. Now fork it over!"

"No."

"You're on thin ice, buster!" I reached toward his hand. Earl pulled on the wheel, and the car swerved. I looked up. The car headed off the road, hit a bump, and then we went airborne. The last thing I remembered was thinking about my pink Sunday dress. Then I blacked out.

I opened my eyes, and slowly Momma's face came into focus. My room. I was in my bedroom! What a dream! There was no Earl Gladstone, no crazy mother, no nakedness, or any other such nonsense. It was all a dream, albeit one leaving my head feeling like it had just been wrung through Momma's wash rollers.

"Momma," I said, a little groggy and unaware.

"You're back with us, dear."

"Oh, I had this terrible dream. I had a boyfriend with a … what do you mean, 'back with us'?" My head pounded.

"We brought you home from the hospital, remember?"

"Hospital?"

"The doctor said you were fine, just hysterical, and that you needed some rest. He gave me these pills to give you," Momma continued, shaking the bottle. "You were alert at the hospital. You don't remember yelling at Earl?"

It wasn't a dream. Earl Gladstone wandered this planet.

Momma filled in my memory from what the sheriff told her. Earl's car landed in a ditch just off Route 17. A trucker found us, bruised and dazed, but nothing serious. Then, I had what was best described as an emotional breakdown. I figuratively lost my head and literally went into a blacked-out tirade. They said I was kicking and screaming and causing all kinds of ruckus. Even though I was conscious, my subconscious controlled my mind, and to this day I still don't remember any of it. Apparently, it was bad.

Supposedly, Earl couldn't remove his foot from the car, which left the rest of his body at my disposal. I first wore his head out with my pocketbook. When I tired of that, I went at him with the heel of my shoe. At one point, I had my hands around Earl's throat, trying to choke the last gulps of air out of him. It was reported that I used foul language to question his father and mother's marital status, but I really don't believe I would say such things. Truck drivers hear what they want to hear. When all was said and done, it took three grown men to pull me off of Earl. I wish I could remember it—it must have been quite a show.

The whole event made sense. At the time of the accident, I had so many emotions coursing through my veins from the previous twenty-four hours that something like that was bound to happen. One thing was certain. I was through with Earl Gladstone—or at least, that was what I wanted to believe.

Now, I could concentrate on important things like school work and the crossword tournament. I could avoid that nasty confrontation with Nelly I'd been dreading since Earl picked me up out of the mud hole. This whole thing was Nelly's fault, anyway. She just had to go window-shopping in South Creek!

Thankfully, there were no visible signs of my accident, which kept the rumor mill around Forbye in the dark. If anyone asked how I spent New Year's Eve, I'd tell them, "Oh, nothing spectacular, just home with Momma and Daddy." So, again, I lied.

Things quickly returned to normal. School was back in session, my preparation for the crossword tournament was going swimmingly, and Nelly had found another boyfriend. Life was right where I wanted it, predictable.

When I came home from school that Friday, Momma greeted me at the door. "Earl called," she said. It had been over a week since that awful day, and just about as long since I heard the name Earl. All week, I could tell Momma had something on her mind. Momma, bless her, was careful not to bring up his distasteful name.

"I've got nothing to say to him! It's over!" I flopped down on the couch and grabbed a crossword puzzle off the end table.

"He wants to come over," she said.

"Yeah. Well tell Daddy to meet him at the door with his shotgun!"

"Daddy wants him to come over, too," she said, "and I wouldn't mind seeing him."

"Let me guess. Daddy needs his tractor fixed, and you've got your logical perception acting up," I grunted.

"Well, the tractor is broken," Momma admitted.

What were the odds that my own parents would turn against me for a tractor jockey and some wild premonition? Daddy always hated boys, and suddenly he and Earl were thick as thieves? And Momma, of all people, just didn't want to be wrong about her logical perception! They'd probably fit right in with Earl's mother. You could round them all up and put them in the loony bin, and no one would question their insanity.

"Then have him over. I'll stay at Nelly's."

"What happened between you two, dear?" Momma asked.

"What didn't happen would be the better question," I said, while trying to look busy with my crossword. Momma sat down beside me and straightened out the fabric on my school dress. Her gentle touch always made me talk. "His mother is half nuts, and the other side of her is crazy," I said.

"Most mothers of boys are. Do I have to remind you of Grandma Baumgaertner?"

"No, Momma, she's not like Grandma," I said, and then I told Momma every last detail of my encounter with Earl's mother. Nothing I said shocked her. She didn't even raise an eyebrow when I repeated that ugly name Mrs. Gladstone called me. Momma just listened and threw in an occasional "uh-huh" when I reached a dramatic part, of which, as you know, there were several. It felt good to unleash a week's worth of pent-up agitation.

I mentioned earlier that I hadn't heard the name Earl in a week, but I never said I didn't think of him. I thought of him often. Oh, I tried to fool myself, quell romantic ideas, and find some reason to hate the man my heart longed for and possibly belonged to. Scared? Maybe. I never liked the unknown, and love was riddled with the unknown, especially when it was attached to Earl and his mother. I wanted the car accident to be God's way of telling me to come to my senses, snap out of it, and stay away from Earl. Did I misread its purpose? Perhaps God was telling me something else—that life was fragile, tomorrow wasn't guaranteed, and true love can survive a bump in the road— literally.

After I finished telling Momma about Mrs. Gladstone's behavior and ethics, we sat briefly without speaking, just letting the story sink in. Momma finally spoke up and said, "Do you want to know what I think?" It really wasn't a question, because she didn't give me an opportunity to answer. "His mother saw it the moment you walked into her house. You weren't like the other gals Earl had brought home," she said.

"Don't tell me—the glow," I sighed, giving her an eye roll.

"Roll your eyes if you want to, dear, but she knew you were special and marked her territory the best way she knew how. Nothing is scarier than a batty old woman, and she expected you to run for the hills. And right now, in her mind, you did."

"I suppose that makes sense, but why fake illness all these years?" I asked.

Momma waved her hand in the air. "Please dear, old women have been fabricatin' illness ever since Eve ate a sour apple. Earl's mother is a sympathy hound, and she'll lap up all the pity Earl will toss her way.

Been that way for years, I'd imagine. It just so happened that it came in handy to make her insanity credible."

"You're a smart woman, Momma. I don't think my brain will ever work like yours."

"Sure it will," she smiled. She tucked my hair behind my ears and then patted my cheek. "No one can make you see Earl. If you don't want him here, then I'll stand at the doorway with Daddy's shotgun. Nobody will mess with my baby."

"I love ya, Momma." I hugged her.

"I just want you happy ... so can I tell ya somethin' I saw today?"

"Doc Peterson didn't get drunk and run over Mrs. Clark's prized petunias again, did he?"

"No, silly. Well, he might have. It is after three o'clock. But this was somethin' I saw on your face when you came home. The second I mentioned Earl's name your expression changed. Oh, you tried to hide it, but a tree full of lemons couldn't remove the way your eyes smiled, and everyone knows the eyes are the window to the soul."

"And the nose is the doorway to influenza," I repeated a line she had used several times.

"How true," she mused. "The body tells us so much."

"So, what are you telling me?"

"To be happy, that's all, dear. Just be happy."

"Well, I did wonder how Earl was doing after the accident."

"He told me his concussion was healing nicely."

"Concussion? Mercy, I didn't realize we crashed that hard!"

"Oh, it wasn't from the crash. It came from your swinging pocketbook, or maybe it was from your shoe. You put quite a wallop on that boy's noggin," Momma said.

"Oh, dear, tell me I didn't."

"You only hurt the ones you love."

"Momma!"

I was outnumbered in my own house. My momma, my daddy, and my heart all wanted Earl to pay a visit. Finally my head agreed. Momma made the arrangements, because a gal never places a call to a boy. It just wasn't proper back then, and it still shouldn't be. Anyway, Earl would come over to the house on Saturday. Momma would cook chicken and dumplings, fried okra, black-eyed peas, and collard greens. Daddy would haul Earl out to the shed. Normally that wouldn't bode well for a boy, but Daddy and Earl had a common bond with the tractors. I guess it was my job to look pretty. Not a hard task, really.

Going to bed that Friday night wasn't a problem; however, falling asleep was. My tossing and turning had nothing to do with Earl. I still held all the cards to our fledgling relationship. My angst was over Miss Nelly Wilkinson. I'd never been a hand wringer. Fretting over uncontrollable outcomes wasn't part of my constitution. That trait came from my momma's side; she never worried. But this thing with Nelly had to be dealt with the right way. All week I'd been accidentally—sort of—avoiding her. We talked at school and so forth, but I didn't want a long drawn-out conversation with her while I was still mulling over Earl and this thing called love. After talking with Momma and listening to my heart, as ridiculous as it sounded, I had stronger feelings for Earl than before. I mean, I really loved the fella. Crazy, I know. That's what I thought, too. Who falls in love after only one half of one date? Well, Emma Baumgaertner did.

Where was I? Yes, Nelly. She cornered me at school and asked to meet with me Saturday afternoon for a sundae and a chance to catch up on our lives since the Christmas break. Catching up to Nelly meant listening to her carry on about boys, her new brassiere size, and telling her if she looked better as a blonde or a brunette. I always told her natural was the way to go, but she loved that blonde-from-a-bottle look. (Still does and she's pushing eighty years old. You ought to see it, bless her heart.)

Another quality I have is honesty. It came from my Daddy's side. Not that Momma wasn't honest—she was, but let's just say she was pleasantly honest, whereas I leaned on the brutal side of honesty. (Thanks, Daddy.) I knew I needed to be honest with Nelly without letting the brutal side rear its head.

I know you're probably shaking your head and crying, "Emma, you've lied throughout this story! You claimed to have a headache when you didn't. You lied about a roach to fool Nelly, and it did. You told your daddy that Calvin spent the night in the yard, but he didn't. You told friends you spent New Year's Eve at home, and while technically true, it was far from honest. What about the lie your head's been telling your heart about Earl Gladstone?" Well, I don't care one iota about what you think! How's that for brutal honesty?

So, back to Nelly. She, naturally and effectively, had moved on from Earl and found herself a fella named Fred Dalton. If you have followed my other stories, then the last name should ring a bell. I hoped this new boy would take the edge off the knife she would surely accuse me of sticking directly in her back, and I feared she would do just that—accuse me of stabbing her in the back. I knew Nelly well, maybe too well.

After I finally drifted off, the morning came quickly. I did my chores, gathered eggs from the henhouse, and then picked fresh collard greens for supper. We had a Langshan hen that Momma was saving for a special occasion. She decided Earl was that occasion, so she commissioned me to fetch the chicken for her dumplings. Chickens are smart creatures, indeed. You wouldn't think it, being their brains are so small, but they know when it's slaughter time. For instance, if I walked out to the pen with a pail full of scratch, those chickens would gather around me like I was a momma hen. However, put an ax in my hand, and they'd scatter like they had cat genes under their feathers. That Saturday morning I had an ax in my hand.

I approached the coop, and sure enough, bedlam broke out. Normally I would sit on a stump and give the birds a chance to say their last good-byes; it seemed like the respectful thing to do. However, time was more valuable to me than the birds that particular morning, so I swooped down on the cornered hen and yanked her feet up in one fluid motion. I held the hen in the crook of my arm and slowly stroked her feathers as a calming tactic. You never want to kill a nervous bird; they end up tough and stringy. She clucked for a while, came to accept her fate, and settled down in my arm. Surprise is always the best way to wring a neck, so between gentle strokes, I quickly pulled down the hen's neck and then jerked it up. *Snap!* She was dead, but a dead chicken still has some energy to exhaust. I put the bird down and it ran around a bit, then finally flopped over. I placed the dead carcass on the cutting stump, in view of the other chickens. *Thwack*! I lopped its head off. A few chickens clucked. I could never tell if they clucked out of relief or if they clucked with anger, but they always clucked. I dropped the ax, and the chickens went about their normal routine, knowing that one of them had till next Saturday. I tied the dead hen's legs together and hung it up on a post to bleed out. Time was getting away, so Momma would have to dress it out. Besides, removing blood from under the fingernails wasn't the easiest thing to do.

I went inside to take a bath. "Momma, I hung supper out on the post. You better dress it before Mrs. Taylor's hound comes sniffing around," I said as I breezed through the kitchen.

"I'll tend to it, dear. I got the slingshot in my apron 'case that mutt shows up," she replied. Momma was a sharpshooter with her slingshot. She could knock the whiskers off a tomcat from twenty paces while wearing a Sunday dress and holding a Bible between her knees. I saw her do it. Remarkable woman, my momma.

After a good lather and a quick soak, I dressed and headed down to the drugstore. I wasn't quite sure how my conversation with Nelly would begin, but I had a good inkling how it would end. I spotted Nelly through the window. She saw me and started waving her hand for me to hurry up. That gesture always meant "I have some exciting news." I saw it when she first kissed a boy, when she got her first pair of nylons, when she received her first monthly, and yes, when she first met Earl. Thinking back, I was always the first one Nelly wanted to tell whenever something exciting or sad happened in her life. A bit of wistfulness hit me as I opened the door. I knew that Nelly would have no one to run to when our conversation was through. I took a deep breath and walked slowly toward her booth—the same booth where I first met Earl.

"Emma, I have the most wonderful news," Nelly said. We hugged and then I sat down across from her.

"Well, I have some news for you too," I said.

"Oh, it can wait. This is important!" she exclaimed. "Fred gave me a ring!" She held up her hand.

"A ring? You're engaged?"

"I think so—well, it's more like a promise of engagement. Aren't you happy for me?"

Suddenly, telling her about Earl didn't seem so hard. *This whole thing might just work out,* I thought. "Of course I'm happy for you. Fred sounds absolutely wonderful," I said convincingly.

"What do you mean, you're happy for me? That's not the Emma I know. I was waitin' for you to say, 'It's too soon,' or 'How well do you know this fella?' Why, you haven't even met Fred, and you're already giving him your seal of approval? What's up with you, Emma?" Nelly furrowed her brow and lowered her eyes on me.

It was true. Throughout our friendship I had been Nelly's conscience, that constant good angel sitting on her shoulder. I talked her out of more backseats than I cared to remember. I preached caution, good judgment, and patience. Nag? Sure. Annoying? Totally. Nelly knew my role, and deep down she loved and needed me to play that role in order to keep a semblance of virtue. If she could get whatever she was selling past the Emma sniff test, then she was good to go. She also needed my resistance, not a quick acceptance. Now, I found myself wholeheartedly endorsing a boy I'd never met and an engagement that seemed flimsy at best. Nelly was right; I wasn't acting like the Emma she knew. I just didn't know she'd catch on so soon.

"There's something different about you," she said, still looking deep into my eyes.

*Don't tell me I'm glowing.* "Well, I just wrung an ol' hen's neck," I said.

"Oh, please, I've seen you wring a chicken's neck before Sunday service and then take the Lord's Supper guilt-free. No, you don't have a guilty look... that's not it. But you sure look a far cry from innocent," she said.

"You're off your rocker, Nell. I said my prayers this mornin'."

"I dunno. Something is off kilter 'bout you." She cocked her head sideways, like a dog ready for the hunt. A hop came over, which broke her gaze. "Oh, Emma, let's celebrate. How 'bout we split a double-large sundae with extra fudge?"

"Sure, and let's do it up right with some fries to dip in it," I said.

"Excellent augmentation, dear." Nell turned to the hop. "Fries and a sundae, the biggest of both, and give us all the fudge in the house and then some. And two spoons."

I wanted the fries for two reasons: one, they really tasted good dunked in ice cream and fudge. And two, with the news Nelly was about to hear, she needed a starch to absorb all the sugar that would be coursing through her veins. Sweets never bothered me. But Nelly? They went to her head like a hobo's breakfast.

"So, you and Calvin want to double with us this weekend?" Nelly asked.

"Oh, I don't think so. I'm not seeing Calvin anymore."

"What? Oh, poor dear. What happened?"

"Nothing really ... look, Nell, there's something you need to know—"

"Calvin was an idiot anyway," she interrupted. "You deserve better."

"Well, that's what I wanted to tell you—" I tried to say.

"Then you can come stag to meet Fred, or maybe he has a buddy. I'm sure a lot of fellas find you pretty." No one was better at a backhanded compliment than Nelly, and no one was more clueless about making one. "In fact," she continued, "if your ears were a little smaller and your eyes a little closer together, then you'd be a catch." See? Clueless.

"Well, I can't because I'm seeing—"

"You know," she broke in again, "it wouldn't hurt if you applied some makeup, and kept your nose powdered." The hop placed our order in front of us.

"Have a few fries first, dear," I said. *Let 'em get a good head start before the ice cream lands,* I thought. Nelly filled her cheeks full of fried potatoes and then jammed a spoon full of fudge into her mouth.

"Thwis swooo gwood," she said. "This is soooo good," she meant. I could translate stuffed-face Nelly-speak.

With her mouth fully engaged, I took one more stab at telling her my news. "So, I've been seeing Earl." She didn't seem to hear it.

"Oh, I just thought of something," she said as she swallowed. "There's a Sadie Hawkins dance next Friday. I'll ask Fred, and you can ask ... Earl who?"

Maybe she did hear it. "Earl Gladstone," I said.

"Barth? My Barth!"

"Well, I'd hardly call him your Barth. You've moved on. But yes, that's him," I said.

"You're joking, right? Oh, I get it. Very funny, Emma." She stuffed more fries into her mouth.

"Look, you have Fred. It really shouldn't concern you anymore," I said.

"You're not kidding, are you?" She stopped chewing. Her mouth dropped open, such an unpleasant sight, really—potatoes and ice cream and fudge.

"No, I'm not kidding. It was really kind of an accident. Us two—"

"Wait, wait, wait just a cotton pickin' minute! How long has this been going on?"

*Oh, dear. Should I be brutally honest or pleasantly honest?* I thought. "Since the day he broke up with you," I said. Brutal. Thanks again, Daddy.

"I'll just turn around, and you can remove the knife!" she accused.

*I knew it.* "Oh, what drama! I can't wait for the second act!" I retorted.

"Barth was my boyfriend long before he was yours!"

"Long before he was mine? How long are your weeks, dear?"

"Doesn't matter. I had him first! How would you feel if I started dating Calvin?"

"Relieved."

"Okay, bad example," she threw off the comment. "I just can't believe you have the scruples to do that. You know Barth broke it off with me. Then on the same day, you waltz in like Ginger Rogers without a care for your best friend's feelings. You're unbelievable!"

"No, it wasn't like that. I told Earl that you were his gal and to leave me alone," I protested, and then realized what I said. Darn that brutal honesty.

"Hold on, missy! You told Barth what? Well, isn't this a fine how-do-you-do! You two set me up. The whole thing was a sham—the crying in the ladies room, telling me he was wrong for me. Oh, that night is coming back to me now. You two were laughing in the theater, sharing whispers, and such. I thought nothing of it 'cause I just wanted you two to get along. And boy did you! Then you fell in that mud puddle, which now, I don't think was an accident after all. It was just a ploy to get Barth's arms around you. Oh, and yes, I caught you sitting on his lap! It all adds up now! What a fool I was, Emma Baumgaertner!" Nelly continued her accusations.

Well, there you go. Nelly finally put it together as she saw it. She was wrong, of course. "Oh, stop this foolishness and carrying on," I said. "That's the biggest crock of nonsense I ever heard. Don't flatter yourself by thinking this was some grand scheme to hurt you. Nobody set you up. Besides, you'd have dumped Earl in a week or two anyway. You know it, and everyone in this drugstore knows it."

"That may very well be the case, but it doesn't change what you did to me!"

"I did nothing to you. Why does it always have to be about you?"

"Because I always get the boys," she hissed.

"Not this time," I hissed back.

"I hate to use the word Jezebel, but it's the only one that applies!"

"Think what you want, but Earl never cared two cents about you! He so much as told me," I huffed. That comment came dangerously close to hitting below the belt, but I was mad.

"You musta done something intimate with him because you're certainly not pretty enough for Barth—or for half the boys in Forbye!" Nelly sneered, clearly throwing a punch below the waistline.

"I've never worried about my monthly visit coming!"

"What are you implying?"

"I'm not implying anything, but you did mention half the boys in Forbye! Now, who could I be talking about?"

Our voices rose above the drugstore chatter and clinging dishes. Our conversation deteriorated with each hurling adjective and pejorative. Accusations, founded and unfounded, were thrown into a festering pot of acid-laced tongues. I was too wrapped up in the monster before me, but I'm sure we were quite a spectacle. Nelly's neck throbbed with each beat of her heart. I felt my nostrils flare to the size of saucers. Our faces reddened and our hair stood up on end. Backing down wasn't an option; an all-out brawl was.

The ice cream we'd long forgotten about was now a puddle in the bowl between us. A few limp fries clung to the scene like witnesses with no place to go. My appetite was gone anyway. However, I did have a weird craving to wrap my hands around Nelly's throat.

"You gals pipe down," the fry cook hollered from behind the counter. His roar meant nothing and was treated as such.

"You wear envy well, dear. It complements your reputation!" Nelly snapped.

"I'll consider that an endorsement coming from the town tramp!" I yelled. Then, Nelly called me the word. I will not repeat it, nor will I hint to what it was. All I will say is—she called me the word!

Without another thought we dove at each other, meeting in the middle of the table. We both had strangleholds around each other's neck, flopping around like fish on a dry dock.

"I've always wanted to choke some sense into you," I managed to say.

"I ... never ... liked you," she gasped.

We rolled off the table and hit the floor. Even though Nelly had a good twenty pounds on me, I flipped her and pinned her shoulders down with my knees. (And you thought the Church Social was the first time I'd sat atop Nelly.) Things happened quickly. A pimply soda jerk came over and tried to intervene. I growled. He saw my fangs and whimpered off. I went to town on Nelly's head while she pulled on my hair and clawed at my face.

"Take everything you said about me back!" I demanded. Then I took my palm and pressed it hard up against her nose.

"Not in a million years!" she shouted. Her index finger found its way near my mouth so I clamped down on it, and I didn't let go until I tasted blood. Daddy always told me that if I was in a fight, I may as well fight to win. He also said there were no rules in a backyard brawl. I assumed he meant a drugstore brawl, too. Nelly's gnawed-up finger only made her angrier. She balled up her good hand and caught me with a right cross to the eye. It startled me for a second, but I quickly regrouped and threw a roundhouse at her jaw. Her eyes spiraled like a pinwheel in a hurricane.

The fry cook who yelled at us earlier must have been on a cigarette break because he came running in from the front door. "I told you gals to knock it off!" The cook was a grisly, greasy, and grumpy man. "Now, break it up!" He placed his arms in between us and pried us away from each other—almost. I popped Nelly in the nose before the cook put a bear-hug hold on me. My legs, however, were free, so I kicked at Nelly, who was still dazed. Regrettably, the only things my feet found were the cook's shins. "Get over here, Chester! We've got a live one!" he hollered. Chester, the pimply-faced lad, returned. "Grab her legs and let's haul her out of here," the cook ordered. I don't think Chester had ever touched a gal's legs before, much less ones that were flying in every direction. He spent a few moments studying the angles from which to grab. Finally, his hands took a dive for my legs, and then he, along with the cook, picked me up. To be honest, I let them because I was plumb worn out.

"Keep the other one inside till I get rid of this one," the cooked barked at a waitress. Truth be known, Nelly was still cuckoo from my haymaker and wasn't going anywhere. They plopped me down on the sidewalk. "Now, beat it, and I don't wanna see your mug in here again!" the cook said with a good deal of force. I turned and started walking home.

So far in this story you've read about two fights that I was involved in. One was a blacked-out tirade that resulted in Earl Gladstone receiving a concussed skull, which I didn't and still don't remember; the other was this little flare up. So, you're probably turning to your friends and saying, "Boy, that Emma is not a very likable character. She bullies her friends and settles things with her fists." Well, yeah, when times warrant such actions. However, I do have a softer side, but that would take all the fun out of reading this story, now wouldn't it? I'll be the first to admit that I'm not perfect, and you might want to tell yourself that as you read through these pages. But never forget, through Christ we all can be forgiven—even Nelly Wilkinson.

I didn't live that far from the drugstore and the brisk air felt good on my open wounds. I felt my left eye closing a bit, and I figured a shiner was coming up. I'm sure I'd looked worse before. My toes were swollen from kicking the cook, which gave me a slight limp as I lumbered down the sidewalk. I heard a loud clatter and popping noise behind me. I groaned; the sound was unmistakable, and it meant that the last person I wanted to see was driving up beside me. *Just keep going; don't stop,* I thought. Unfortunately, the driver couldn't read minds.

"Hey, Emma ...goodness, what happened to you?" Calvin Tibbs called from his car window.

"I slipped and fell," I said still walking.

"Looks like you were in a fight," he said still rolling his car beside me.

"You're gonna make an excellent investigative journalist, Calvin." I kept walking.

"Get in. I'll give you a ride home. I need to talk to you anyway." He stopped the car.

My feet did hurt, and I needed ice on my eye, so why not. "Okay." I went around and pulled on the passenger side door.

"Uh, that door don't work," Calvin said. I took a step backwards and pulled on the backseat door. "Uh, it don't work either," he said. I rolled one eye because the other one was just about swollen shut. I walked back around to the other backseat door, and pulled. Yep, you guessed it. "It don't work, either," Calvin said.

"First, Calvin, the door *doesn't* work! You keep saying 'don't work' which is incorrect. Second, why did you have me walk all around this vehicle knowing good and well that the doors don't work?"

"You just said, 'don't work,'" he said.

"The doors, plural, don't work! The door, singular, doesn't work! You know, to be a journalist you do need to take an English class!" I didn't want another fight, but I felt a second wind coming. "So, why did you let me pull on all doors, without saying a word?"

"I dunno. I forgot?"

"You just said that like a question. Are you asking me if you forgot?" Through my one eye I could see Calvin's head trying to sort out the obviously complicated question. "Never mind, just get out so I can get in."

"Oh, this door doesn't work either." He smiled over his grasp of the word *doesn't*. "Just climb in any window," he said, still smiling. I don't know why I did it, but I climbed through the backseat window. Now Calvin was my chauffeur, and I wasn't about to hop the seat and sit by him.

"Emma, I'm glad I found you," he said.

*I didn't realize I was lost,* I thought. "Yes, Calvin, thanks for the ride,' I said.

"Emma, I don't know how to tell you this, so I may as well come out and say it. We cannot see each other anymore," he said. "Though I find you attractive, and in some ways fascinating, your manners are frightening and downright overwhelming. I can no longer deal with the rambunctious aspects of your character," Calvin said. It sounded like the boy had swallowed a dictionary.

It took me a while to understand what he was saying, and then I realized Calvin Tibbs was breaking up with me. Of course, a break-up normally requires a couple to be going steady in the first place, so Calvin's speech was baffling news to me.

"I wanted it to work. I really did, Emma, but I can't stomach our volatile relationship." Calvin kept talking, but my emotions started to catch up with the physical pain my body felt. From the backseat, I glanced into the rearview mirror and saw my face. Then it hit me—Earl was due in a few short hours and I looked hideous. My left eye was puffy and closed. I had two claw marks running down my cheeks, and my hair was sticky and matted down with clumps of dried-up ice cream. I felt my lower lip begin to tremble.

"Why did you do that?" I said to myself. My eyes clouded up, which didn't help the swollen one. As the tears rolled down my cheeks, they found their way into my open wounds on my face. Emotions gripped me and I cried like a child. I had just beat up my best friend; I was banned from my favorite hangout; I couldn't hide my injuries from Earl; and now, the boyfriend I didn't know I had was sitting in the front seat breaking up with me.

Calvin heard my sobs. "I didn't mean to upset you," he said.

"Oh, it's not you, Calvin," I groaned.

"I've never seen you cry before. You do have feelings," he said as he pulled into my driveway. He pulled on the hand brake and turned around. "Maybe I was too rash in my judgment. How 'bout we go out when that shiner heals?"

Part of me wanted to kick the back of his seat. I didn't want his pity, and I surely didn't want him! But the other part of me, the softer side you didn't think I had, took over. I dried my tears with an old napkin I found on the backseat, I straightened up my blouse, and cleared my throat. "No, Calvin dear. You've put up with me for far too long. You're a nice fella, too nice, really. Find yourself a gal at college, someone with a little less, what was the word you said? Rambunctious; yes, rambunctious. You deserve it." I patted Calvin on the head and then leaned forward and pecked him on the cheek. Finally, Calvin received a kiss from me, a kiss he'd been coveting for years. I guess it was a poetic conclusion to our relationship. I crawled out of the window, gave him a wink with my good eye, and then watched him drive away.

Momma was in the kitchen rolling out her dumplings when I came through the back door. She didn't stop or look up at me. "I put an ice bag in the freezer for you," she said.

*That darn logical perception,* I thought. I didn't bother asking how she knew about my eye because I wasn't in the mood to hear her retell a story I had just lived. She would've, too, probably right down to the word Nelly called me. That was the good thing about Momma—I never had to tell her how my day went. She always knew.

I stopped in front of her. "Does it look as bad as you thought?" I said.

She looked up. "Oh, dear. Your face is scratched, too." She wiped the flour off her hands with a dishrag and then touched my face, turning it side to side. "They're not that deep. Grab the ice bag and lie on the couch. I'll doctor up those scratches," she said.

About that time, Daddy came through the door. He was just passing through, looking to grab a drink of tea and a cookie. He saw my face and stopped. After a brief wordless stare, he said, "Goodness, girl, tell me the other fella looks worse!"

"The other fella was Nelly, and she's probably still trying to remember her name," I informed him.

"That's my gal," he crowed.

"Charles!" Momma said. Charles was my Daddy's name, but Momma never used it unless she was mad. "We don't condone fighting in this house!"

"We don't condone losin' either. I'm sure Nelly had it comin' to her," he replied.

"That may be the case, but we don't reward rambunctious behavior," she shot back.

*What is it with this word, rambunctious? Does everyone see me that way?* "I need to lie down," I said.

"Yes, honey, go lie down. We'll talk about your pugilistic endeavors when you feel better."

"What time is Earl gonna be here?" Daddy asked.

"Seven o'clock," I said as I plopped down on the couch.

"Good, I'll have time to get in the tub before he gets here," he said.

That statement was unbelievable, coming from Daddy. He never took a bath before supper, and that held true even when Preacher Babcock would be coming over. Of course, the preacher just repaired souls, not tractors.

Daddy started to head out to the farm for a few more hours of work when I called him and Momma over to me. "I know we always tell the truth, but do you think we can keep my fight with Nelly mum tonight?" I asked.

"Sure; I'll tell Earl you got out of line, and I backhanded you one," Daddy teased.

"Charles!" Momma yelled.

"You're right, Earl might not fix my tractor if he thought I gave you the what-for," he laughed.

"Honey, we'll just tell 'em you fell down some steps. How's that?" Momma said in a soothing voice.

"Thanks, Momma."

I drifted off to sleep with an ice bag on my eye and apprehension in my heart. Even though I really didn't know Earl all that well, I knew I loved him. The fight with Nelly confirmed it. Not only did I fight for my good name, but I fought for Earl's honor as well. Subconscious crossed into the conscious when I chose Earl over a life long friend. Inner thoughts ran without guilt, and exposed happiness. Nothing Nelly said or did could change that glow on my face. Now, if I could only make that glow cover up my black eye!

I rolled over and glanced out the window; it was dark. *Oh, what time is it? Dark? Wait! What time is it?* I turned and looked at the clock. "Six-thirty!" I screamed.

"Momma, how come you didn't you wake me?" I hollered as I got up.

She poked her head around from the kitchen. "I was going to just as soon as Daddy gets out of the tub," she said.

"Daddy's in the tub?!" I ran down the hall and banged on the bathroom door. "Daddy, get out of there. I gotta get ready!"

"In a minute," he said without urgency.

I ran to my room. Quickly I rifled through my closet. *Red dress? No, too suggestive! Pink dress with bow? No, too little-girlish ... oh, think, think! Green dress? No! Ah, blue dress; it will match my black eye!* I grabbed the dress and then I ripped open my dresser drawers. I took a handful of unmentionables and ran back down the hall. Daddy was just coming out of the bathroom. And what a sight! He was clean shaven, hair combed in a Sunday-go-to-meeting fashion, and he was wearing more than just a hint of aftershave.

"Daddy, you do know Earl is coming to see *me*," I reminded him.

"What? Can't a fella get spruced up?"

"That tractor must really need fixin'." I slammed the door before I heard his response. My bath was quick. I'd never been a long soak gal anyway. However, fixing my face was an entirely different story. Usually makeup went on light, if any at all. I was blessed that way. But desperate circumstances called for extreme measures, so I took a page out of Nelly's book and followed the directions under dolled up faces.

The technique worked well on the scratches. From ten feet away you probably couldn't see them. I wished I could say the same thing about my shiner. That thing, pardon the pun, stuck out like a sore thumb. Picture an overripe summer squash planted firmly in my eye socket. You think makeup would help? Of course not, it was pointless to try. Earl would have to accept me for who I was: a fascinating gal with a black eye from time to time.

I was completing my ensemble when Momma hollered from the kitchen. "I think I hear a car pullin' up." I bolted from my bedroom, Daddy bolted from down the hall, and then we bolted into each other.

"Daddy, keep your shirt on! Your eagerness to see Earl is starting to frighten me," I scolded.

"Just want the boy to feel welcome," he said. I'd never seen Daddy act like this. Making boys feel unwelcome was his hobby. At the rate Daddy was going, I was sure by the end of supper he'd hand Earl a dowry of some sort. I beat Daddy to the window and peeked outside.

"Momma, that's not Earl. There's a hearse parked out front," I said.

"A hearse?" Momma asked.

"No. Wait. It is Earl."

"Maybe he has Nelly in the back," Daddy teased.

"*Charles*!" Momma said. That was three in one day for Daddy. One more and he was on the couch tonight.

Earl knocked on the door. "Act natural," I told my parents. "Daddy, quit smiling." I opened the door and without beating around the bush I launched into the longest run-on sentence in the history of grammatical fanfare: "I have a black eye because I fell down some steps it should be fine in a couple of days no lasting scars or anything you know me clumsy I'm sorry for hitting you I really don't remember it I have no idea what got into me crazy huh and how is your mother hello by the way good to see you again and why are you driving a hearse?" I said with no commas, which resulted in a blank stare from Earl.

"Uh, okay ..." Earl said. I think I lost him somewhere between my black eye and "How is your mother?"

"Oh, come in, Earl dear," Momma said. He stepped in with flowers in his hand. "Earlier today I picked out a lovely vase for those flowers to go in." Sometimes Momma liked to flaunt her logical perception.

It was really good to see Earl—really, really good. His Spencer Tracy grin, his wonderful blue eyes ... and what do you know, he had run a comb through his hair. He looked like he was happy to see me as well.

We sat down, ahem, the four of us in the living room. With my one eye, I pointed in Momma's direction to the kitchen. She took the hint and popped up from her seat. "C'mon Daddy, I need your help in the kitchen," she said.

"Okay," he said, but he stayed in his chair. "So, Earl, why the hearse?"

"Oh, uh, I'm waiting on a part for my car. My boss let me drive the company vehicle," Earl said.

"Company vehicle? I thought you were a tractor mechanic?" I asked.

"I am. I work for Bleaker Brothers Funeral Home and Tractor Repair," he explained.

"You work for what?" I said.

"The Bleaker Brothers," Earl repeated.

"Hey, I've heard of 'em. They play their commercials on that bluegrass station out of South Creek," Daddy said. Then he got a big grin on his face and started singing a jingle:

*Unexpected death or tractor out of breath,*
*Bleaker Brothers is above the rest.*
*Your grief will be brief;*
*Our talents are balanced.*
*From steering wheel vibration to an economical cremation,*
*We're here to comfort your despair and we guarantee our repairs.*
*Let Bleaker Brothers—bop—bop—serve you!*

Then Earl and Daddy intoned in unison, "Don't forget, free tune-up with headstone purchase!"

"I sing that on my tractor all the time. Bop—bop—serve you!" Daddy sang the hook again. "You think I can get one of them tune-ups?" Daddy asked.

"Maybe so, Charles," Momma said standing with her hands on her hips. "You might need a headstone after I'm through with you. Now get in here and leave them alone!" That was the fourth *Charles* of the day. Daddy jumped up.

"Gotta go, kids," he said.

I was somewhat alone with Earl. "So, how," we both said at the same time. "You go first," we said again at the same time. We giggled. Earl put his hand over his mouth as a signal that he wouldn't talk.

"I'm glad you came," I said. "After what they said I did to you, I'm surprised you wanted to see me."

"Well, I've been hit harder. Maybe not as many times, but harder," he replied.

"Oh, I feel just terrible. I really don't remember a thing."

Earl moved a little closer. "You're all I've thought about since that night," he said. My face felt flushed, and my bad eye started throbbing.

"Me, too," I giggled. Earl kissed me on the cheek. It was really a tender moment—Earl next to me, near enough for just a whisper. And then the phone rang. We jumped apart. Momma came in to answer it.

"Hello ... no, Blanche. No one is dead here ... Oh, that's Emma's boyfriend's car ... No, he's not an undertaker; he works on tractors ... Oh, you've heard of 'em? That's right, the Bleaker Brothers." Momma held the phone away from her mouth. "Blanche is singing that jingle," she said. Then she went back to the phone. "That's right, Blanche; bop—bop—serve you ... Okay, I'll ask him. Bye." Momma hung up the phone. "Blanche wanted to know if the tune-up offer was good through February. She said her mother isn't feeling well and she might be dead by then."

"I think so," Earl said. "I know our spring special begins in March. Coffins are half-priced with a brake and clutch job. You know what? That's a better deal. She might want to ask her momma to hold off till spring."

Daddy materialized in the room. "Speaking of clutch jobs," he began, "you think you can give my ol' iron horse a look see? Been smelling funny out of the rear end."

"You or the tractor?" Momma asked.

Daddy thought for a moment. "Well, you just work on tractors, right, Earl?" Daddy said.

"Yes, sir," Earl said.

"Then I reckon I'll just worry about the tractor for now," Daddy laughed.

"Y'all ready to eat?" Momma asked

*Am I related to anyone in this room?* "Please, anything to move the conversation along," I groaned.

We had a lovely supper, indeed. Momma bragged on the tenderness of the chicken. She said it was because of the way I wrung its neck, and Earl seemed impressed. Her collard greens were the best, as always. Okra is only good one way, fried, which Momma did with lard. Earl fit right in with our happy family. Our conversation was easy and natural, like we had known Earl all our life. There was one awkward moment, though. We all were sitting at the table when Momma asked, "So, Earl, what church do you go to?"

"Oh, I don't go to church," he said. The rest of us dropped our forks; they clanked down on our plates. No one said a word in the resulting uncomfortable silence. "Well, I do take my mother when she needs a ride."

"What church does she ride to?" I asked.

"Baptist, of course. Did God make another religion?" Earl replied.

"The boy's got a point," Daddy said. We picked up our forks and resumed eating. Earl was a Baptist, even if he didn't know it.

Over peach cobbler, Daddy asked, "So, Earl, what do you want out of life?" That was a pretty deep question coming from a man who sometimes favored grunts over dialogue.

"Well, sir, a farm with a sweet woman for my wife is my ultimate dream. Pretty much your life, sir." Momma and Daddy both blushed. "And I reckon the army is the best route for that to happen. I'll send my mother some money, but I figure on saving every other dime I make until I get out. Then I just want to grow crops and have a few cattle."

"Ya know, that Korea is a hotbox. Truman ordered a withdrawal from the north. All signs are pointin' to a war," Daddy said.

"Oh, let's pray that doesn't happen," Momma said quietly.

"If it does, I'll keep my head down. I should be all right. My recruiter told me with my experience I'd probably work on airplanes in Milwaukee," Earl said.

"During the Great War they told me I would shuffle papers in Denver, but I got shrapnel in my side that said somethin' different," laughed my daddy.

"Let's change the subject. War talk makes me nervous," Momma said. "Emma, are you prepared for the crossword tournament?"

"Three letter word for affirmative: *yes*," I said.

"Crossword tournament?" Earl asked.

"It's a big shindig, Earl, with all the trappings of a carnival. We call it the Forbye Olympics. Daddy even brings his tractor down and gives hayrides to the kids. On contest row there's a pickle-eating contest, a jelly-making contest, and a wood-choppin' race, just to name a few. But the big event is the crossword tournament," Momma proudly explained.

"I've heard of the Forbye Olympics, but I didn't know it had all that. I figured it was just a couple of hicks gettin' together for a sack race," Earl said.

"We have that, too," Momma said.

"Sounds fun. When is it?" asked Earl, smiling at me.

"Next Saturday," I said.

"Doggone it! My train leaves at 1:30 in the afternoon on Saturday. I told Mother I'd spend the day with her. I wish I could see you in the tournament, though, Emma," Earl said.

*Yes, the crazy woman, of course.* "Oh, that's okay. I'll just win the tournament without you." I acted like it didn't bother me. But it did.

"Emma has won the tournament three years in a row," Momma bragged.

"Then I guess the fourth year is in the bag," Earl grinned.

"Not so fast," Daddy said. "Emma moves up to the adult division this year. She'll have Marge Rosenberger to contend with."

"Marge Rosenberger. Please, Daddy. I'll have twenty-eight down and ten across solved before she pulls out her bifocals," I said confidently.

"The overconfident coon ends up with a belly full of buckshot," Daddy warned.

"Maybe you're right. I'll just have twenty-eight down solved before Mrs. Rosenberger pulls out her bifocals," I stated.

"All right, enough talk with us old folks," Momma said. "Daddy, let's clear the table and let the kids alone."

"You want to go for a drive, Emma?" Earl asked.

"Sounds lovely ... wait, in a hearse?"

"Sure. She rides smooth, and she's quiet, too."

I always figured the first time I rode in a hearse would be the last time I rode anywhere, but death and true love did have odd similarities: they happened once, they were final, and at some point, there would be tears. So, I didn't blink an eye, the black one or the other one. "Okay, let's take a drive," I said.

I kissed Momma on the cheek. Daddy wanted to go outside to take a peek under the hood, but Momma pulled him back. Poor Daddy, I think he wanted to go for a ride, too.

We stepped outside. It was a perfect evening for a drive; the sky was clear and the air was cool. Earl wrapped his jacket around my shoulders as we walked to the hearse. I know, *hearse*. It sounds romantic, doesn't it?

"Don't get any ideas about gettin' me in the back of that thing," I said.

"Oh, I can't. There's a body in the back," Earl said with a straight face. "You wanna see?"

"Earl Gladstone, I don't even know who you are! No, I don't want to see, and I'm not going on a drive with a fifth wheel, especially when the fifth wheel is dead!"

Then Earl flashed me his Spencer Tracy grin. "Just kidding. I love it when you get all riled up."

"Oh, you do, huh? Well, I'm not leavin' until you open the back of that thing and show me it's empty! If it's not, then I'll show *you* riled up!"

Earl opened the backdoor and proved the hearse was empty. So, Earl, I, and the Bleaker Brothers' hearse went for a drive. It was kind of nice, actually. Cars moved over for us, men bowed their heads when we went by, and a couple of old ladies crossed themselves while we waited at a stop light. We received all the accolades due a corpse while enjoying the benefits of breathing. Life is good when you're dead.

We drove out of Forbye Township and headed down a stretch of road where headlights were few and far between. I scooted a little closer to Earl, willfully violating my own matchbook rule. It was time I discarded that antiquated law anyway. Earl touched his shoulder as a sign to rest my head. I did. "Earl, am I rambunctious?" I said softly.

"Oh, yeah," he said.

"You say it like it's a good thing."

"It is. That's what caught my eye the first time we met at the drugstore."

"And all this time I thought it was my good looks," I playfully said.

"Your looks weren't far behind. In fact, there are pretty gals and feisty gals, but rarely do they stand in the same body. Emma, I knew you were unique from the moment I first saw you. Even before you sat down that night, you know what I said to myself?"

"These straws are hurting my nose?"

"What? Oh, the straws I had up my nose," Earl laughed. "You're a quick wit, too, Emma. But seriously, I said to myself, 'I'm gonna marry that gal.'"

"Hold on, buster. I haven't said *I do* yet."

"Well, you haven't said *I don't* yet, either."

"You move that hand any further up my knee, and you'll hear it," I said. Earl put both hands on the steering wheel.

"I'll tell ya somethin' else. I don't believe in coincidences," he said.

"What a coincidence! Neither do I."

"Now you're being funny when I'm tryin' to make a point," he scolded.

"Sorry, dear, but you get what you see," I said. "I get that from my momma."

"Anyway, the point is, our meetin' wasn't a fluke. So, laugh it off if ya want to, but I'm gonna marry you, Emma. You watch," he insisted.

"Well, we'll see. There's still some courtin' to do. Besides, you wouldn't want to marry a clumsy gal who trips over her own feet." I lifted my head off his shoulder and looked at him with my black eye and then laid my head back down.

"No, I wouldn't. But I would want to marry a gal that packs a good wallop and stands up for what she believes," he said.

I jerked my head up. "What are you talking about?"

"I know you got into it with Nelly."

"Daddy told you?"

"Nope," he said.

"Don't tell me you have logical perception, like Momma."

"I wished. No, I stopped for some gas on the way to your house. Some gas hops were talkin' 'bout a fight between two gals across the street at the drugstore."

"And you naturally assumed it was me and Nelly?"

"Not at first, but when I heard them say stuff like, 'Emma had Nelly by the throat,' and 'Emma bit Nelly's finger,' and 'Emma took a punch to the eye, but she returned with a wicked blow' then I..."

"Okay, okay, I don't need a play-by-play recap. You know there could be two Emmas and two Nellys in Forbye."

"Then I'd like to date that Emma. The gas hop said she was a pretty thing."

"Really?" I blushed. "Then I guess it was me."

"You're a fascinatin' gal. There ain't too many gals that can wring a chicken's neck in the mornin', knock her best friend silly in the afternoon, and then go on a romantic drive in a hearse later that evening. Unique indeed. Hey, what say we head over to the drugstore for a cherry coke?"

"You better add 'banned from that establishment' to my repertoire of uniqueness," I told him.

"Oh, I reckon that makes sense," Earl paused. "You never got in any fights over at the Forbye Diner, have you?"

"Nope," I said. I was almost certain I hadn't.

"Good, we'll head over there."

Earl and I spent a lovely evening driving around Forbye and parts of Wayland County. He was the perfect gentleman, keeping his hands mostly on the wheel. I won't tell you how much we smooched or even if we did. And for good reason. Through this story you have already encountered brief nudity, a few suggestive innuendoes, and a lengthy make out scene, which took place in my bedroom. If I were to describe every provocative detail and tantalizing event between myself and Mr. Gladstone, then this book would be in the same company as that trashy pulp you find in a dime store, or worse yet, wrapped in a plain brown cover. Of course, some of you would get a charge out of it, and I'm sure there are several outlets for you to find such rubbish, but I do have standards. Okay, he kissed me goodnight. There!

The next day, Earl actually wanted to go to church with me. And I wanted him to as well, but there would be a problem—Nelly Wilkinson. I decided, and he agreed, that it would serve everyone better if he made himself scarce around Nelly. Since I would be seeing her at church, I figured our meeting wouldn't come to fisticuffs, but it would be cool, if not downright cold. I planned on apologizing, even though the whole scene was her fault. She would pout and tell me I was discourteous to her feelings, that type of thing, but I always felt we'd eventually work through it.

I arrived at church early just in case Nelly was there. Hopefully, we could put this mess behind us before Preacher Babcock told the congregation we were all going to hell. He liked to do that sort of thing, especially if he caught wind of Gus Miles selling moonshine to some of the parishioners.

I waited on the church steps for Nelly to arrive, but she never came. Instead, up walked Doris Glosenfoot. You may know Doris by her married name, Humfinger. Funny, she traded a foot for a finger. Anyway, Doris walked up and handed me an envelope. "Nell came to my house this morning. She shoved that envelope at me and said, 'Emma must positively have this,'" Doris said in a dramatic voice. "What on earth is eatin' that child this time?" Doris asked. She and Nelly never really got along.

"Oh, her feelings got bruised, along with her face," I said.

"Looks like you got a pretty good taste of it, too," Doris said looking at my black eye.

"Nah, it looks worse than it feels. I'm over it."

"From Nell's description, I don't think she is," Doris said.

"She'll come around," I replied. Doris pretended to dust off her hands, indicating her mission was through, and then she went inside the church. I took the envelope and pulled out a letter.

*Dear ex-best friend* was the opening salutation. I thought it was bit dramatic, even for Nelly. Here I was ready to forgive and forget, let bygones be bygones, and say all the things we say, and sometimes mean, to keep a friendship alive. Apparently, Nelly was not. I continued to read:

> *I really shouldn't even call you an ex-friend, because the more I think about it, you were never a friend in the first place! A true friend would never get fresh with my fella like you did. You can deny it all you want to. It's probably how you can sleep at night. So go ahead and convince yourself that you're little Miss Innocent and it was all just one big coincidence. Do whatever it takes to clear your guilt over this blatant act of betrayal! However, I will always have a constant reminder for you, and it's called Alabaster Heaven. That's right, not only is it a wonderful smelling perfume, but it will be a symbol for double-crossing. You gave me Alabaster Heaven as a gift, a so-called act of friendship, but now I realize it was nothing more than a Judas kiss. How foolish of me. Well, dear, now I will turn the table on you, and that smell will haunt you for the rest of your life because I will never go anywhere without liberally applying that scent! That should give you something to think about. I know we will cross paths eventually, and when we do, betrayal will be your first thought!*

Well, there you have it. Now you know why Nelly has continued to wear a perfume throughout the years that was really better suited for lamp oil—and cheaper, too. She calls it betrayal; I call it nuts.

I went into church, sat down on a pew, and scribbled a little note. After service, I found Doris to deliver my reply:

> *Dear Nelly,*
> *I don't believe in coincidences.*
>
> *God Bless,*
> *Emma*

It may sound insensitive, but I didn't concern myself too much with

Nelly's wild claims. I had other things on my mind, like Earl and the annual county crossword tournament. If Nelly wanted to reconcile, then she knew where she could find me. If she wanted to hold a baseless grudge for the rest of her life, fine. But I wasn't about to let bitterness eat me up. My life was falling into place nicely, with or without Nelly Wilkinson.

The week before Earl left for the service, he spent every day at my house. The Bleaker brothers gave him the time off with a week's pay because of his commitment to the military. They also allowed him to use the hearse all week—as long as no one died. Thankfully, no one did. It was a really nice gesture on their part. Those were the days when companies weren't afraid to show their patriotism. But I digress.

Earl arrived at five o'clock each morning and didn't leave until a good three hours past supper. After reading that, you may think that we spent a lot of quality time together, right? Wrong. Remember, I was still in school. And after school I had my studies in addition to my chores, plus my preparation for the crossword tournament. So why did Earl Gladstone spend all that time at my house? Daddy.

Those two became quite a pair that week. They overhauled Daddy's tractor. Well, Earl overhauled it while Daddy watched, and fetched wrenches, and made iced tea runs. Earl was the son that Daddy never had, or maybe the brother, because one day I caught them sneaking smokes behind the barn. (Yes, Daddy smoked, too; that is, when Momma didn't see.)

During that week, Earl and I came to the same agreement that my folks had on cigarettes. No smoking in the house, cars, or around us. A man had to have his vices—Eve saw to that. Like Eve, we had the power to set the parameters in which a habit can be indulged.

Of course, it wasn't all school work and tractor repair. Earl and I did catch a few moments together. After supper each night we sat on the porch swing and talked or just looked at the stars. I found that words sometimes got in the way of a good conversation. If you've ever been in love, then you know what I mean. You become adept at reading facial expressions. You communicate through a squeeze of a hand, a slight brush down the arm, a nod of the head. You're able to hear a smile through darkness, when the only light is sparkling from the pair of eyes sitting next to you. Nothing matters but the creak of the porch swing and the sound of your beating heart. Words are really useless tools when building a romance. I guess that was when I knew I truly loved Earl. It wasn't what we said; it was what we didn't have to say.

Spending that week with him was a wonderful courting experience. It was nice to give him a peck on the cheek each morning as I left for school and a more formal form of affection when he went home each night. The neighbors got used to a hearse in our driveway, so the calls stopped, as did most of the flower arrangements. Somehow, it seemed that just when things became routine, it was Friday and time for Earl to leave for boot camp. On our last night together we sat out on the swing holding hands and not wanting the moment to end. Earl could tell that I was sad by the way I rocked back and forth on the swing. "It's only nine weeks," he said.

"May as well be nine years. Then who knows where Uncle Sam will send you," I mumbled. "I wished we could hit a button to rewind the whole week."

"Not me; I'm tired of working on your daddy's tractor," Earl teased.

"You know what I mean, silly. You're gonna leave this hick town and forget all about little 'ol Emmaline Baumgaertner. I reckon you'll find a new gal before your boots are broke in."

"Why do you worry your pretty head over that nonsense? I told ya that from the first time I saw you, I knew I was gonna marry you."

"Well, Nelly told me one time that we would be friends for life. Forever seems to have a short memory 'round these parts," I said.

"Listen, do you hear that?" Earl whispered. Through the screen door I heard the faint sound of dishes rattling together as my momma and my daddy's muffled voices carried out from the kitchen. In one instance, Momma would start to giggle, and then Daddy would say something else. Suddenly, Momma's laughter would bolt out of the house and fade away somewhere in our yard. They were just washing dishes together, nothing special. You could tell that neither one of them wanted to be any other place than right beside each other.

"It's sweet, isn't it?" I said.

"That's us in twenty years," Earl said.

"If we're together in twenty years, the only sound coming from the kitchen will be my frying pan against your head," I chuckled. It felt nice to smile.

"That'll be fine as long as we're together," Earl said. *Could this man be any sweeter?* My smile turned into a frown, the kind of frown one has right before they well up in tears. I lowered my head on his shoulder.

"I love you," I whispered. The words just came out. With no forethought and without hesitation, they popped out of my mouth. I was quite stunned. I had thought it for a long time, but never actually said it to him. It was like an uncontrolled force moved my lips. *I just told Earl Gladstone that I loved him!*

"I'll always love you, Emma." *Earl Gladstone just said he loved me!*

We both said nothing after that. We didn't need to. The sound of Momma and Daddy carrying on in the kitchen melded with the creaks of the porch swing and our beating hearts. Everything seemed right, secure, determined—and it was.

Twenty minutes passed, maybe longer, before a word was spoken. I really didn't want to leave the crook of his arm because it would mean one thing: our last night together was coming to an end. It was late though, and we both had a big day ahead of us. My head made my heart remove Earl's hold. "It's gettin' late, honey, and I need a few winks before the tournament tomorrow," I said as I peeled myself away from Earl.

"I reckon so. You're gonna win that thing for me, aren't ya?"

"I had planned on winning it for the Baptists, but I'll throw your name on the list, too." We walked hand in hand to the hearse, and then I leaned against the driver's side door. "I guess this is it then?" I said.

"Wait, I just realized somethin'. My train makes a stop in Forbye!" Earl exclaimed.

"What?"

"My train, it has a fifteen minute stop in Forbye to pick up passengers. We might be able to see each other one more time. What time will your tournament be over?"

"Uh, it starts at noon, so probably around one-thirty," I said.

"Hold on," Earl said and then dug out a thick billfold from his back pocket. "I keep everything in here."

"Apparently," I said as he started handing me things. I collected his birth certificate, an out-of-date library card, a ticket stub from a circus that came through town two years ago, a title to a car he no longer owned, and a coupon for a free kiss at the county fair. "What's this, buster?" I demanded, waving the coupon.

"Oh, reckon I don't need that anymore." Earl tore it in half. "Here it is," he said unfolding a piece of paper. "Arriving in Forbye at two o'clock, and departing at two-fifteen."

"So, if I win the tournament by one thirty, it would give me plenty of time to make the fifteen-minute walk to the train station."

"And that would give us ten minutes or so to smooch or do whatever," he said.

"Yes, like you'd pick that whatever over smooching."

"Just don't bring your daddy. He'd want me to fix somethin' between kisses."

"Between his kisses or mine?" I asked.

"Funny, Emma, but your daddy did take a shine to me."

"You're just one polished up fella, aren't ya, Earl Gladstone?" I said, snuggling up to his neck.

"So, we got one more date. Don't be late," he said after a soft kiss.

"Nothing will keep me away from that train station."

We spent a few more minutes together, just not wanting the evening to end. We cuddled looking up at the moon. Cupid rode its romantic beam down and tethered our hearts as one. Earl softly brushed my hair away from my face. I held onto his shoulders like there was no tomorrow, and at the time I really didn't care if there was. Tomorrow meant he would be gone. Tonight meant I could still feel the warmth of his breath and the softness of his touch. We stood in a quiet embrace, stuck in the moment, confessing our love through unexpressed words.

"You're not leaving without saying good-bye!" Daddy said. His voice surprised us and separated us.

"Daddy! How long have you been standing there?"

"Oh, long 'bout the time Earl said he'd be passing through Forbye tomorrow."

"Daddy, how could you?"

"What? This is my yard too, and I agree, that moon up yonder sure is pretty," Daddy said.

"You're unbelievable. You know that, right?"

"You kids were gettin' ready to break it up anyway," Daddy said and put his hand out. "Earl, son, you've been a blessing 'round here this week. My tractor ain't never run better, and no one had to die to get it that way."

"It was nothing, Mr. Baumgaertner," Earl said.

"Please, son, you've earned the right to call me Chuck," Daddy smiled. *Whoa, call him Chuck? Only his close friends call him Chuck.*

"Okay, Chuck," Earl said and it sounded odd coming out of his mouth. "Now, be careful of those gears. Since I tweaked it, I'm afraid that tractor might get out of hand when you slip it into high."

"Ah, no worries, my boy. I'll just use that gear on the highway," Daddy said, and then he looked at Earl. His bottom lip shook a bit. Daddy was always emotional for his size, and his fondness for Earl was apparent by the moisture that gathered up in the corner of his eyes.

"Take care of yourself, son." Daddy cleared his throat. "And you best not be a stranger when you get back."

"No, sir, I'm afraid you'll be seeing a lot of me," Earl said as he shook Daddy's hand one last time.

"Good, good," was all Daddy managed to get out. He turned away in an attempt to hide his feelings and then walked back to the house with his head down and shoulders sagging.

"So, who are you gonna miss more? Me or Daddy?" I asked.

"Your daddy is a good egg, but I love you!" Earl said. "You smell better, too."

The only way that evening could have ended any better was if it never did, but it did. Earl slid into the hearse and I poked my head through the window. Let me clean this up the best way I can. Earl happened to be chewing gum at the time. When I finally removed my head from the inside of his car I was chewing gum, and I hate to chew gum. I waved and watched Earl drive away. One more day, perhaps one more stick of gum.

In the year 1913 the first crossword puzzle was printed in the Sunday *New York World*. It was quite popular and became a weekly feature. However, the sport of crosswords really didn't catch on until 1924, when Simon & Schuster published a book with a collection of crossword puzzles. The crossword craze happened to coincide with the town of Forbye's creation of the Forbye Olympics. The town leaders wanted games the average farmer could compete in; hence they had hog calling, seed spitting, wood chopping, and such. The women folk would have pie baking, dress making, flower arranging, and so forth. However, the grand game was the crossword tournament. It was open to men and women, but there wasn't one man in Forbye who ever entered the tournament. I believe it was from fear. Can you imagine what it would have been like in those days to lose to a woman? Anyway, after a few years the county got involved with the tournament and it became a Wayland County sanctioned event. It was pretty big deal around these parts. If, on occasion, you ever find yourself passing through Forbye, be sure to stop by the Town Square and look for the giant plaque hanging inside city hall. There, you will find a list of all the past county champions. Then do one more thing—count how many times you see my name.

The morning of the crossword tournament brought excitement and anticipation to my heart. I was finally going to have the chance to put my skills to the test. Crossword puzzles are the ultimate game of spelling, memory, and analytical dexterity, and I happened to have all three. It's really an odd gift. I can read words backwards, upside down, and of course, sideways. Momma thought it was because she had a difficult pregnancy with me which required bed rest. She killed time by doing crosswords, and many times she'd fall asleep with a puzzle on her tummy and with me right there underneath soaking it in. Momma might have been right, because I'm rarely stumped by a puzzle. Furthermore, the speed with which I solve them is on record, too. I had three trophies to prove it; but that was in the youth division, and things were about to change.

The morning also greeted me with another emotion, sadness. My Earl would be leaving for Fort Jackson, South Carolina, and I missed him already. Momma cooked my favorite brain foods: grits, fried ham, and two eggs, slightly runny. It was a tradition that went back to my first tournament, but I just sort of picked at the food while thinking about Earl. Two emotions like excitement and sadness wrestling each other didn't rest well in the belly.

"You better eat 'em, sugar," Momma said. "You need your strength for the tournament."

"Oh, I'll be fine. You reckon the tournament will end on time?" I asked.

"Why, Miss Emma! When did you ever care when a crossword tournament ended? Oh, I remember, now. There's a certain G.I. that'll be passing through the Forbye train station around two o'clock," Momma said.

"And the tournament had better be over by 1:30." I took a bite of grits. Daddy came in through the back door.

"Got the trailer hooked up to the tractor. That Earl. Boy, he got that thing runnin' fine as frog hair," Daddy said. "Y'all gals ready to go?"

"I suppose so," I said.

Daddy looked at Momma. "What's eatin' her? She's usually rarin' to go."

"Earl's leaving today," Momma reminded him.

"And I thought I was taking it hard," Daddy teased.

"Ha, ha, very funny, Daddy," I said and flicked a little grits his way.

"Well, that put some fire under ya. Now, go take it out on Marge Rosenberger," Daddy encouraged.

Marge Rosenberger—a crossword champion extraordinaire, a bully, a Pentecostal. She was in her mid-fifties and built like a German tank. Marge had held the county crossword title for ten years. Before Marge, there was Ruby Moore, a Pentecostal, and she held the title for three years. Before Ruby was a woman named Annie Jacobs, a Pentecostal, who held the title for five years. Then there were several other women before her, all from the same Pentecostal faith, who won the tournament. The Pentecostals believed God was on their side because no one outside their religion had won the tournament since its inception. The Baptists put up a good fight. Mabel Grover, for example, was an excellent crossword solver, but the bright lights of a tournament caused her brain to freeze. Poor thing, one year all she needed to win the tournament was a three-letter word for ball of fire. The middle intersecting letter was "u" to help with the clue. Did you guess the word yet? *Sun*, of course.

Now, the Baptists had put their hopes in me. I didn't mind the pressure either. I was groomed for this. I knew it, the Baptists knew it, but most importantly, the Pentecostals knew it. When I was competing in the junior tournament, the Pentecostals would scout out the talent and then send recruiters over with Bible tracts and so forth, trying to get the best and brightest converted to their side. I was always at the top of their list. Once, they even went as far as sending their preacher over to our house just to see if we were happy with the Baptist faith. Daddy told him in no uncertain words that we would never join a group of jibber-jab-talking, snake-handing holy rollers! Since that moment, the Pentecostals had feared this day—the day Emma Baumgaertner would be old enough to compete in the adult division. On a side note, rumor had it that Marge Rosenberger had been a Baptist at one time.

The morning was clear, the air cool, as we made our way to the Forbye Olympics. Our mode of transportation to the event was Daddy's tractor. It made sense, because Daddy supplied the hayrides to the kids. I was in the wagon with Momma while Daddy pulled us along Main Street with his newly refurbished tractor, courtesy of one Earl Gladstone.

The Forbye Olympics took place in Battlefield Park, which was just outside Forbye's city limits. Most folks parked near the town square and then took a leisurely stroll to the park. Vendors of all sorts were out selling their goods along Park Boulevard: popcorn, peanuts, cotton candy, and everything under the sun that could be baked, fried, or boiled. From the wagon, I'd occasionally hear shouts from the crowd: "Go get 'em, Emma!" or "Give Marge the what-for!" It felt good knowing I had the support of so many people. The town was alive. Red, white, and blue bunting had been draped over telephone lines. Jerry Randolph and The Country Swingers were playing bluegrass music in front of the courthouse, and if tradition held true, Gus Miles was selling moonshine behind the courthouse. It was just one of those things everyone in Forbye knew, but did little about.

Daddy pulled up to the reception tent, and I hopped out to sign in for the tournament. It was a little after nine o'clock, still three hours away from the contest, but the line was already deep with crossword hopefuls. Hobbyists, most of them, with no real chance of winning, but the tournament gave them something to do on a Saturday morning. I walked slowly down to the end of the line. It was a calculated tactic on my part, used merely as an intimidation ploy to let the others know I was there and that their odds of winning just dropped like a burnt biscuit. Suddenly, my eye caught sight of Marge Rosenberger standing only a few feet away. She had a huge homemade ribbon pinned to her dress that read, "Crossword Puzzle Champion." Obviously the ribbon was faux, because the county didn't give out ribbons. The winner received a five-dollar savings bond, a trophy, and a sash. Her flaunting didn't stop there. She also was wearing that red sash across her chest. It read "1948 Wayland County Crossword Champ." Talk about vain! A peacock had nothing on Marge. Also, talk about tacky! My colorblind daddy could have picked out a more pleasant ensemble. I couldn't help myself; I rolled my eyes.

"Well, if it isn't Emma Baumgaertner. So, you think you're ready for the big leagues, honey?" Marge taunted. Not "Hi. How are you doing?" or "Good luck and welcome to the adult division." No, she chose to belittle me in front of a line of women that stretched a good twenty-five feet.

I had two choices; I could run away like a shrinking violet, or turn the tables and come back with a biting comment of my own. You can probably figure out what I did, but I'll tell you anyway. I looked her in the eye and said, "So, you think you're ready for second place?" Women gasped up and down the line. One didn't speak to Marge Rosenberger that way, and certainly not a seventeen year-old rookie at her first rodeo.

"Did your momma raise you to disrespect your elders?" she questioned.

I dug my heels in. "If I'm not mistaken, we're all the same age in this tournament. It's called the adult division. I do hope you start acting like one," I stated and then settled in at the back of the line. Some women groaned, some snickered, but they all knew that I would not and could not be intimidated by a sash, a ribbon, and a pompous windbag who needed dethroning.

I signed up for the tournament without any further incident from

Marge. I walked the Olympic grounds just soaking in the atmosphere. Usually, I'd kill time with my best friend Nelly. We'd stand by the corral and watch Buddy Scruggs lard up the hog for the greased pig contest, or we'd sit in the grandstands and talk nonsense while sharing a bag of popcorn. She'd whistle at boys, I would cover my eyes, and then we'd giggle until we cried. Nelly was also my biggest fan when it came to the tournament. I could always count on her to give me a pep talk right before I hit the stage and a big hug after I won. What times we'd had.

Now, I walked the grounds alone—alone in so many ways. I would be the youngest contestant in a contest full of women. It was unheard of for a seventeen year-old to make it to the finals, let alone win. So I had that on my mind. Also, Earl was probably all packed and headed to the train station. I wondered if he was thinking about me as much as I was thinking about him. And, of course, Nelly. She was not with me.

The weight of everything hit me. Suddenly my confidence dropped. I stood there and looked around. I was between the greased pigs and the pickle barrels, and nothing mattered. I had waited for this day since my first junior tournament. I used to pretend that I was the one battling it out with Marge Rosenberger for the county title. I sat in the bleachers and watched her every move like a chess player's understudy picking up little nuances. I'd have my momma grill me on crossword trivia. I spent days doing nothing but puzzles. I ate it, I slept it, and I didn't date many boys because of it. Funny, isn't it? Suddenly one boy comes along, and this thing that was so important now rang hollow in my soul. It was more than missing Earl. I was even beginning to doubt my abilities and regretting the comment I had made to Marge Rosenberger. I was standing there feeling sorry for myself when Momma brushed by me, toting a vat of pickles for the eating contest. "Emma, honey, grab the side of this thing before I lose a hold of it," she said. I gripped one side of the handle and together we dumped a load of pickles into a barrel. "I reckon we got enough pickles for the contest," she said, "unless your daddy enters the event."

"Yes, ma'am."

"Emma, dear, what's wrong? You're moping like you've lost your best friend," she said. Then Momma realized what she had said. "Oh, dear, I'm sorry. So goes my logical perception."

"It's not just Nelly. I don't think I could spell my name right now, much less compete in a crossword tournament," I muttered.

"Oh, that's just the jitters talkin'. It's okay to be nervous. Now forget about the pressure. The Baptists ain't won it in over twenty years, so one more won't hurt." Momma patted me on the head. "Now, I'm gonna go help set up for the musical chairs. You know they want me to be the judge this year." Momma left. As pep talks went, that one fell like a half-cooked pound cake. I loved my momma, but all she did was acknowledge the fact that I could lose. It really didn't matter to her if I did, but I didn't need that. I needed a kick in the pants to get my competitive juices flowing. If someone or something could just slap some solid sense into my beleaguered spirit, then maybe I could shake that gloomy troll off my shoulder and get on with the tournament.

Just then, I got a big whiff of Alabaster Heaven. No, I didn't think of betrayal. "Oh, it's you, Nelly," I said. "From the smell, I thought Daddy's tractor broke down again."

"You think you're so funny! Well, missy, watchin' Marge Rosenberger mop up the floor with you will be a treat beyond satisfying. I wouldn't miss this for the world!" Nelly huffed.

"You imagine so, huh? Dream on; I just want to see your eyes when the mayor hands me the county trophy! And I'll be sure to give ya a wave when they place the sash over my shoulder!" I slammed my heel down, and turned away. Unbelievable! Without knowing it, Nelly came through with just the pep talk I needed. My will to prove someone wrong surpassed my desire to have a pity party. I channeled my anger to one objective—to win the tournament at all costs. Twelve o'clock could not come too soon, but my watch said I had another hour and a half.

I thought about heading over and watching the junior tournament. I was, after all, the reigning champion. But on second thought, I decided to keep myself out of sight and wait until the last minute to enter the arena. It would add more drama to a day that was already filled with theatrical scenes. I figured the best place to go unnoticed was on a hayride with my daddy. He was just pulling up front, letting out a group of kids.

"Hey, Daddy, got room for one more?" I asked as more kids piled into the wagon.

"Sure, honey." Daddy looked at his watch. "You're not boning up for the tournament?"

"No, sir. Fresh air is what I need most." I hopped into the wagon. The rumble of the old tractor seemed right. Maybe it was the swan song to my fleeting youth. I'd been on countless hayrides as a child, and there was always something special about their nothingness. Hayrides were just a few bails of hay scattered loosely on the bed of a weather-beaten wagon with a hitched-up old tractor pulling it to no particular place.

However, from a child's point of view, the destination wasn't important; it was all about the ride. I looked around at the kids on board. It wasn't that long ago that I was in their shoes. One boy had a frog in his hand, playfully teasing the girl beside him. Once upon a time, that was me and Calvin Tibbs, except I had the frog teasing him. Things were so simple then, with youth's uncluttered juvenile dreams and grown-up thoughts still so far away.

Daddy made the circle around Battlefield Park and the ride ended where it began. I hopped out. "Thanks, Daddy," I said and waved.

"I've got one more trip to make, and then I'll be in to watch your tournament," he said. I smiled and watched a new pile of kids jump into the wagon. Hayrides—what joy indeed!

The tournament was still forty-five minutes away, so I found a secluded bench under an oak tree and used the time to gather my thoughts for the contest. I liked to visualize the event. The rules were quite simple. The tournament consisted of three rounds. The first round was used merely to thin out the herd. Everyone thought they could be a crossword champion; the first round shattered most of those dreams. The puzzle was simple and would have only about twenty clues with easy words that rarely went over seven letters. The first ten contestants who solved the puzzle went on to the next round. Round two was the proving round. Clues were more indirect, and the answers could have a tricky vowel or two. The first two solvers went on to the final round. That was the round for all the marbles. It was also the round I pictured myself in, going head to head with Marge Rosenberger, the Pentecostal.

I sat under the oak tree. I thought about the tournament, and I thought about Marge. I'd be lying if I didn't admit I also thought about Earl. I had to make it to the train station to see him off, so not only did I have to win this tournament, but everything had to run on time, which could be out of my hands. I'd never pray to win—I wasn't that brash, although perhaps the Pentecostals were. However, I did call on God for a favor. *Dear Jesus, I ask thee for a guiding hand in this tournament. I would never ask for a victory, but if I'm going to win, can thou make it be done quickly? Thou hast given me this gift to use in your name. And the Baptists would like this gift to be used in their name as well. I say these things in the name of the Baby Jesus ... oh, and can you delay Earl's train just a bit, so I'll have time to see him off? Amen.*

I checked my watch. I had just enough time to make it over to the tournament tent without breaking into a sprint. The closer the tent came into view, the more my heart pounded—a good sign indeed. I felt alive for the first time that day. My feet hardly touched the ground while I maneuvered past the spectators waiting in line for a seat. I happened to see Momma and Daddy standing by the entrance. "There she is!" Momma called out.

"I told ya she'd make it," Daddy said. I gave them both a quick hug. "Knock 'em dead," Daddy hollered to the back of my head as I kept moving. I went to the back of the tent, where all the ladies were waiting to go on stage. They saw me and started milling around nervously. They reminded me of hens that just saw an ax in my hand. Fitting, when you think about it. Word spreads quickly when you're a child prodigy. I glanced over to Marge Rosenberger. She was chatting with another woman and acted like she didn't see my arrival, though I knew she did by the way she shifted her eyes. I started thinking about her intimidating move earlier in the day. Then I thought of Nelly and the satisfaction I would have in proving her wrong. It was time for me to do some intimidating of my own. I implemented a little trick I learned from Daddy—an old-fashioned stare down.

From fifteen feet away, I fixed a gaze at Marge. I focused on nothing but her gray pupils and bushy eyebrows. *Look at me, Marge. Look at me, Marge. Look at me, Marge.* Finally, she did. We locked eyeballs. The chatter around me faded into the background. My expression remained motionless as I continued to send a laser beam into her eyes. Drunken Doc Peterson could have run his car into the tent, and if it fell down around us, it still wouldn't have broken my stare. I don't know how long we stood there, and it wouldn't have mattered anyway because I wasn't looking away until Marge looked away first.

I saw her weakening, though. Little beads of sweat gathered in her bushy eyebrows, and her head swayed ever so slightly to the right. She was losing the battle and she knew it. *You can look away, Marge. You can look away, Marge. You can look away, Marge.* Finally she did. The poor woman looked like she'd just run a mile. She reached into her pocketbook to grab a handkerchief, and she mopped her face. What just happened between us didn't tell me that I would win, but it did tell me one thing: Marge Rosenberger had a breaking point, and she could be beaten!

"Ladies, please go to the stage and find a seat," a man with a megaphone said.

We all huddled near the stage entrance, and slowly the women filtered into the arena. I hung back, being the current junior champion. Marge waited as well, being the current adult champion.

"I've got nine more of these old things layin' 'round the house. But it's always nice to pick up a fresh one," Marge said, tugging on her sash.

"Maybe they'd stay fresh if you didn't wear them out in public. Was the word *crass* ever a clue in one of your crossword puzzles?"

"Well then, I'll just do all my talkin' with my pencil!" she bristled.

"I'll write with mine, thank you." I turned on my heel and headed for the stage. There were about forty school desks lined up in a row, and most of them were occupied by the time I stepped up to the platform. When I came into view, half the audience erupted with applause. "That a gal, Emma!" I heard my daddy shout as I found a desk. I was used to performing on stage, so the crowd didn't bother me. The spectators only increased my resolve to win this tournament. I glanced out into the audience. It was split down the middle. On one side sat the Pentecostals, or as Daddy sometimes called them, the Pentehostiles. Their women wore long dresses, long hair, and long faces. On the other side sat the Baptists, a little less drab, but at least I could tell they were breathing. Well, some were holding their breaths with hopes that the outcome would finally fall in their favor. My daddy appeared more nervous than me, but then again, he could never spell.

Marge made her entrance, and the other half of the audience clapped politely. Of course, that was the Pentecostal half; they're more reserved in public. However, get them in a room with a bag of snakes, and you'll find all kinds of carrying on! But that's another story.

Two judges walked down opposite ends of the line and placed a puzzle face down on each desk. Forty women waited on pins and needles for the bell to ring. I suppose this would be a good time to tell you about crossword strategy. Some say, start in the corners and work to the middle. Others will tell you to start in the middle and work your way out. I say balderdash. Find the longest word, then the next longest word, and so on. When doing this, you'll find the smaller, trickier words will fill themselves in. Never try to tackle short words first! That's what the puzzle maker wants you to do. Trust me—you'll be there all day.

The bell rang and I flipped my puzzle over. I had two clues solved, *Mayday* and *winter*, before some women had their puzzle turned over. *Three down, Oscar winner Humphrey—six letters—Bogart. Judge and—four letters—jury. Six across, Nineteenth President— five letters—Hayes.* The puzzle was easy, fast, and finished. I dropped my pencil and held up my puzzle. Then I glanced at Marge; she was just finishing her puzzle. I beat her by a good fifteen seconds. She glared, I smiled, and we waited for eight other women to solve their puzzles.

It was just past twelve o'clock, a good sign that this tournament would be completed by 1:30, perhaps no later than 1:45, which would leave me plenty of time to meet Earl at the train station. Except for one thing: the other women were not cooperating with my timetable. Mabel Grover, a Baptist, finished her puzzle. Now, the three of us waited as time ticked. It was truly unbelievable for such a simple puzzle. Frankly, if you couldn't solve that puzzle in five minutes, then you had no business being in the tournament. A few more women finished their puzzles as the clock pushed toward 12:30.

Since I was stuck with absolutely nothing to do, I scoured the crowd for Nelly. She wasn't hard to find because there she sat among the Pentecostals with her blond hair, red lipstick, and gum-smacking self. Her arms were folded like the rest of them, but that was about the only similarity. She looked completely out of place. I never wanted to win a tournament more than this one, and Nelly was fueling my desire with each breath she took behind the enemy's line.

Without much fanfare Bess Pendergrass finished her puzzle. The judges quickly reviewed all the answers and then dismissed the rest of the group. Finally, the stage was set for round two. It was 12:45—not good.

Ten ladies sat ready for the bell to ring. Only two women would move on to the final round. I closed my eyes, and waited ... the bell finally rang.

The puzzle had forty clues across and forty-six clues down. The longest word was in the middle of the page, twenty-five down, and it had eleven letters. Clue: *shortened*. I filled in the word: *abbreviated*. I moved to fourteen across, a nine letter word, the second letter, a. The clue read *silly or inappropriate*. I filled in the word: *facetious*. That word was the key to the puzzle; it contains every vowel, a, e, i, o, u. Look it up! Intersecting clues were as good as solved. I was on a roll.

The puzzle was falling into place, but then I did something stupid; I took the puzzle for granted and let my mind wander. I thought about Earl boarding the train. I thought about the clock moving faster than the tournament. I thought "football" was a six letter word for field game, when actually the right word was "baseball." I dug my eraser in, cleared the boxes, and corrected my mistake. It was a small hiccup, but it was enough to throw my rhythm off kilter. The next few clues tumbled around in my head longer than I wanted them to. I had no choice; I stopped looking at the clues, closed my eyes, and took a long deep breath. I opened my eyes, and the answers starting popping off the page,

*Genesis—Dickens—needle—luau.* My brain was clicking faster than my pencil could write. Through my focus, I heard faint applause, and I knew Marge was finished with her puzzle. But I didn't care because I had filled in my last box and I was finished as well! The Baptists erupted!

The match everyone anticipated was a reality: Emma Baumgaertner, the Baptist, versus Marge Rosenberger, the Pentecostal. It was a contest for all the holy marbles. I looked out and saw Momma and Daddy hugging each other. On the other side of the aisle, Nelly, with her newfound Pentecostal friends, gave sour expressions. They knew a Baptist had finally come to play.

One judge came over and placed a puzzle on each of our desks. I glanced at my watch; Earl's train was due in thirty-five minutes. I quickly ran the numbers in my head. The walk to the train station would take fifteen minutes. The puzzle, if everything fell into place, should not take any longer than twenty-five minutes to solve. That still left five minutes, maybe more, that I would have to make up somewhere along the line. So not only did I have to win this tournament, but I had to win it in record time. In order to do that, I needed concentration, a sharp pencil, and a little help from the Lord. I reached for the small pencil sharpener on my desk and shaved the pencil down to a fine point. I closed my eyes and envisioned my hand filling up little boxes with little letters. The words or clues didn't matter at the moment; they would come to me. What mattered most was visualizing my hand and mind moving as one. Again I took a deep breath, and the bell rang.

I flipped the puzzle over. The longest word had sixteen letters. The clue was *Confederate victory.* My mind raced, for so many letters, it might be two words scrunched into one. I started thinking, *Battlefields, two words, Confederate victory, ah yes, Cumberland Church, it fits!* Then I broke my rule of moving to the next longest word because this clue caught my eye. *A locomotive captured in April 1862? The _____.*

I couldn't believe my eyes. This was a Civil War themed crossword puzzle! The one thing I knew everything about. I smiled. *I knew the Lord likes Baptists*, I thought. Themed puzzles, though not unheard of, were rare in tournament play. The puzzle masters always wanted to keep the contestants off their guard, but today, for some reason, they came up with a puzzle that was right in my wheelhouse. I quickly filled in the word, *General,* which was the name of the captured locomotive. It was downhill from there. Just like I envisioned, my pencil was filling in tiny boxes with tiny letters. I wrote *Chickamauga, Bullrun, Bragg,* and *Muleshoe* without much thinking. The puzzle was as easy as saying my

ABC's. The length of the puzzle was the only thing standing in my way. Imagine repeating the alphabet one hundred times. Sure, you know it, but it takes forever to get through it.

I heard Marge cough, which broke my concentration. I had completely forgotten about her and the fact that I was sitting in front of a crowd, my focus was that great. I briefly allowed myself to look up. Marge was scratching her head and mumbling to herself. She must have looked my way at some point and saw my nimble fingers racing through the puzzle. Obviously, Marge Rosenberger wasn't a Civil War buff. I went back to work.

The puzzle was halfway solved, but after observing Marge's body language, I knew I had it in the bag. Still, it was no time to get sloppy. I slowed my pace down a notch, just so I wouldn't have another football/ baseball mix-up. One slip and the tides could turn. Not really, but I told myself that anyway. It was hard, though. Slowing down only made that clock on the wall speed up. It seemed to be moving twice the rate of normal time. I had to fight off the urge to glance at it every few minutes. Yes, the puzzle was becoming that boring. So, methodically and meticulously, I perfectly finished the puzzle, undoubtedly.

I dropped my pencil, raised the puzzle in the air, and the Baptists exploded with cheers. Marge jumped from the eruption and then looked at me with a blank stare, she realized I was finished. Then, she went back to work on her puzzle just in case I made a mistake.

The Baptists started chanting, "Emma! Emma! Emma!"

"Not official! Not official!" a judge yelled from the stage. The crowd died down after a few boos. "The puzzle has to be graded. Please consider the other contestant and refrain from cheering until we declare a winner," the judge shouted. Regardless of what you've heard, the Baptists are a well-mannered lot, and they settled down while the judges went over my puzzle as the clock moved.

Earl was due in fifteen minutes. The walk took fifteen minutes. The judges were taking forever! They huddled, they conferred, and they whispered back and forth. They even went as far as holding my puzzle up to the light, of all things! Who knew why, because I have excellent penmanship. *It's a puzzle, not an x-ray, for crying out loud!*

I knew without a doubt that my puzzle was correct, but what I knew didn't matter. My victory waited on the fat man with a magnifying glass, and his trusted sidekick, Mr. Cross-all-the-T's-and-dot-all-the-I's. The clock ticked. I glanced over at Marge. From what I could see, she was about halfway through with her puzzle, but the Pentecostal in her wouldn't let go, and she kept at it like the tournament wasn't over.

The fat man rose up from his desk. His face took on a somber look as he walked toward me with my puzzle in his hand. The quiet in the hall became even more deafening. Tension built with each step the fat man took. He seemed to enjoy it because he took very slow steps. The clock ticked. Finally, he arrived at my desk. "Ladies and gentlemen," he said and then paused for dramatic effect. He looked at me and said, "The 1949 Wayland County Crossword Puzzle Champion is Emma Baumgaertner!" I jumped up, the Baptists jumped up, and Marge dropped her pencil. I never heard such a ruckus. The Baptists were clapping and stomping their feet so loudly that the Pentecostals probably thought a bag of snakes had been turned loose.

The mayor of Forbye, Big Al Forster, rushed to the stage and handed me the crossword trophy. His lovely wife, Annie, placed the championship sash over my neck. I had arrived. I turned around and gave my promised wave to Nelly. Her reaction was predicable—sour. She made her exit before my hand went down. Then I saw Momma and Daddy. What a pair, those two. Momma was shouting and whooping it up with the other Baptists, while Daddy was doing every thing he could to hold back his tears.

I was caught up in the moment but not in the time. Could you really blame me, though? After all, I just did something that no other seventeen year-old Baptist had ever done before. I really don't expect you to understand what it meant to be Wayland County's crossword champion, but you should know there would be parades, interviews, and that five-dollar savings bond for the spoils. Life was grand, and I wasn't riding in a hearse!

I was halfway through my victory march when I realized the time. Earl was pulling into Forbye Station right that very minute! I stopped mid-stride. Cinderella had to leave the ball. *I gotta get out of here!* I thought. I rushed down the stage and past the waiting press.

"How's it feel to beat Marge Rosenberger?" one of them shouted as I blew by.

"Delightful!" I kept running. Earl's train called for a fifteen-minute stop. Even if I ran as hard as I could, the only thing I would see was his train leaving the station. That wasn't good enough. I wanted to see him. I needed to see him.

I pushed through the crowd as nicely as a newly crowned queen could. A frozen smile plastered my face. I waved and glad-handed through a parting sea of Baptists. I needed a miracle to make it out of there. Suddenly, I heard my daddy's voice over the rest. "That's my gal!" he hollered.

"Daddy, daddy," I said. We hugged. "Pick me up and get me out of here!"

"What?" he said.

Momma was there, too. I pleaded to her. "Momma, Earl is at the station right now. I have to get out of here!"

"Charles, pick your daughter up and run out with her!" Daddy launched me on top of his massive hands like I was first prize at the biggest pumpkin contest. The crowd was clueless and loved it. I'm sure they thought it was just a move by a proud papa. I continued to wave. Daddy was an agile man for his size, and we were outside in no time. He flopped me down.

"I'm taking the tractor, Daddy!" I said.

"Wait! My tractor?"

"Yes, now go give it a crank!"

"But—"

Momma was close behind. "Charles, crank the tractor!" she said.

"All right, I'll crank the tractor. Wait, let me unhook the wagon," he said.

"No time, just crank it!" I yelled. I hopped up to the seat, and pulled my dress up just enough to find the gearshift between my knees. Daddy stood in front, gave the rod a good twist, and the old tractor roared to life. "See y'all at the house! I love you!" I said. With a forceful punch, I jammed it into high, the gear Earl feared. The tractor hesitated a bit and then leapt forward causing the front wheel to rise off the ground. Luckily, no one was standing in the way because I had no control over the runaway tractor. I traveled a good twenty yards before the front wheel settled down and I was able to steer the blasted thing.

Of course I knew how to drive a tractor. I'm a farm girl, remember? But there was a learning curve to Earl's modification. It was funny how a speeding tractor seemed to draw a crowd. People just appeared before me. As soon as I dodged one, there was another standing in the way. Mommas were yanking kids off to the side, and dogs didn't know if they should chase me or run away. Most of them ran, and the ones that didn't wished they had, but I kept it in high gear. Someone decided a lemonade stand would be a nice feature for a thirsty mob. And I'm sure it was—past tense. I never liked lemonade anyway.

The park exit was a tricky maneuver. Gus Sabatini had just finished stacking tomatoes next to his produce stand. One problem: he stacked them in a precarious spot, the same spot where my tractor was heading. To my left there was a pond, on the right a ditch. A narrow opening between the pyramid of tomatoes and Mrs. Finch's new Cadillac was my only option. I gripped the wheel and gave a hard turn to the right. The wagon behind me followed suit, tipping on two wheels. The tractor cleared the vegetables and Mrs. Finch's Cadillac with a few inches to spare, but the wagon did not. It sideswiped the lower portion of the tomatoes, just enough to shake loose an avalanche of rolling ripe love apples. *I'll write Gus a letter of apology; more practice for my penmanship,* I thought as I left the grounds and charged for the main highway. *Better write one to Mrs. Finch, too, and the owner of the lemonade stand ... I wonder who owned that dog?*

The open road was a breeze. Obstacles were few. There was an occasional maneuver here and there, but nothing to get excited about, unless you count the dairy truck that chose the ditch over the front end of my tractor. I glanced at my watch. I had eight minutes at best to arrive before Earl left the station. Up ahead, the only traffic light between me and the train station was red. The sensible thing to do, slow down, didn't come to mind. The only other thing to do, keep it in high gear, took over my mind. My sash fluttered in the wind as I factored in the cars ahead, the sidewalk, and a little old man sweeping his storefront. The best available route had a detour through the old man. *Surely, he'll be able to hear this tractor coming.* I made a swift turn and bounced up on the sidewalk. The old tractor gripped the pavement and raced down the walkway. *Turn around, old man,* I kept saying to myself. Fortunately, someone in one of the stopped cars saw what was going on and started blowing their horn. The old man looked up in the nick of time and dove into his store. Yet, I wasn't out of the woods. That pesky red light still stood in the way.

Sometimes you just have to trust in the Lord. Other times you have to trust that everyone can see you when you decide to run a red light. Hopefully the former would take care of the latter. My firm grip on the wheel tightened. I locked my elbows in—just in case a car was coming—and then braced for impact. I had no idea what was over the hill that was just a mere twenty yards ahead.

I did know one thing. If I were to survive this, then Earl and I were meant to be together. I also knew I had a lot of apology letters to write. *I think the name of old man sweeping the sidewalk was Mr. Cosgrove.*

The tractor, with me holding on for dear life, sprang from the sidewalk and cut through the intersection. One vehicle brushed by the wagon's backend, while another car nearly grazed the tractor's grill, but I made it through, lickety-split. I bounced around on the seat until I reached the bottom of the hill, my skirt flopping up the whole way. Finally, the train station was in clear sight. I could see steam rising up from the train's stack. My watch said I had four minutes until the train left; my heart pleaded for more.

I turned into the depot and downshifted when I hit the gravel parking lot. I drove right up to the front gate and slammed on the brakes. Smoke rose from the old tractor, and a few lemons and tomatoes rolled out of the wagon. I hit the kill switch. The engine knocked and popped as I jumped off and sprinted through the gates. I happened to catch my reflection in the window of a ticket booth. Quickly, I stopped and dug out my red lipstick that I had tucked inside my blouse (never mind where). I painted my lips up, pushed my windblown hair down, and then took off for train number nine, leaving Forbye.

I ran down the long corridor, and then skidded to a stop at the gate to the number nine train. I burst through and the train was still there. A few people were milling about; obviously they had already said good-bye to their loved ones. Frantically, I scoured each car looking up to the windows. Up and down I went. A man with a pocket watch stood at the train steps watching the time. "Two minutes," he yelled.

Suddenly, I head a banging on a window. I looked over by the train's platform. It was Earl, God love him, with all his Spencer Tracy smiling charm. *I've found him.* I raced to the platform and bound up its steps. "Hold on missy, gotta have a ticket," the man with the watch said.

"No, I'm not going. I'm just saying good-bye."

"Well, you'll have to do it outside, and you only have a minute to do it," he said.

It was apparent the man had never been in love with anything other than his watch. At least I was on the platform, which would get me closer to Earl. I quickly traveled down the side of the train until I saw my man again. He was fidgeting with the window when I came into his view. He stopped and our eyes met. The tractor drive was worth that alone.

He was saying something—I think it was about the window being stuck, but I really could not tell. Those train windows were awfully thick. He threw his hands in the air and gave up trying to open the window. Then he pointed to my blouse and started clapping his hands. For a second I thought that maybe my buttons had come undone when I reached for my lipstick and he was applauding the show. No, I realized he saw my crossword championship sash that I was wearing. Of course, I played it off like it was no big deal.

"Clear the platform," the man with the watch called out. My heart sank. I just wanted to hold Earl's hand, hear his voice, and, yes, give him a long kiss good-bye. Earl held up a finger as if to say, "Hold on." The he took out a pen and started writing on his arm. The train's horn blew, and the car moved slightly, but it didn't start rolling. Earl pressed his arm against the window. Down the length of his arm were the words "Will you merry me?" Some men get down on one knee; other men may put a ring in a dessert at a fancy restaurant. Earl Gladstone chose to scribble it down his bare arm, and he misspelled marry. I don't think I would have wanted it any other way.

I stood on my toes and kissed the window leaving two perfect red lip marks for Earl to view all the way to South Carolina. I still had the lipstick in my hand, so I pulled off the top as the train slowly rolled forward. Walking and reaching for the window, my hand found a place right by my lip marks. I took the lipstick and wrote—*Yes*.

# RECIPES

## Earl's Hamburger Gravy

Earl could eat this dish seven days a week and ask for seconds. Serve it over white rice or, for a real treat, heap a ladle-full on top of my skillet biscuits.

**1 pound ground beef**
**½ chopped onion**
**2 cloves minced garlic**
**1 tablespoon chicken bouillon granules**
**2 ½ cups milk (divided)**
**1 tablespoon butter**
**¼ cup flour**
**Salt and pepper to taste**

Brown hamburger with onion and garlic in a large skillet, and then drain grease.

Pour 1 ½ cups of the milk into the skillet. Add butter, bouillon, salt and pepper, and mix well. Bring to a boil and cook for 5 minutes, stirring frequently.

Mix flour with remaining milk until smooth. While stirring, slowly pour milk into skillet. Simmer until thickened.

*Emma's tip: For a richer flavor, add about ¼ cup of whipping cream while the gravy is simmering. If gravy is too thin, add extra flour.*

## Momma's Turnip Greens

(Can also use mustard or collard greens)

**A mess of turnip greens**
**3 or 4 slices of bacon, or a chunk of salt pork**
**¼ cup of red or cooking wine (don't worry; the alcohol cooks right out)**
**4 Tbsp sugar**
**2 Tbsp baking soda**
**4 Tbsp butter**
**6 cups water**

Bring water and bacon to a boil, and then lower temperature and cook for 10 to 15 minutes. Add greens and roots and bring to a slow boil for 15 minutes.

In a separate bowl combine wine, sugar, and baking soda in ½ cup of cold water. Mix well and then pour over greens. Simmer until greens are tender. Add butter and serve. If greens are bitter add more baking soda.

*Emma's tip: Fresh greens are sweeter if you pick them after the first frost.*

## Skillet Buttermilk Biscuits

Over the years I've used several biscuit recipes, but this one is the best. If you like your biscuits crispy on the outside, you'll love this recipe.

**6 Tbsp unsalted butter, for the skillet**
**1 1/2 cups of all-purpose flour, sifted**
**1/4 cup cake flour, sifted**
**1 Tbsp sugar**
**2 tsp baking powder**
**1 tsp baking soda**
**1 tsp kosher salt**
**1/4 cup vegetable shortening, cut into cubes**
**1 cup buttermilk**

Preheat oven to 500 degrees. Melt butter in a large cast iron skillet over low heat. Keep hot until you're ready to bake the biscuits.

Sift flour into a large bowl. Add sugar, baking powder, baking soda and salt. Mix well. Add shortening and toss to coat. Use a fork or your fingers to cut the shortening into the flour until the mixture is coarse, then add buttermilk.

Stir quickly until the dough is combined. Do not overmix.

Use a large spoon to drop the dough into the hot skillet. Place 6 mounds evenly apart. Quickly turn each biscuit over to coat with butter. Place skillet in oven and reduce temperature to 475. Bake 12 to 14 minutes until golden brown.

## Doris Humfinger's Banana Pudding (Cooked)

**1 cup sugar**
**1/3 cup all-purpose flour**
**2 egg yolks, slightly beaten**
**2 cups milk**
**1 tsp vanilla flavoring**
**1 tsp butter**
**Vanilla wafers**
**About 3 bananas**
**2 egg whites, beaten**
**1/4 cup sugar**

Mix sugar & flour in saucepan. Combine egg yolks & milk & slowly add to sugar mixture, stirring to mix. Place over medium heat & stir constantly till thickened.

Remove from heat & add vanilla & butter.

Layer casserole dish with vanilla wafers, then bananas, then about ½ the pudding mixture. Repeat.

Beat the egg whites until stiff & add ¼ cup sugar & continue beating till it holds a peak. Top the pudding with the meringue & brown in a 350-degree oven.

## Flaky Pie Crust

**¾ cup chilled butter**
**4 Tbsp chilled lard**
**2 cups flour**
**1 tsp salt**
**½ cup ice water**

In a large bowl, mix together flour and sugar until well combined. Wash hands.

Add butter and toss until coated. Mix butter with hands until flour mixture is coarse.

Add lard, then rub into flour mixture until mixture resembles pea-size pieces.

Sprinkle in half of the ice water and comb through mixture with fingers until moistened. Add in remaining water 1 tablespoon at a time and comb through mixture with fingers to moisten. Keep working until dough starts coming together. Do not overwork dough.

Push dough between bowl and palm while rotating bowl until dough forms a ball. Divide the ball in half and place each ball onto a sheet of wax paper. Press each into a flat disk.

Cover and place in refrigerator for at least 30 minutes. Remove and roll each disk into a pie crust.

*Emma's tip: Use leaf lard and Goldfields Baking Butter.*

## Emma's Boysenberry Pie

Yes, that's right—the pie that made Forbye famous and me the talk of the town is here for all the Nelly Daltons of the world to steal. So go ahead, gals, and give it a go if you want to be a hit at the next church social.

I do hope you will use my pie crust for this recipe. However, I understand that today's modern mom might want to use a store bought crust—speaking of Nelly Dalton.

**4 cups fresh boysenberries (if boysenberries are hard to find in your neck of the woods, you may substitute with blackberries)**
**1 cup sugar**
**1/3 cup corn starch**
**Almost, but not quite 1/2 tsp ginger**
**About 1/4 cup of corn syrup for coating berries**
**2 Tbsp butter**
**3 Tbsp whipping cream**

Preheat oven to 425 degrees.

Wash berries and place in a bowl. Pour corn syrup over top of berries and gently toss to coat. Set bowl aside.

In a large mixing bowl, add sugar, corn starch, and ginger. Mix well. Gently add berries to mixture. You can smash just a few to get a little juice flowing.

Form your pie crust inside a pie dish and bake the bottom crust for about 10 minutes, let cool. Pour berry mixture on top of bottom crust. Cut butter into thin slices and place evenly on top of berries. Cover berries with pie crust and seal up the edges. Cut off dough around dish. With a knife, make about 6 slits around top of pie. Brush whipping cream on top crust and sprinkle with sugar.

Bake for 10 minutes on lower rack, and then transfer to middle rack and bake for an additional 30 minutes or until brown.

*Emma's tip: Form aluminum foil around crust edge before baking to keep the crust from burning.*

# *All About Forbye* Crossword Puzzle

**Across**

2 – Emma's given first name
4 – Heaven-to-Hell ______
6 – Scottish word for near or beside
7 – Emma's daddy
8 – Jed Burton's occupation
10 – Earl is from
14 – Dean Martini and the _______
15 – British preacher Alistair _______
17 – Championship puzzle theme
18 – Emma's rival religion
20 – Town gossip
21 – Klan member
23 – Forbye's sacred water
24 – Earl's sergeant
25 – Earl's nickname
26 – aka Bill Webber
27 – Axle grease

**Down**

1 - Died at the pulpit
3 – Pentecostal crossword champ
5 – Toxic punch
9 – Earl served in this war
11 – Hiram and Doris
12 – Antagonist
13 – Good looking preacher
16 – Funeral Home & Tractor Repair
19 – Ace reporter
22 – Forbye is in this county

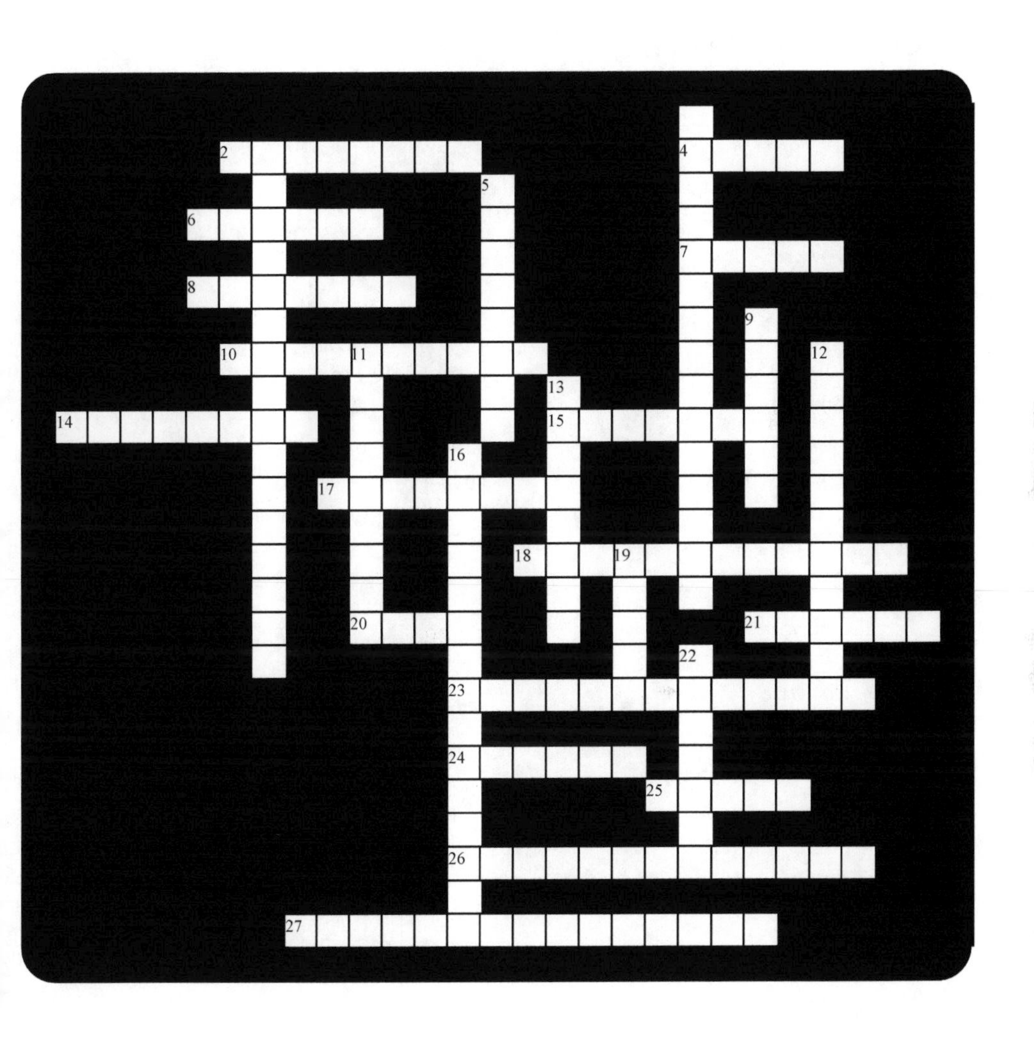

## Crossword Solution

### Across

2 – Emmaline
4 – Ratio
6 – Forbye
7 – Chuck
8 – Sheriff
10 – South Creek
14 – Ice Cubes
15 – Colgate
17 – Civil War
18 – Pentecostals
20 – Rose
21 – Kotter
23 – Baptismal Pond
24 – OBoyle
25 – Barth
26 – Earl Gladstone
27 – Alabaster Heaven

### Down

1 – Preacher Babcock
3 – Marge Rosenberger
5 – Planters
9 – Korean
11 – Humfinger
12 – Nelly Dalton
13 – McGreevy
16 – Bleaker Brothers
19 – Tibbs
22 – Wayland

# Preacher Scorecard

Dear friends, chances are good that at some point you will serve on a pulpit committee. When that day arrives, you should be prepared. On the next page you will find a well-thought-out Preacher Scorecard. You do not merely have my permission; I actively encourage you to make copies for everyone on your committee. Simply put a check mark after each action from your prospective preacher. Refer back to my story "The Pulpit Committee" to calculate the preacher's overall score.

# Preacher Scorecard

Date ______________________ Attendance for service ________
Preacher's name ____________ Actual minutes preaching _____
Name of church ____________ Time of dismissal ____________

Pounded the pulpit ______________________________
Raised voice for affect ___________________________
Shook his Bible ________________________________
*Amens* from the congregation ____________________
Read from the *Book of Revelations* ________________
Told the congregation that we were going to hell ____________
Referenced eternal damnation _____________________
Referenced the devil, Lucifer, or Satan ______________
Referenced sins of the flesh _______________________

## Heaven/Hell ratio

Said the word *Heaven* ____________________________
Said the word *Hell* ______________________________

**Notes**: ____________________________________________

I hope you enjoyed reading my stories as much as I enjoyed telling them. I have many more stories and perhaps they'll find their way into another book or two. Until then, you can visit emmagladstone.com for more information and merchandise. You can also friend me, Emma Gladstone, on Facebook, or follow me on Twitter.

God Bless,
Emma

# About the Author

Ron Hosea is a freelance writer and the author of the Emma Gladstone short story series. He contributes to online publications with articles on running, pop culture, and politics. He grew up in Florida, where he still lives with his bride of over twenty-five years. Ron has two sons and a granddaughter.